THE
HIAWATHA

Also by
DAVID TREUER

Little

THE

HIAWATHA

DAVID TREUER

Picador USA

NEW YORK

"The Lamentations of Jeremiah," translated from the original Latin, courtesy of Gimell Records Limited.

Library of Congress Cataloging-in-Publication Data

Treuer, David.
    The Hiawatha / David Treuer.—1st Picador USA ed.
    p. cm.
    ISBN 0-312-20313-6
    1. Indians of North America—Minnesota—Minneapolis—Fiction.
2. Ojibwe Indians—Fiction. I. Title.
PS3570.R435H53   1999
813'.54—dc21   99-12842
                                          CIP

First Picador USA Edition: May 1999

10 9 8 7 6 5 4 3 2

for   M e g a n   a n d   M i c a h

h e l d

You would love me because I should have strangled you
And because of my infamy;
And I should love you the more because I mangled you
And because you were no longer beautiful
To anyone but me

—*The Love Song of Saint Sebastian*, T. S. Eliot

How desolate lies the city that was once
Thronged with people.
The one-time queen of nations
Has become a widow.
Once a ruler of provinces,
She is now subject to others.

—*The Lamentations of Jeremiah*

THE
HIAWATHA

PART
ONE

1

They let it pass. The deer is so close they can see in its eyes the dawn light seeping gray over the rotten soffits and pooling there in the parking lot of Saint Steven's Church.

By 1981 death is not interesting to the Southside of Minneapolis, but this sliver of life, wild and strange amid the parked cars, this is news. When whole families freeze to death in abandoned houses, stacked like cordwood to share what heat they have, no one is surprised. When cops shoot teenagers point-blank, people shrug. When social workers and bill collectors come to ply their trade among those who have neither society nor money anymore, they turn back thwarted and tired. Tired more than anything. If a bill collector happened to park across from the Institute of the Arts, thinking that there his car wouldn't be broken into, and walked along Twenty-fourth Street or up Third Avenue, he could see something. He might look at the faces in the green smear of park, or clustered on what steps the crumbling apartments offered, and see something behind the studied neutrality of the Indians who moved into the neighborhood in the fifties and sixties. He might glimpse an awareness, an acknowledgment of the tide of misery that sweeps the neighborhood and bends for neither mood nor season. The collector might notice that despite what the weather, society and the government throw at the city transplants, they are determined to endure. But it is March and the streets are dirty with sand and salt and the veneer of frozen exhaust. After all, it is March and the bill collectors and door-to-door men have kids and pets, they have Edina and Maple Grove, White Bear Lake and Bloomington, strung like pearls around the withered heart of the city.

They do not see the interest the homeless men take in the deer as it strides wild and alert through the church parking lot. They do not see the men reach out but stop short of actually touching the deer.

They let it pass. The men sitting on rolled foam or piles of rags stand and scoop their bedrolls from its path, and when their palms are placed out and pulled short they feel its animal warmth. They hold their hands there, fingers splayed, stealing its heat. The line forms, men and their benedicting hands, a channel of men through which the deer walks, concerned, but certain.

Those inside the church sense something happening outside. Because of the silence they have ruled out the police, who always come wearing a mantle of noise, and so they are unafraid to stand clustered and steaming on the cement steps.

They let it pass. When it leaves them behind they do not lower their hands, do not shift or move, as if asleep.

The deer approaches the end of the channel of men, its small hooves click on the frost-hardened asphalt and steam plumes from its nose. It pauses then, preparing to leave this human forest. As it steps clear, the last man reaches out and gently places his hand flat against its fur. In an instant it is running. It jumps once, and then again. In two leaps it is over the fence. The men drop their arms and rush to the chain-link, hook their fingers and watch the deer bound down the weedy and trash-strewn slope to the freeway and into the traffic.

The first car clips its legs from under it and it flies into the air, rolled up the ramp of the windshield. The yearling lands on the hood of the second and the men hear the bone mulch. Again, for what seems an eternity, it is sent toward the leaded sky. The legs mill on broken joints, a gout of blood erupts from between the pages of its ribs. The deer is lofted once more before it falls limp on the litter-strewn shoulder, its head among the brown winter weeds where black garbage bags have caught fast and flutter like crows. The deer is dead.

Some men stare at the tangle of fur and gritty flesh, others turn but do not walk back into the soup line.

"Good job, Simon," says one as he kicks at the broken glass by the fence's edge. "Good job," he mutters again.

With that they all turn in various angles of regret and spread back out over the pavement until only Simon remains at the fence. Then he, too, drifts back to the parking lot and since he has nothing to carry, moves on from their midst, crossing the street with his head down, along the alley next to the old Windsor Hotel, his face hidden in the folds of his jacket.

At eight years old Simon woke before the others. He rose shirt-less in the blue light and listened to the stovepipe clink, contracting in the cold. The fire was reduced to a nest of dying coals sheathed in powdery ash inside the barrel stove. He stepped over the others, conscious always of the shifting human architecture that patterned the one-room cabin, a thief stealing a moment of privacy as he moved into the new day.

The plastic-coated window made the weather seem soft, the cold not so deadly, though the pine walls were spangled with frost, and the water bucket next to the door was skimmed with ice.

He lifted the pail, the handle sheathed in the tatters of an old shirt, and poked off the skim ice with his fingers before he tilted it, tinkling softly, into the bucket on the stove. He slid his feet into the oversized boots of his sleeping father and lifted the wooden catch to the door and in one motion he was outside, taking shallow breaths against the sharp sub-zero air, grainy with ice. The half-moon was bright enough to light the snow, casting shadows of the other cabins skyward, broken only by scattered trees. The frozen lake spread out unhurried and full between the jack pine. Simon went without a lantern. There was no wind and the pressure of his booted feet made the freshly blown snow crackle as he stepped past the mounds along the walk to where the high drifts lay unseeded with fur and the guts of snared rabbits. He dipped the bucket full. He stopped when he noticed holes punched in the snow. A jagged line of fist-sized craters zagged past the cabin, crossed the narrow road, leaped the bank and continued on the other side. He set the pail down, held his hands in his armpits and stalked out to where the tracks crossed the road. There, on the packed snow, he saw the perfect arrowhead shape of deer tracks, like marks on fine porcelain.

He stood and wondered down the tracks, knowing that with each step he was moving forward in the life of the deer, moving closer to its present. If he followed it long enough, he would catch up to it and be there at the time of its death, somewhere in the woods, impassable now because of the snow.

He walked back to where the bucket shone like lead in the moonlight and picked it up again. The coldness contained there should have weighed more, should have strained his boy shoulders. But the bucket was light. He packed it with his hand, scooped and packed until it was full, and carried it back inside, a boy holding a bucket of snow to melt on the stove for tea and oatmeal.

Simon crosses the street lined with cars that hulk in the morning cold, ice welded to the mud flaps. Even now, when Simon looks
at objects bigger than himself, he seeks out their center, calculating
what it would take to balance them spinning through the air, where
the cables could be clipped and on what the nylon webbing could
rest to hoist it, passed like a puzzle high over the city. After ten
years of not being allowed to lift anything heavier than a sack of
potatoes or hold any tool that had heft or edge he is still building
skyscrapers.

He passes the cars and skips over the snow-crusted curb and
looks with sudden shock next door. The other houses have disappeared, replaced with two poorly constructed apartment buildings,
each a study in how to charge more for less.

He shakes his head and mounts the sagging wooden steps. He
pauses, not sure anymore of the etiquette of visiting, the choreog-
raphy of knocking and waiting, of entering someone else's space. He
stands poised, knuckles raised. He is spared when she opens the
door, sensing him there, wanting him to do it, to close the distance
of ten years and his brother's blood. Three inches between flesh and
wood, ten years between touch. She opens the door and steps forward so now she is what he will have to step through to enter the
house.

"Simon," she says. Her voice speculative. She could have
pointed beyond the fringe of brick buildings over the skyline and
said *Cloud* or *Orange*. She doesn't move.

"Ma," he says.

She moves back a step, her hand on the doorknob.

"Ma. You look good."

She smiles a little and turns. She isn't prepared for this. She
does not expect the soft humor the boys have inherited from their
father. They were never much for loudness in either anger or love.

7

"Don't lie straight off," she says.

She leaves the door open and slides farther back. He raises his foot over the metal-cased step and sets it inside the house, his weight still cocked onto his back leg.

He won't remember stepping in, his hands shoved deep in his pockets, Betty's slow retreat to the kitchen. He won't remember how the house has changed. It will stay in his mind as it was when he lived there: the living room with two tattered couches someone was always passed out on, sleeping off a binge or "just setting for a while" after a fight with wife or husband; the old oak floors clear and waxed, not covered with carpet to hide the blood-soaked wood; the kitchen and breakfast nook still painted white, with white linoleum tiles. So memory always murders the present. All he will remember is sitting there in the cramped kitchen, the coffee swirling to a standstill in the chipped mismatched rummage-sale mugs as the silence coasts between them. It isn't a shared silence, not one tended, as fires are, throwing off invisible warmth.

"Ten years," she says, shaking her head and then steadying it as she purses her lips to meet her coffee cup.

"Ten, yeah, well, that's a long time," he agrees.

He shifts his weight, broad shoulders dipping and leveling like the wings of a large bird.

"Where are the girls?"

"Irma's off in San Diego, married. Got a kid, too."

"Caroline here?"

"Oh my, my baby, no," whispers Betty, her hand flying to her cheek as if she's forgotten an ingredient in an often-used recipe. "No, she's gone. Died three years ago now."

"Ma, no. Really? How?"

"She was in a car. Got hit on the tracks up north. She didn't hurt none. At least that's what the doctor said."

Four children, she thinks. Two of them dead, one ran off as soon as she could with the first white man who said he loved her, and the last one, Simon, lost somewhere in between. At least they lived long enough to outgrow their kid clothes. Seeing all the jumpers and tiny pants would be too much. At least they didn't die when they were sucking on her tit or tugging at her skirt. They had more personality as children. After they hit their teens she can't remember much about them, their dislikes and their loyalties, their habits. Merciful, maybe, that her mind deprived her of knowing her children when they were old enough to create their own hurt.

"Aw, damn," says Simon, shaking his head. "I'm so sorry, Ma. I'm so sorry."

"Ain't got nothin to be sorry about. You couldn't help that."

They both breathe in heavily, great drinks of stale house air. As if such breathing were enough to shake out the chill of young death. Simon feels anger rising. Betty's refusal of his sympathy makes him feel that his sister's death is something Betty wants all for herself. Lester is one thing, but he is mad at her for denying him the right to be sad for his sister.

"You got anyone for yourself?"

"Naw, not me." She grimaces.

Then Simon hears the stairs squeak, a shift of feet on the aging wood, the risers gapped back from the tread like poorly set teeth. Simon shoots her a look with raised eyebrows and then urges them down toward the surface of the table. The stairs continue to let out their warnings and Simon, who still knows the whispers of this house, can hear whoever is walking down them swing out on the newel post, take three steps to the kitchen door and stop. Betty looks up from the table.

"Lincoln, get in here. Why you hangin your head like you was slow?"

Simon shifts in his chair and sees a boy enter the rare fluorescent kitchen light. Unsure, doe-eyed.

"Come on. Say hello to your uncle."

The boy moves his eyes from Simon to Betty and back. He is

careful of a joke at his expense, the potential for embarrassment. Even at ten he charts each room, mapping the dangers nestled within people.

Lincoln has known only this quiet house, empty of the traffic of people. He was six when his sister Irma flew in the door with the white man she announced to Betty she was going to marry. The man stood to the side of the door and looked at his feet, pinned against the wall by Betty's withering gaze. "Well, good for you," drawled Betty. "I just came back to get my clothes," said Irma defiantly. Betty laughed. "From the looks of things it doesn't seem like you've been wearin them too much. Go on then." The man said nothing in his defense. Perhaps it was only then he realized Irma was using him to escape her mother's gravity, that she clung to him only to break her orbit around that sad house and its history. Lincoln sat on Irma's bed while she hurriedly stuffed her battered suitcase full. "We gonna move away from this cold-ass town," she said. "San Diego. You know where that is?" Lincoln shook his head. "Well it's a hell of a lot warmer than here, that's for sure. Later on you can come live with us." Lincoln said nothing. "Later on" held no meaning for him. With her suitcase in one hand she stomped down the stairs without looking at Betty. Lincoln followed her to the door, and she ruffled his hair. Irma stepped out and the man fell in behind her, swinging the door shut meekly, in pathetic deference to Betty. His blue Electra spat to life, coughed once as it idled down at the intersection, and was gone. After that Lincoln was left in a home packed to the rafters with stories Betty would never tell and trouble she'd never share. The house was full but silent.

He takes another hesitant step forward. Simon can tell he wants to hide under the wing of Betty's arm, or in the cave of her skirt but is too old and doesn't want to do that in front of a stranger.

"Didn't know you had an uncle, huh?"

The boy shakes his head. His eyes rest on the scratched linoleum floor.

"Well I didn't know I had a nephew, neither," says Simon and he tries to laugh, hacking out a few quick sobs before turning back to his coffee.

"Ten years old. Eleven this May."

"Damn. Damn it." Simon shudders in his chair.

The boy speaks. "I know what you did."

Simon stiffens, his knuckles wrapped white around the coffee mug.

"Lincoln!" Betty half rises from her chair. "What's the matter with you?"

"I saw. I saw it. I know."

"You'd better get quiet."

The boy keeps looking at Simon.

"I saw what you did. I saw you touch him and he died."

"Goddamn it, Lincoln!"

Betty rises and slaps him across the cheek.

"Leave him alone," Simon whispers. "It's okay. Really."

He looks over and sees the boy's lower lip trembling. Lincoln is trying not to cry. The three of them look in opposite directions. Their gazes jut out from their gathered bodies like spokes on a wheel, turning slowly around the kitchen.

Betty sighs.

"You'd better get to school."

Lincoln bolts across the room, swoops up his jacket and slams out of the house.

Betty looks at Simon.

"I never told him," she says. "I never told him. I didn't."

Simon looks up at the sagging ceiling tiles and shrugs his shoulders.

"Can't help it if he finds out what everybody already knows."

Betty tries to keep her eyes steady, locked on her son. She has told herself she would look at him. At his forearms braided like old willow. His river-stone eyes. The bevel of his smooth jaw. She has told herself she would look at him. That she would give him neither her shredded love nor her hatred. That she would hold him with her eyes. Not with her hands, not with those, surely. But she can't, and instead watches *his* hands, the quiet hands of a murderer.

Instead of turning up Third Avenue and then over to Twenty-fourth, Lincoln looks at the blank front window over his shoulder and jumps the curb and runs down the alley. His feet slap the concrete, the shock running through his thin tennis shoes and into his thin body. He is already used to the cold. He snaps his head from side to side before shooting across Clinton and slows to a fast walk as he enters the church parking lot and skirts the edge of the church. The homeless men gathered earlier for breakfast have floated away to predestined spots in the city and the asphalt is rippled and empty. He reaches the chain-link fence and slows down, his heart beating wildly, his nose pressed against the rigid mesh. He finally sees what wasn't visible from the upstairs window: the deer twisted from impact into an unnatural sleep, the once smooth fur pink with road rash and blood, and studded with ribs.

Lincoln wants to scale the fence, furt through the weeds and trash, the layers of Crown Royal and Ripple bottles losing their labels to the wet like old skin. He wants to walk down the hill and touch the deer, too. To feel the last shreds of its body heat before it turns cold, then stiff, then is picked up by the highway department and thrown in the back of an orange truck. He wants to hold its head in his lap but it is too late, it is always too late. After living for ten years without knowing, for certain, who his mother is and how his father died, he wants to be present when something happens. He wants to claim the right to say, *This is what happened. See? This is how.*

He turns away, crosses the parking lot again and walks, miserable and cold, to school.

2

Betty and Simon sit in silence for a while longer, not sure, as the morning cracks open around them, what should happen next. As soon as Lincoln made his frantic exit they both thought, both hoped, that when the front door slammed, other, more secret doors would open between them. That without Lincoln present they would have no choice but to speak about him and so be forced into the past by talking about Lincoln's future. But they couldn't. Talk of smaller things, facts that fit into the palm of the hand, were equally unavailable. Mention of work, or no work, the weather, specific aches or injuries beginning to plague them both, were of no use, were too small, to plug the cracks through which loomed a terrible silence. They sat caught between a history entirely too large to admit and a present too small to mention, and were unable to call forth the in-between, could not strike a balance that would rock them into each other as woman and man, as mother and son.

"I'd best get on, Ma."

"You just got here," she says with a mixture of relief and anger. Silently furious because he doesn't ask for her help.

"I jut got out and I gotta find myself some digs."

"Got any ideas?"

"Some. I got some. Curtis Hotel, maybe. The parole officer gave me some names."

"You gonna come by again?"

"Yeah, Ma. I'll be by." Simon leans back and stretches his arms above his head.

"You got money? Least I could give you that."

"No no no," says Simon quickly. "No. Ain't nothin I need."

"Sure?" asks Betty, reaching toward the sugar jar.

"Really, Ma. It's okay," he says, almost pleading, as if accepting anything from her would break something inside him.

"Well," her motion across the kitchen arrested, "if you say so."

She crosses her arms and leans against the kitchen counter, her hands folded in her armpits for warmth.

"You still workin at the hospital?"

"If you call what I do work," she says.

"We both been doin the same thing for the last long while, huh?" he says with a rough chuckle.

"Seems so," she says, a chill clicking along her neck.

Simon notices and quickly adds, "But for different reasons."

"That's true, too." She glances at the grease-spattered stove clock. "But I got to get to work."

Simon starts to rise.

"You can set as long as you want," says Betty.

"Naw. I gotta get on."

"You sure?"

"Yeah, I'm sure."

They make their way to the front door with Simon shambling in the lead. They don't know if they should embrace or not so Betty takes a step back, crossing her arms again. Simon grabs the door

14

handle and opens the door. He half-turns and reaches out and touches Betty's elbow. "I'll be seein you," he says.

"You'd better," she replies, and they both laugh nervously. Simon steps out and closes the door behind him.

Simon is too chilled by the cold and by his memories to take the scattered blocks through Whittier to Uptown where he has a room at the Twenty-eighth Street YMCA. He stomps his feet on the rotten porch boards, turns left, and walks up Third Avenue toward the Curtis, the first place on a list of seven given to him by the parole officer.

A few people are on the sidewalks, stepping carefully, as if testing uncertain ice over a deep lake. They cluster at the bus stop or run with gloved hands held over their mouths from the grim doors of apartment buildings to salt-splattered cars idling at the curb.

Simon crosses Franklin keeping to the inside of the sidewalk, his hands thrust from view in his coat pockets while the buses and cars hiss through the slushy soup of snow on Third Avenue. He recognizes no one as he walks. No one looks at him. He searches them, their various faces, postures and strides. Most concentrate on the sidewalk or the curb with their chins welted down into their collars, their eyes purled against the cold. Simon looks for the familiar someone who can anchor him to the old lazy grid of the city, but distant enough not to know his crime or recognize the guilt he keeps knotted safely against his heart. But he finds no one in his neighborhood from the old days.

His hands find nothing in his pockets. Nothing he carries that can satisfy their aching grip, there is no loose change tumbling there in the linty nose of his pockets as the result of some humble or casual purchase. No lighter taken on purpose or by accident from the tabletop jumble of a raucous party. He has no keys to doors either past or present. His cold fingers do not close on an errant tube of lipstick held for a girlfriend whose new outfit harbors no pockets. None of the small things everyone on the street around him takes for granted. No torn movie ticket stubs or rubber bands from the morning paper. No grocery list scrawled on the back of a deposit slip or any other reminder of harmless domestic responsibility.

Simon passes the Third Avenue Market and a couple emerge with a brown paper bag of groceries that the woman carries in both arms like a baby. The man stalks ahead in the blue uniform of a delivery man, bus driver or mechanic. The woman is bundled against the cold so Simon can't see her form very well. She takes mincing steps on the ice. Her man wears the weariness of a night's work sliced into his forehead.

"Baby, wait up," calls the woman. "Wait."

The man marches ahead, daring the ice to make him slip.

"Wait honey. I'm sorry," says the woman.

The man stops abruptly and cocks his head to the side in exasperation.

"I don't wanna talk about it," he says and lifts his eyes to nod at someone across the street.

"Okay, okay," she says, resting the bag on her hip, "just wait up, okay?"

They move forward together and pass Simon. The man takes the bag from his girlfriend and Simon can hear him chuckle at something she says as they retreat into the distance.

Simon crosses 94 and the Curtis Hotel looms suddenly. The brown brick is slicked with grime and stained with rust from the oxidized window casings. Simon gauges the approaching structure. It never had a proper launching, and despite the grand plans its architect had envisioned, it was built the same way the city took shape—in ill-formed stages. Still, it used to be a good hotel. The limestone sills are worked into nice relief, but not over-worked. The flesh-colored corner stones contrast the brown brick to make the building look secure but not scary or fortress-like. As with all good hotels, the architects saved lavishments for the interior so guests felt included, pampered instead of awed.

Simon pushes open the brass-plated oak doors and enters the lobby. There is less light and he stands at the entrance until his eyes adjust. Despite recent renovations the lobby smells of mold and rotting newspapers. The air is glazed with cigarette smoke. The tan carpet is shreft of the class and elegance its pile suggests. It is spotted and worn, with what looks like dried vomit or blood ranging from the desk to the front door. A rubber mat has been laid over the carpet at the entrance to protect it from the snow and salt, but the slush slips over the edges to pool on the carpet like dried semen. Two men sit in quiet conversation on adjoining couches whose red velvet clashes with the tan carpet. The walls had originally been paneled in wood but successive decorators had painted them first red, then gray, and finally, in desperation, covered them with paisley wallpaper, like throwing a blanket over a corpse. The paper splays from the top of the wall in unreachable and hopelessly cobwebbed corners.

The lobby is united in neither theme nor color. The decorators, like poor parents, tried to pave over their mistakes with new approaches to discipline but gave in too soon so that their child bears all the scars and none of the good effects of their efforts. Simon looks over at the desk and realizes that a clerk has been standing perfectly still behind the counter all the while, his ill-fitting red vest blending too well with the wall behind him. He casually watches Simon.

Simon shifts, aligning himself to the clerk like a compass finding north, and ambles slowly over to the counter. He clears his throat and places his hands palms down on the aged wood but quickly withdraws them when he sees that his long nails sport crescents of gray-black dirt. The hotel clerk says nothing. Simon clears his throat again. The clerk blinks.

"Hi," mumbles Simon, "I'm here to see about some work."

"Here?" the clerk asks.

"Yeah, here. Umm, I was supposed to talk to the maintenance manager."

"Dougan."

"What?"

"His name's Dougan."

"Okay," offers Simon.

The clerk unclasps his hands from behind his back and folds his arms across his chest.

"Well," says Simon not knowing what else to say, "is he here?"

"Yes," says the clerk. "He's down in the boiler room. There's no phone down there."

"Oh," says Simon. A whoosh of cold air hits him as the front doors open and in the mirrors over the key rack he sees the hotel admit a bum who totters in on legs that look as if they have been broken and never properly set. Somewhere in a back room a phone is ringing.

"Can I go find him?" asks Simon.

"Sure, just take the service elevator down to the basement and follow the noise. You'll find him." He pauses and looks down at his feet as he uncrosses his arms and takes a confidential step forward. "My name's Eric."

"Eric."

"Yep."

"Okay. Thanks."

Simon walks down the narrow neck of the lobby, past the elevator doors to the scabbed steel service elevator and makes his way down. The doors open into the bright bustle of the laundry room where steam curls the paint from the ceiling. The machines hum, and the clicking of the steam presses is steady and numbing in the background. A gaggle of women stand around a long steel table drawing sheets from a castered canvas hamper. They throw them out over the table and fold them in pairs, then stack them in bins behind them. They talk over the noise in Spanish and laugh in the wetted air.

Simon approaches them and he has to shout to be heard. His words clash with the turbulent air. He says "Dougan" three times into the cocked ear of one of the folders but she doesn't understand, so he shouts "Boiler room" and she nods and smiles and points him toward a blackened doorway which leads to a set of chipped cement stairs lit with a single dusty bulb.

He takes the stairs and at the bottom hears a new, deeper set of sounds, Jurassically low, and follows them down a narrow hall into a cavern filled with archaic machinery. He descends the rusted metal stairs into the crevasses between the huge boilers, walks them like a maze, not even bothering to shout above the din. He finds Dougan soon enough, hunched in a corner on an overturned milk crate reading a tattered and smudged back issue of *Hustler.*

Simon stands before him but Dougan says nothing and instead continues to puzzle out the tangle of flesh in what can only be a lesbian scene, judging from the number of breasts dangling at angle.

"You lost, chief?" asks Dougan in a cigarette-scarred voice. Simon bristles but doesn't say anything.

"Just kiddin, dad. You must be Simon."

He closes the *Hustler* and slips it into the cage of the crate. He stands and swipes his cap from his head, freeing the fringe of red hair around his bald pate. His pustular nose is even with Simon's shoulders.

"How'd I know your name?" he answers Simon's unasked question. "Well, we don't get a hell of a lot of Indians down here."

He rocks back on his heels in obvious pride at his own acumen and hitches up his sagging pants with his thumbs.

"Besides, your parole officer called and warned me you'd be comin."

Simon nods and starts to speak but Dougan claps him on the shoulder and pushes past him.

"So," he bellows over his shoulder as Simon falls in behind him, "so, you're a murderer, huh?"

Simon stops.

"Well, at least you're not a thief." He stops and glares at the hotel above. "Nobody'd give a damn if you knocked off some of the scum stay up there. But stealin the towels'd piss off the management plenty."

He sets off again and climbs the metal stairs, Simon in bewildered and shameful pursuit. They pass the stairs to the laundry and Dougan turns the brass knob of a water-swollen door and kicks it open with his foot. It swings on blackened hinges into a cement room with a sink and plywood counter lit by a single bulb on a string. Nothing is in the room except a rust-colored mattress on a low steel frame, with the ticking molding like cattail down into the windless and dank air. Dougan turns sideways so Simon can view the interior and gestures expansively with his red-knuckled and callused right hand.

"As you can see," he says grandly, "we've been expecting you. It ain't much, but all you got to do is sweep down here and record the pressure gauges, the ones that work. Dress clean, take a shower once in a while. And, most important, only I get to drink on the job. Okay. Any questions?"

"Well—"

"Towels, sheets and pillows is upstairs. So's the shower."

"When do I start?"

"Now."

Dougan turns to go. Simon squeezes past him into his new room.

"By the way," asks Dougan, "who'd you kill?"

Simon looks at him blankly.

"My brother," he whispers.

Dougan nods thoughtfully and turns to leave. As he passes Simon he gently touches his elbow and makes his way down the dim hall.

3

Back at the house Betty shuts the door and casts around quickly to the spare living room, the doorway to the kitchen. Pale winter light leaks through the gray windows. It wasn't always like this. Life never seemed this long. So unbearably, so unshakably long and even and sad.

The house used to be a good home. The foundation was square, not pushed from level by the stubborn frost, jagged lines between the cinderblocks. The walls used to be smooth and flat. No cracks or watermarks showed. The studs were set evenly, sixteen inches on center, and the ceiling joists were adequate. Humble, but sweet. And it was hers. She made the payments, not HUD. She chose it, and for the first time choosing had meant more than simply opting for something over nothing.

People had come. They dropped by. There was no phone in 1961, when they moved to the city. No phone, but when Betty saw the other scattered families at the Lake Street Market or at the Wednesday service, no one ever warned her they would be coming over. No one said they would show up. Doing so would signify to the host that the guest—church friend, cousin, or bus driver—felt uncomfortable visiting, that they did not feel welcome at any time or in any condition.

They stopped by with hams or haunches of deer meat they brought back from up north, with children and smoke and gossip. They dropped by with stories of whose son had been arrested and who had narrowly escaped. They arrived with news of the next batch to come south packed tight, four kids, parents and clothes, in an old Fairlane that burned oil. Sometimes they dropped by and did just that: sat heavily in the metal chairs with loud sighs or hangovers or both, with nothing in their hands to offer except their aching heads. Betty fed them, coffeed them and in that home they felt better, had been cradled by the bickering of the kids and the rush of weak coffee, had been given straight mac and a little love, but not too much. Not so much love that it felt like pity. Sometimes when they came over—mirthful, distressed or lovelorn—they entered to find the household caught in the middle of some domestic distress: Betty pulling Irma and Caroline apart, fighting over their favorite book, or berating Lester and Simon for skipping school and stealing milk from the nicer porches in Kenwood.

These outrages were mild ones, were normal and strangely comforting because no matter what bad luck or situation had brought the visitors up the steps and through the door without knocking, the familial whirlwind they found was predictable and therefore safe. They nodded into the tussle and politely excused themselves to make coffee, content to let the trouble die down.

It changed, though. It changed and they stopped coming. Lester's death was a tragedy that affected them all. But after the terse funeral held in the living room, during the close of which the police brought Simon unshaven and weeping in leg irons, they began to leave their condolences under tinfoil on the porch and written in cards bought at Woolworth's and slipped through the mail slot. What Simon had done lost Betty two sons and her neighbors, and along with those losses the joy of what was once her home, her life. In its stead the house grew cold, it settled and groaned, and the walls cracked and colored.

Now, as the city spits Simon back into her life, Betty leans against the door and scans the house to see if anything has changed. As if crocuses will suddenly send their waxy fingers through the warped floorboards and bloom, as they do, early and violently in the otherwise gray and slow-coming spring; or honeysuckle dance through the heating vents, daffodils and tulips through the sink drain. But no. The living room which hasn't lived up to its name still doesn't. The drapes hang lifeless at the window margins as the morning spills over. Betty sighs and eases off the door, which after all, is not going to burst open with good news, or any news.

She shuffles back into the kitchen, unplugs the aluminum electric perc pot, takes a plastic bag from under the sink and shuts off the light. She places her shoes in the sack, puts on her coat and steps outside.

Betty turns left onto Third Avenue and the short slope brings her to Franklin. She turns right again and walks the level stretch to Chicago. It isn't a long walk to Northwestern Hospital, but today it takes her longer to cross that small space of the city that has been hers for twenty years. Once she starts walking she tunes out the trucks and commuter traffic. With the snow and ice completely covering the cement it could be any path or road, her feet any feet, her anguish that of any mother contemplating the murder of one son and the incarceration of the other. The tragedy has felt like hers alone. Lester is dead and Simon has his guilt and punishment to comfort him. *You have driven me this day away from the ground; and from your face I shall be hidden; and I shall be a fugitive and a wanderer on the earth, and whoever finds me will slay me.* But her? Hate is a pale substitute for Lester's shy smile and Simon's head-hanging. Death was not a choice for her. Irma and Caroline cowered and held each other in their sweaty sleep, and they needed her. No amount of explaining would be enough, nor was soothing with tender tears or hard love the antidote. So Betty had made her bed wide and shored it with discarded plywood and piled the blankets on. She fluffed the pillows and brought each girl in there with her, where they listened to the radio until they fell asleep. It was in that fraught rest that she was finally of use to them, was finally the mother they needed. She placed one arm around Irma's rigid body and coaxed her, as the night drew on, into a more relaxed slumber. When Caroline curled into a ball on the far edge, Betty held her so she wouldn't fall off. The bed was quiet, empty of the loudness and tumble of men. And who held her as she slept? The quiet house and silent girls made her long, just long for the man beds had been made for. She yearned for Jacob's chiseled back and tender thumbs that pressed her here. And here.

On their first night together he spoke with his hands. He had changed the shape of her flesh. Lovers can do that. Like snowshoe makers they can turn what is knotted and hard into the grace of a curve.

"*Iw ina giwaabandaan?*" he asked as he pressed her hip. Her dark, milk-smooth skin held the shallow shape of his thumb. Lover's talk.

Yes I do. There wasn't much light, for which she was thankful. Though even she, through her modesty and tight-eyed look, could see her flesh hold his touch.

"*Giwaabandaan ina iw? Endaso-giizhig igo ge-izhi-izhichigeyaan.*" Every day?

"*Gabe-giizhig,*" he said, and he pushed again and held her ribs, his fingers resting in their grooves as on the top of another pair of hands.

That is what beds are made for. Jacob had cut the ash and split it lengthwise and soaked it, split it finer and cut it to size. He took the lengths and in an old oil drum steamed the bed into shape with the legs curving up and joining, the headboard a shallow point like a temple dome. The rawhide lacing held it tight like a net in which they struggled with each other, not against. That's what a bed is made for.

His brothers had laughed as he spent the nights sanding the runners, though the young couple's skin would never touch the wood. They teased him as he laced the headboard. To them it looked too much like a net, and he, the most self-sufficient among them, afraid she would struggle free.

"Aaniin ge-izhichiged giwiiw? Giwii-ozhimig ina?"

"Gaa wiikaa," he said.

He came back from Normandy with no stories to tell, no scars to exhibit, nothing to say except *Ingii-ayaa iwidi.* That's all he said when pressed. He left silent and came back the same. He towered above his squat brothers when they gathered around him as he bent over the gaping hood of a steadily chugging engine. He was as silent among men as he was around his young wife, so at least she could tell herself it wasn't just her. Though he rarely spoke she learned to hear him through the rattle of her own girlish fear. A wonder: she was only sixteen.

When he came back from the war he moved out of his parents' thin frame house and built one out of logs. He cut Norway pine in the winter and peeled them so that by spring they were seasoned and straight. He dragged them by himself to the site on which he chose to build. The corners were dovetailed, the cracks chinked with wire and cement instead of clay and moss. The floor was planked with maple he had cut and had planed at the mill in exchange for labor. The cabin had a re-blackened cookstove he had rescued from the charred tumble of a burned-out hotel. A winter's worth of firewood leaned comfortably under a corrugated tin roof supported by peeled tamarack poles. By the end of the summer the cabin was finished. In early fall, when the lakeside poplar shook loose their gold, he walked the smooth path from the highway to Betty's house with a cardboard box of packaged deer meat in his muscular arms and a bank statement in his back pocket to show her parents. He'd saved everything he'd earned in his three years in the army.

Betty remembered him. When he took the freight train to Duluth in 1942 in order to sign up she was thirteen, five years younger than Jacob. She had seen him around and though he'd nodded hello, they were both too shy to say it. She was only thirteen and so she merely watched him. She admired the snakelike curve of his back as he caned the felt during moccasin games at the powwow, eyed his easy stance in the back of his mother's canoe as the village gathered at the lake on the opening day of ricing. She'd watched him disappear into the tan fuzz of the rice stalks with his mother until all that was left was the splunk of the pole, the click of her knocking and the scattered shouts and laughter of the other ricers.

When he came back from the war she was sixteen and looked at him differently. She'd stamped her feet like a horse and stared hard from under the screen of her lowered lashes. She watched him with hunger but could not, would not, give him more than a loaded, husky hello.

But there he was, with a home of his own and a box full of venison, walking up the path to her house. Her mother saw him first from where she was plucking ducks in the dusty yard. She brushed off her skirt, took the step and leaned in the open door.

"*Nashke na, indaanis. Indaga nibinaadin!*"

"*Aaniin dash igo? Mooshkine akik,*" Betty said, peering into the bucket. The water was full to the top, shuddering with each of her mother's impatient footsteps.

"*Ziigisen.*"

"*Aaniin?*"

"Bizaan igo!" her mother snapped. *"Mii geget igo bi-dagoshing waa-wiidigemad!"*

Betty blushed and took the pail and dumped the water in the slop bucket. As she hurried from the door she passed Jacob on the path. She didn't acknowledge him. She kept her eyes on the red hand pump down the trail.

Her father roused himself from where he was oiling his gun and cleared the table without having to be told.

When Betty came back with the water, Jacob was gone and her mother was lugging the box of meat into the makeshift icehouse next to the woodpile.

Two months later, after it had snowed twice and the lake was skimmed with ice and all the trees except for the red oak had shrugged loose their clothes, Jacob and Betty were married. There existed between them a similar nervousness; both were shy and overly gentle with each other, with that hesitant tension, that blend of tethered-dog quiver and dove-soft moan.

On their first night together, in their new house and inventive bed, Jacob poured out his words, each one a measured passion. With those bright promises coasting in the dark comfort of the cabin like finches, with the delicate punctuation of his thumbprints on her skin, she finally knew what a bed was made for. That bed, anyway, lashed down and ready to move.

After Lester died and the girls slept with her while Simon slept with his grief waiting trial, that was just a bed. Nothing special, nothing different. The frame was iron and the box spring and mattress like all the others across the city, torn and slanted, bought cheap at the Salvation Army. Without Jacob, lacking the various poses of her terrified daughters to hold it to the floor, to warm its winter-chilled reaches, Betty felt it yawn open, the kitchen shrink back and the living room floor cough uncomfortably when Simon walked in the door.

It is a relief to close that door and walk the anonymous sidewalk to the hospital lit savagely with fluorescent lights that brighten the clear linoleum and spotless steel of the kitchen. She sits down heavily to change out of her boots and begin again the long day's work.

Much of the kitchen machinery isn't functional anymore. The great Hobart mixer squats dusty and unused in the corner, the curved steel arms protecting a mixing bowl large enough to hold a bouquet of small children. Now, instead of baking at the premises, they contract for the starchy white bread and brown dinner rolls that no matter how sick or hungry the patients are, remain uneaten, steeped in the curdled gravy. Turkey and roast beef come wrapped in plastic and are considered safe only after they have been blasted by the steamer at four hundred degrees. The vegetables they used to uncrate and spend hours chopping by hand, over which Betty and the other cooks would chatter and gossip, arrive now in great plastic sacks, like body bags.

The peas are as hard as deer pellets, the carrots as bleached and tasteless as blocks of wood. Over the years the kitchen staff has been diminished from a squad of twelve to a patrol of two. Betty managed to stay, out of charity and design. As the arrival of packaged goods sent the staff packing, Betty said less and less until she became part of the process, just another machine that transfers the frozen food to warm places and the dry to the wet. Even at its best, the food the hospital provides makes no difference to the patients there. Perhaps it is fitting. The hospital sees no extravagant diseases or conditions. It does not merit food of that order.

The sick or hurt who sink slowly into the rough bedsheets or stumble through the door are afflicted with conditions either too late or too sudden to treat. The diabetic amputees are wheeled scowling from their beds to the row of dialysis machines as their extremities and organs begin to fail. The victims of gunshot, frostbite, or beatings are patched with even temper and professional attention instead of caring and concern. Their condition is, to the doctors, a challenge of form; satisfaction in the performance beats out the pleasure of helping. The tricky run of stitches becomes the object itself instead of the life that pulses underneath.

There are no lingering sicknesses in the hospital or neighborhood. No exotic diseases that draw specialists from conferences or shake families from their vacations to stand in the crowded rooms and dirty hallways. The doctors see no diseases that kill the patients but leave them their minds and tongues so they can give the family a blessing before they die, diseases that enable them to heal a quarrel or come clean with the whereabouts of an illegitimate child, or even to die peacefully, silently, with dignity.

Instead, people die exhausted. Everyone is tired—the patient, the tattered families, and the doctors who have long ago given up healing and instead focus on containment. No one dies whole. They move on missing limbs, or blood, or bone, or memory. They are hit by cars, sugar diabetes, fractures, evisceration and strokes. Since they die this way, die because they lack a part of themselves, they have nothing to bequeath to the living. No fortune or advice. No tender words or harsh regrets. Instead, the sick take from the living the remainder of their sympathy, energy and tenderness, all of which they use to make themselves whole as the sheets they incarnadine while they creep like thieves from the living.

It hasn't always been like this, surely. Betty ties on the apron and takes the bucket of prepared cookie dough from the freezer. She has only to dollop it on the baking paper with a number-two ice cream scoop and stick it in the oven.

She moved down from the north, minus a husband and a bed, plus four children. She'd arrived in a neighborhood that jumped. At the same moment the disease that struck the cities was given a name, urban blight, Eisenhower hatched a plan to bring Indians there. His idea for relocation, with color brochures and an official

name in capital letters, had sounded so worthwhile. Relocation. A
new place. A new location. They'd left in the summer and the six-
hour car ride brought them to the city, where for the first time
Betty had noticed and loved the color green. Maybe it was just the
season. But the trees exploded and the grass looked sweet enough
to drink. Against the brown and gray brick and cement, the buds on
the branches of elm and dogwood seemed greener than up north.
And the neighborhood was jumping. She tucked one girl under
each arm and made the boys hang onto her skirt as she stepped out
of the car on Lake Street. She thought she'd never seen so many Indians in one place before. They were all poor and struggling, but
they were making it.

She found the house and the schools, and with family looking
after the girls, she found a job. A real job. She was paid regularly.
Every two weeks. No more collecting stray dollar bills—some for
rice, more for pine cones, a little for syrup or berries. It was regular,
she thought with amazement, when she received her first check.
Her name was typed on the top. Her name spelled out with a dollar amount below it. For the first time her name was there, official,
for something she'd worked for, instead of on the rolls or allotment
list, which meant she was being done to. She wasn't the only one.
The Indians worked as bus drivers, as janitors, as clerks and waitresses. They brought home the bacon instead of killing it at the
yards or out behind the shed. They worked as carpenters and me-
chanics, plumber's assistants and high steel workers who made the
city, who urged it from the ground.

When Betty landed the job at the hospital she made the food.
She put the ingredients together and people ate her food in order
to get better, to heal. So, with a new house, a small but regular
check, and the ability to create, she could forget about her abandoned bed and its sweet shipwright for a while and start fresh. It
was hard but it was hers, she thinks, as she puts the cookies in the
oven. I made all of that.

4

From here to there is a space traveled alone, too far to walk but not so far as to beg for subways and trains, for the elephantine blunder of diesel buses that replaced the old streetcars. So the city sleeps and rises without the grumble of its workings to annoy or comfort those who need a bit of edge to their lives, just a little bit of sound or tremor to urge them, smiling or frowning, from their front steps into the tide of life that trickles past the neatly spaced elm and borders of tulips planted carefully at the margins of domestic sight. The absence of rushed spin that comes with most cities has turned Minneapolis into a city of secrets. A city where a dentist can meanderingly chip packed snow from his walk while his wife bakes cherry coffee torte in the morning, and in the afternoons the dentist fucks his drooling, anesthetized patients. A city of secrets. When a particular patient had a higher tolerance for nitrous than most and the plainclothes police led the dentist to a brown Caprice with his moleskin trench draped like a mantle over his failed shoulders: when this happened, the anonymous neighbors (who came into focus only when Halloween unfurled the larval appetites of their sticky children, the PTA came looking for cake-walk donors, or the cat needed to be fed during the July trip to the lake) shook their heads as they watched the news, and said over tuna casserole or spaghetti, *Well sometimes you just don't know, you know.* That's what they said until it was their turn, and they accepted their own crimes with Lutheran fortitude; aware that they had done wrong, but strong enough to admit it in front of God and jury, although they broke down in front of the chiseled stares of in-laws and social workers. Until then they just shook their heads slowly and looked sidelong at wife or husband, or at the children who slept in their moist beds dreaming of their own crimes, looked sidelong but short and kept reading the paper or picking at the remains of meat loaf and pineapple upside-down cake and hoped, prayed that what they'd done would stay locked behind the gates of service berry and juniper, that no matter how well they prepared for winter always emerged slightly smaller and frost-seared around the edges come spring.

Yes. A city of secrets. Suburban crimes are hushed into backyard whispers and reported earnestly on the evening news where the newscasters stand on street corners for live broadcasts. Afterward the viewers go to bed and listen to the house groan under the pressure of winter. Their own thoughts move from what is happening outside their houses and take the carpeted tread of the stairs and pass the almost-closed doors to the children's rooms. The family was spared this time and the moans of the children crying out in their sleep surely aren't so serious as to make mother or father rise to crack the door and check, just to be sure, to crack the door and see if the children are okay. The parents, surrounded by the groans of the house and the moans of the children, let themselves wonder instead about the house. They fret about the pipes being strangled by tree roots and worry themselves about the wooden soffits that should be torn out in early spring and replaced with aluminum so the yellow jackets and paper wasps won't breed in the arms of the house, to descend and light on the lilac, stinging the children into screams and raised flesh soothed only by careful parental shushing and dabs of baking soda. Surely the parents can fix that, can do that, because the nighttime moans of their children tell them nothing. The sweaty toss of sleeping children sometimes grows so loud that it shakes the parents from their beds. They tiptoe into the sanctuary of the children's rooms to sit lightly on the edge of the bed and speak at the coiled child and say it's all right, it's nothing, nothing really, just a bad dream. The parents wonder if this is a lie, although they aren't speaking to the children but to themselves. It is better to control the bees and spiders, the carpenter ants eating away at the floor joists, because as parents they can fight those, can see the battle being fought.

The morning after, the usual domestic babble is smoothed over the lingering domestic terror of the night. They ease out the door and into their cars and back out cautiously although the other motorists stop and cheerfully wave them into the wake of traffic and they coast downhill into the city from the vantages of Lowry, Diamond Lake, and Saint Louis Park. They roll around the lakes and along the straight shot of Lake Street or Franklin. The family disbands in different directions into the thrill of their daily lives: to jobs, grade schools, and hockey rinks. There are always errands to run after work, to the hardware store to price siding or to buy another rattling package of D-Con for the mice that winter in the walls, nesting in the newspaper left there as insulation by the first owners who didn't have enough money to buy rock wool. It is of these things they think as they near the rutted apartments of South Minneapolis, not of the people who live in the faded glory of the Windsor, in the redbrick town houses on Portland, rat-holed, and broken-into cells where children sleep on the floor. If they do look up from the thin space between the steering wheel and the visor, they don't notice much but once in a while the Pillsbury Mansion strikes them as strange, misplaced, out of step with the rest of the neighborhood, set there by a strong force of nature.

It is only this kind of thing the drivers notice; the building seems alien in its surroundings. They note this instead of the people whom they pass, folded tightly into their clothes during their brutal wait at the bus stop. The drivers pass these people and then turn onto Third Avenue or Eleventh Street, over I-94 into the wide tunnels of steel and downtown offices that sweep them up over the city. Their own houses wait empty to greet them and their failures at the end of the day. Ready to begin again the terror muffled by the lawn and the hedge, planted this time with ornamental cedar so winter cannot lower its skirt to show what is really going on, quietly, in these houses.

5

Lincoln tells himself stories. They aren't wild, or especially good. He tells himself stories because he has to. It started with the Gale Mansion; if the small house Lincoln grew up in could have as many worries as it did, then the huge stone house was bound to have more. By the time Irma left, he had stories for most of the buildings on his route to Andersen Elementary School. In the Gale Mansion he has placed a starched white woman who is so old and so mean she could be part ghost. No one really knows. What is certain is that small children regularly disappear forever along that stretch of Stevens Avenue.

On the corner of Twenty-second Street and First Avenue, in an old Victorian that now houses an accounting firm, Lincoln has created a mortician who solemnly and wordlessly prepares the dead. In the three years since Caroline's death, the spell of that redbrick house with the carved white gables has grown so strong that he can no longer remember her real funeral. Caroline died on the reservation. "At least she was convenient," said Betty miserably. "May have raised my kids in the city, but they gonna be buried up next to the lake." Lincoln's mortician interfered. When he recalls Caroline he thinks of rows of mourners in black suits and a viewing room draped in black crepe and lit by candles.

When Caroline died, Betty and Lincoln took the bus up north. Irma was already there, but hadn't been in the car when the Burlington Northern freight train folded it in half. It was the only time he'd ever gone to the reservation. They left the city on the freeway. After every stop, every turn, the roads got narrower, the bus stops shabbier, the houses set along the road smaller. What took six hours by car stretched into nine on the bus. Betty sat with a straight back, her hands clasped tightly around her sequined black purse. Her wedding purse, she called it. "I got this my wedding day. This and a whole lot more," Betty told Lincoln as they packed one small suitcase with both their belongings. She shook her head. "Didn't have a clue it'd turn out like this. No idea at all." The black purse covered in glittering black sequins was to accompany them to the funeral but they had no proper mourning duds, as she called them. Instead, she put on her darkest skirt, forced Lincoln into the shower, dressed him in the cleanest jeans in his dresser and bought him an almost-black work shirt on Nicollet on their way to the station. They'd entered the store before she realized it was a uniform store for nurses and deliverymen.

"Can I help you?" the clerk asked doubtfully. She stood behind a rack of Carhart overalls and looked reluctant to come out.

"I need the smallest black shirt you got," said Betty, all business.

The clerk stepped from behind the rack and pursed her pale lips. "You look like a twelve," she mused, tucking a patch of greasy bangs behind her ear.

"It ain't for me," snapped Betty, "it's for him," she said, and pointed at Lincoln, who stood absently fingering a pile of sun-bleached socks that sat in a dusty plastic bin.

The clerk eyed Lincoln and turned back to Betty. The disdain in her eyes familiar, the surprise at seeing two Indians in the city quite new. Not today, thought Betty. God, just not today.

"Man's small still gonna be too big. Cuffs are gonna be draggin on the ground."

"Man. Woman. He's only seven, who cares which one is which. We're goin to a funeral, not a pageant."

"It'll look funny if he wears a woman's shirt," said the clerk.

"I don't care how it looks so long as it's black and it don't fall off his shoulders."

The girl walked over to a rack of button-downs. She looked through them casually before she spun around to face Betty.

"See here, lady. This is the problem. All our women work clothes is white. You know, for nurses and such. Does it have to be black?"

"Yes," said Betty wearily. "Just give me the smallest man's shirt you got."

"It'll be too big," objected the girl.

"Don't care. We'll worry about that."

The clerk threw up her hands in defeat and walked to the back of the store. She was gone a few minutes before she returned with a shirt wrapped in plastic. She took off the wrapper and unfurled the shirt with a flourish.

"This here's the best we got."

"That there's brown."

"It's the darkest we got," explained the clerk. "Most companies don't want their employees wearing black. Too somber."

"Somber, huh?"

"Yep. And, if you look here, you'll see it's got a logo on it. Can't take it off. It's embroidered right on there."

Betty looked closer and saw UPS sewn in yellow thread on the left breast. She shook her head.

"We'll take it."

"Sure?"

"Yes I am."

The girl scribbled out a receipt.

"That'll be two dollars and thirty-five cents."

Betty handed her three dollar bills. "Lincoln," she said, "go put this on."

The clerk looked up with wide eyes.

"He gonna wear that now? All that packing starch'll drive him crazy."

Betty said nothing. Lincoln took the shirt and stood behind the Carharts and buttoned it up. When he stepped out he was trying to manage the cuffs that drooped over the ends of his fingers. Betty stooped and rolled them up and tucked the tails into his pants.

"Let's go," she said, taking him by the arm. The clerk said nothing and they hurried out into the warm June air to catch the bus.

Lincoln was miserable the whole ride. The polyester fabric bunched and gathered in his armpits. His neck was red and raw. He looked with envy at Betty in her worn clothes and sleek black purse.

Finally they pulled into the depot on the reservation, nothing more than an extra room tacked on to the gas station, filled with plastic chairs with RESERVATION BINGO lettered on the backs, and old issues of *Scientific American* and *National Geographic* on the vinyl-topped side tables. An old Buick sat in the gravel parking lot, and when Betty and Lincoln stepped off the bus two men got out of the car and stood waiting for Betty to notice them.

"These here your cousins," Betty told Lincoln, "Ned and Boo. Say hi."

"Hello," said Lincoln, suddenly shy, sweating in the UPS shirt.

Boo leaned down. "You must be the deliveryman."

"Huh?" Lincoln was now hot, shy and confused.

"Says so right there," he said, tapping Lincoln's chest. "UPS. So you must be the deliveryman. What'd you bring us other than your old grandma?"

"Leave him alone," said Betty. "Let's get to the church."

"Okay," he said. He turned to Lincoln, "But from now I'll just be callin you Delivery."

Once they were inside Betty patted Lincoln on the knee and leaned over.

"Don't let him bother you. Reason they call him Boo is he's as white as a ghost. Sometimes he acts that way too."

Boo laughed. "That's right, Delivery. That's for damn sure. Up here we got mixed-blood Indians and purebred dogs. In Canada they got mutt dogs and purebred Indians."

Betty laughed and Lincoln found himself giggling and secretly amazed. He has never seen her act so loose and easy.

Try as he might, he cannot remember the funeral. Perhaps it is because they did not let him see the body during the wake or at the church, where they'd closed the casket for good. When he tries to see it, to form it in his mind, he sees the mortician's house. Memories of Caroline are fading fast. If he tries hard he can see her curling her bangs in the messy bathroom before a date. Other memories are harder and harder to come by. The touch of her hand. The sound of her voice when she argued with Betty, or told him stories when she came home drunk. He barely remembers how she'd crack his door open and stick her head inside his room.

"Hey, little guy. Hey, you awake?" she whispered. She tried not to trip on his toys as she plopped down on the bed. She felt warm, her breath sticky and sweet. She stretched out next to Lincoln and groaned.

"Good God, I'm drunk off my ass."

Lincoln curled into her and put his arm across her stomach. *Tell me a story.*

"Jesus. I'm too drunk to tell you anything, except never, never get this drunk."

"Tell me something," he murmured. "Tell me how I got my name."

"Good God, again? I don't really know. Truth is, your daddy's dead and your mamma run off. Them's the facts. There you were, though, right in the middle of all of it. So we named you Lincoln. Cause Lincoln, Nebraska, is smack dab in the middle of the whole damn country."

He tries to retrieve more, but can't. He is invaded by his present and his fictions. Stories of his own origins never work. He is unable to create a father out of nothing. He does not appear as a janitor in the apartment building across the street or as a rich man in Kenwood. He knows there is a real story dormant within Betty, so no fiction will do. Any mother he fashions always ends up looking and acting like his aunts. They are still talked about as the most beautiful Indian girls in South Minneapolis, even though one is dead and the other so distant and hateful, she might as well be. Instead of making unsatisfactory stories out of his life, he pins them on other people and on the decrepit houses that line his walk from school. Not that they help. He knows his father must have walked the same walk, must have seen the same houses, but they don't hold anything of him. He knows his father went to Greeley Elementary, which stood on the site of Lincoln's own school. But it was knocked down the year before Lincoln started the first grade, and so he was unable to plumb it for clues, or even to be able to take comfort in knowing his father had been there.

He hurries by the Institute of the Arts deep in thought. The morning was something to puzzle out. He nears the house and looks to see if the lights are on. They're not and he is relieved that he has some time before Betty comes home from the hospital. He will have time to look for a clue about Simon, for some trace, the way high clouds prefigure a storm. He knows he won't find anything. Theirs is a house with no pictures. No photo albums spill off the coffee table, laden with blurry and bleaching pictures taken at picnics or graduations. They have no lopsided snapshots from parties where people hold aloft beer bottles like trophies. There are no wedding pictures pressed into scrapbooks. There are no plaques from the speech team or old football banners. The mantel above the disused fireplace sports no tobacco tins filled with movie stubs or playbills. They have no yearbooks collecting dust on the single bookcase in the kitchen with gaudy portraits of graduates over-dressed in ill-fitting clothes borrowed from older siblings or parents. There is nothing to prove that Lincoln had a father who'd once been a boy like him. There are no copybooks or report cards tucked into shoe boxes with canceled checks. Surely nothing to show he has an uncle. Irma once said that the closest thing they had to a family album was the face book at the police station.

He bangs his shoes on the first wooden porch step and hears his name shouted out across the street. He turns and sees One-Two waving from the south door of the Windsor. He is waving Lincoln over.

Lincoln turns and crosses Third Avenue while One-Two takes a final drag on his cigarette. He is the biggest Indian, the biggest person Lincoln has ever known. He is six feet two and three hundred pounds. He fills the doorway to the old Windsor Hotel. *They call me One-Two cause that's all it took when I was bar fightin,* he'd said. *But I don't do that no more on account of my bad back.*

"Well now, Delivery. You look like you're guilty of somethin. Might as well work off the guilt. I need a hand downstairs."

Lincoln nods and follows One-Two down the steps into the basement. One-Two and his shadow eat up all the light ahead of Lincoln. He looks like a huge mole squeezing his bulk along the narrow hallway.

"Got to fix some ducts. Insulation's been ripped off," he explains. They stop and he points up at the pipes by his head.

"See? I need you to hold this here trouble light."

There is ample light for the work but Lincoln holds it anyway and directs the beam toward One-Two's huge hands as they nimbly wrap insulation around the pipe. He holds it with one hand and secures it with a piece of duct tape.

"Did you know I got an uncle?" ventures Lincoln.

One-Two doesn't look at him.

"Yep. Used to work with him before I took that fall. Worked high steel with him. Went from workin at the top to workin at the bottom."

Lincoln can't help asking more.

"What'd you do?"

"Built skyscrapers. Me and Simon did the IDS Tower downtown. Indians built all a them. But I took a three-story dive off the IDS and busted up my back."

"Did my uncle ever fall?" The words "my uncle" are strange and exciting on his tongue.

Oh, he fell, fell about as far as a man can, One-Two thinks.

"Him? Naw. He was too good to fall. He never fell off no building, that's for sure."

"You know my dad?"

This time One-Two looks down at Lincoln. He can tell he is on uncertain ice.

"They must call you Delivery cause you serve up too many damn questions."

Lincoln blushes and hangs his head.

Softer now. "I knew him, too. But I don't remember all that much. He wasn't but eighteen when he died."

He finishes taping and takes the light from Lincoln and clicks it off. His face is cast in darkness and Lincoln feels him looking straight down at him.

"You remember this, Delivery. You remember that your uncle's the one who stood over me and wouldn't let them move me till the ambulance got there. He comes around again and you remember that. He saved my legs, you hear?"

His voice comes out ferocious, echoing down the basement hallway.

"Well," he says lightly, "your grandma's probably wonderin where in the hell you are. Go on now and tell her 'hi' from me."

Lincoln turns and walks back up the hallway. One-Two watches him and shakes his head. Ain't no stoppin it now, he thinks. It's out and rolling.

6

In 1958 there were no more furs left, and no one was buying the few stray beaver that remained tucked into boggy ponds away from trappers on snowmobiles or the poorer ones breaking temporary roads under the rawhide web of their snowshoes. The fisher and marten were long gone and since muskrat and weasel only gave twenty-five cents each, they were ignored and left to rut in the broken slashings and rice beds.

Simon and his father took the minimal logging roads along the river and cut pulp off their family allotment ignored by the white land-grabbers because the surrounding lowlands were impassable in the summer months. They left the cabin at dawn. Betty was just waking to feed Irma, newborn in the cradle of winter. Caroline and Lester barely woke for anything, not until Betty shooed them outside to collect kindling. Simon and Jacob left the waking house with the saw rolled tight and tied together with string and their lunch in a tin pail that banged against Simon's leg no matter how he held it as he tried to stay on the hard pack left by his father's snowshoes.

They cut off the logging trail and headed toward the river. The land descended and under the snow the short brush gave way to frozen clumps of grass that tilted their snowshoes off level and so, slipping and cursing, they made their way over the winter-stilled swamps.

Jacob's shoulders swayed under the greasy plaid of his wool jack coat. His bare hands seemed impervious to the cold. They were squares of muscle that could clear a bar of drunks and pull off a frozen deer hide without a knife to separate the neck skin, that could lift two full rice sacks, one hundred pounds each, and set them on the scale gently.

They weren't across the swamp when Simon's legs began to burn and his calves knotted as he tried to keep his snowshoes from landing on top of each other. They were almost across when the nose of one of his snowshoes caught a branch and he pitched head-first off the trail into the three-foot-deep snow.

Their meager lunch wrapped in flour sacking sailed out of the bucket and disappeared in the drifts, leaving only craters on the surface. Jacob stopped and looked over his shoulder as Simon flailed in the snow.

"*Miikaan gimiijiminaan,*" he said.

He continued and Simon looked after him as he made that human road on top of the snow that the next day or the day after would be pocked with the tracks of deer trying to use it but failing. Only fox, light under the flame of their fur, could coast on it, leaving the faint impression of their feet like rose petals.

Simon removed his snowshoes and stuck them tail-first in the snow. He wiped at the powder above their buried lunch parcels with his bare hands until he found them, like frozen jewels, and set each on the packed trail. Once he had found them all, he placed them back in the pail and rolled onto the snow pack, careful not to bring his full weight to bear on any one point. He set the shoes side by side on the crust and stepped onto them and with a numb finger stretched the rubber tubing around his ankles. Brushing the snow from his clothes, he lifted the bucket and moved forward, sweating under the rough wool of his coat.

His father's trail snaked past the bouquets of dead diamond willow and elm, a level plane stamped on the surface of the snow crosshatched like beaver tails. Ahead he saw the churned-up snow where Jacob had stamped the crowns of hazel brush flat as he left the swamp and made to higher ground.

Simon heard his father cough, and as he rounded the skirt of the hill saw his father springing loose the coiled metal blade and testing the teeth with his wide callused thumb. Once he was satisfied that it was sharp enough, he took an oil-soaked rag from his pocket and oiled the blade so it wouldn't catch and bite as the resin in the trees heated up. Simon trudged to his father's side, sighed, and set the bucket carefully on a stump upwind of the section they would be cutting. Without stopping Jacob glanced down at him, a play of a smile on his kissing-thick lips.

"Good job," he said.

Once the saw was ready, Jacob and Simon tramped a circuit around the first twenty trees they would cut, unstrapped their snowshoes and stuck them like crosses in the snow. Jacob gauged the wind again, circled until he stopped in the right place and, with Simon hanging on the other end of the saw, shunted it back and forth loosely. The chalky outer layers crumbled away to reveal the green inner bark. Jacob stopped and checked to see if the cut was at the correct angle, nodded to himself and they began to saw in earnest.

Simon planted his feet as far apart as he could so that his father's long strokes wouldn't pull him off balance. He struggled to keep the blade straight on the back stroke, and on the fore he pushed down with all his weight so the teeth would dig, and his father wouldn't glare at him and rush the saw back to his side. Simon was glad they were just cutting pulp, not pine or hardwood for rich vacationers' fireplaces.

Once the saw passed through the first half and the teeth bit the core, they slowed down. The sawdust freckled the snow, then grew into short piles. Simon felt his father easing off the blade as the tree began to sway and they jumped the saw out before the tree pinched it as it fell. Simon glanced up and the tree wavered, paused, was nudged by the wind and began to arc toward the earth. Gravity was balked by the trees. They seemed to float down until four feet from the ground, when the branches doubled and snapped and were driven in like stakes.

Jacob grabbed the ax and straddled the trunk facing the stump, and with speed he began to limb the poplar. Simon took the saw and by the time he stood at the next tree his father was finished and swiped the wool cap from his head.

"*Bezhig*," he said, as he looked out at the endless forest.

They moved to the next tree, angled the saw and took the guide cut. Jacob swore and spat in the snow as the bark peeled off to expose punk wood and inner bark the color of tobacco. He set his end of the saw down and scored the bark with the ax so they would remember the rotten tree. As they worked, the light grew stronger and the washed-out winter sky hung threaded through the skeletonized canopy. There were no birds, not even when they broke for lunch. The usual whiskey jacks that barked from the middle reaches of the trees and swooped down for the frozen bread were absent. The chickadees and grosbeaks that courted the shriveled pin cherries at the river's edge and in the swamp bottoms were gone too. There was only the rustle of their clothes stiffening in the cold, the slide of their fingers over the parcels that held the old bread and chunks of salted venison.

When they had finished they shoved their hands back inside their stiff threadbare mittens and continued cutting. Already there was a swath leading away from the swamp that would eventually double back. After they were done cutting they would size them in eight foot bolts, stack them, and in early spring would peel and drag them one by one to the edge of the logging road, where the skidder would load them and cart them to the pulp mill.

The saw had begun to dull and Simon was relieved at the pause while his father slid the rasp from his belt and began to put a new edge on the worn teeth.

"Well. What you doing standing there? Why don't you crown some of those downers before we get going again?"

Simon almost groaned as he grabbed the ax and trudged sullenly to the nearest prostrate tree and paced out sixteen feet, allowing for two eight-foot bolts, and began chiseling into the tapered end of the tree. He cut at thirty degrees one way and then the other, and when he was deep enough finished it off by lifting the ax straight over his head and driving it into the wedged cut in the trunk. He crowned three before Jacob whistled him back. He swung his arms as he kicked his way through the trampled snow to ease the steady burn lodged in his forearms and between his shoulder blades.

Since the saw was sharp Jacob walked over to an especially thick tree and they started with the usual cut. Jacob bit his lip and Simon grimaced as they worked the cut deeper and deeper. At one point the saw jerked through Simon's numbed fingers and Jacob stumbled back without Simon's weight on the other end. Simon lunged for the handle and once he had it they kept cutting until they were through, both of them huffing in the frozen air. They pulled the blade free and began a level cut that would intersect the angle. They worked it through and when they were done Jacob leaned the saw against a set of hazel brush that bowed under the saw's weight. Then he lifted the ax and knocked out the triangular block of wood from the base of the tree with the butt end.

They both looked up, waiting for the tree to fall, but it just swayed there, reluctant to move. Jacob shook his head, looked down at the cut and then craned his neck to look up again.

"Must not be cut deep enough," he said to himself. They lifted the saw again and started cutting from the other side.

After five passes of the saw they popped through, roughing the stringy fibers on the outside, then pulled the saw clear again and stood back and watched the tree for motion. It hung without tilting one way or the other and then its weight caused it to slide off the cut toward the space where they'd knocked out the wedge. The butt of the tree slammed down and Simon and Jacob felt the ground shudder. Still the tree didn't fall. Instead, the mass of branches on one side caused it to rotate slightly, and its whole motion, the drop and turn, looked like a slow arboreal curtsy. After that it began to fall.

They both saw at once that it was going in the wrong direction because of the twist, or maybe a lick of wind wound its way through the bare branches above their heads. They gauged its fall and stepped away from it to watch as it gathered speed. The outer branches caught in those of the trees surrounding its upwind side and it spun away from them. With a scrunching slide the forked upper branches caught in the rough-barked limbs of a jack pine and the tree groaned and popped and hung there twenty feet above the ground. The sounds died down again and Jacob and Simon stood motionless, steaming into the chill, as a slight wind began and the uncut trees swayed and scraped one another, singing out where they grew too close together.

Jacob leaned the saw against one of the trees and set the ax next to it with the head up so it wouldn't rust in the snow and pulled off his gloves to reach into the hip pocket of his wool pants for his tobacco pouch and starchy five-cent rolling papers. Simon shuffled over to him and sat on the stump. Jacob didn't look at his hands while he rolled the cigarette between the cups of his palms, straightening and flattening it with his thumbs, strong and shallow like small boats. He didn't look at the result of his work when he tucked the cigarette in the corner of his mouth and rummaged again in the welted wool for a match.

Instead, he kept looking at the deadly embrace of the trees, the angles and lines of force, and tried to conjure the proper attack which would send the poplar groundward and keep the two of them out of danger.

He puffed and Simon sat patiently picking out kernels of snow from the folds of his pants, secured by the cold like burrs in a dog's coat. Jacob held his gloves in one hand, the cigarette smoking yellowly in the other, while he paced around the tangled trees. Simon stayed seated.

The wind knackled the upper branches together, and Simon and Jacob heard the clickering of red squirrels who imagined the falling branches into formless predators. They blustered and chattered from short perches at a danger they could not see. Jacob continued pacing and reached out with his gloved hand to touch the gnarled trunk of the jack pine, as if he could feel through the cold-brittle bark, into the waved grain, as if in there, there was an answer to which way it would fall when he tried to free it.

Simon sat and watched, his fingers cramping from the cold, his booted heels knocking together absently. The cigarette burned down and Jacob juggled it so his mittens wouldn't burn, puffing on it twice before dropping it in the snow. He beat his muscled arms against his sides and walked back to Simon and the tools. Simon stood but Jacob sat him down again with a wave of his wide palm as he bent to grab the ax.

"You stay here," he said.

He walked back to the base of the jack pine and cast a glance skyward at the widow-maker. He stood next to the trunk and scooped as much loose snow away from the base as he could, then he scalped the bark from the chosen side with the ax so the angle and depth of the cut would be more visible. He looked up once more and then down again before he raised the ax, turned sideways and then spun at the top of the back swing. Simon watched his father's top hand slide up on the handle and pop back down as the blade thudded into the trunk.

The tree shuddered and in an instant the poplar slid free and screeched toward the ground. Jacob had raised the ax for the second stroke and as he heard the branches popping overhead he raised his head. He dropped the ax, spun around and started to run. His feet slipped and he fell facedown in the snow just before the poplar landed on him. The snow whooshed out from the impact, then all was still.

Simon jumped and tried to run but floundered and went down. He rose, pumped his knees to his chest and fought his way there.

Jacob didn't move as Simon dropped to his knees and scooped the snow away from the buried shape of his father's head. He trenched through the snow and cleared it from the corded neck muscles. It steamed off his father's skin as Simon whispered over and over, *Dad Dad Dad Dad Dad,* but there was no movement. Simon lay flat to reach under his father's head and swept the snow away but he couldn't hold it up. Simon put his hand on his father's forehead and swept the snow some more and kept saying *dad dad.* Jacob said nothing back and Simon pinched the snow from his eyes and nose and mouth. Still Jacob didn't move. Blood bubbled like soap from between his lips and leached into the snow.

Simon was frantic. He scooped the snow away from Jacob's body. Then he saw what the tree had done. The branches had snapped against Jacob's body and two of them had broken and pushed through. One had been driven through his left shoulder blade and the other by his right kidney.

Simon scuttled back to his father's head and looked at the blood trickling slowly from his mouth. One eye popped out of the socket and hung on his father's cooling cheek. Simon said it again—

dad dad dad—but it was all over. Simon stood and the woods took on a comforting indifference. Simon strapped his snowshoes on and began the walk back to town where he sat numb and unblinking next to the crackling barrel stove. He told Betty, and explained it again to his uncles who gathered there to hear it. Afterward they patted him on the shoulder and went out with a tarp and rope to bind and drag the crushed body of Simon's father back to town, trussed like an oversized package from the butcher shop off the reservation.

7

One-Two showers and squeezes himself into a clean pair of jeans and a flannel shirt. He runs his hand through his brush-cut hair, a style he hasn't been able to abandon since the fifties, and pulls on his Dan Post cowboy boots. He takes the bread from the oven, bangs it out on the makeshift counter in his basement room and smokes a cigarette while it cools. Carefully now, he wraps it in tinfoil and without gloves or coat he takes the steps and crosses the slick road with the heels of his boots spinning on chunks of ice until he stands on Betty's porch.

The air is cold on his still-wet skin but the bread is warm, like the blanketed form of a small animal held softly between his fleshy fingers. Betty opens the door.

"Hmmmm."

"Got some bread for you Betty."

"Get outta the cold."

One-Two ducks his head from habit and walks in. He clicks his boots together to dislodge the snow.

"Got some bread here."

"You said that," says Betty, taking the offered loaf.

"Fresh."

"Yeah, you always was."

"Come on, Betty. Play nice."

She laughs. "You hungry? Got some mac on the stove."

"Got enough?"

"Not for an Indian your size. But I can spare some."

"That'd be nice, then. Real nice. Should I take off these here boots?"

"Leave them on. Leave them on. Christ, don't know why all you men want to go around lookin like cowboys. You take them off you might have an identity crisis."

One-Two shakes his head as he follows Betty into the kitchen. The floor shudders with each step. Lincoln sits at the small table copying out his homework in the pinched cursive he is learning in the fourth grade.

"Long time no see, Delivery." One-Two eases into one of the chairs, which groans under his weight. Lincoln looks up and smiles.

"Howdy, One-Two."

Betty ladles the macaroni into a bowl and sets it in front of One-Two. He waits while she cuts the heel off the loaf he brought over.

"Heel okay?"

"So used to gettin the heel of the boot, don't even know what the middle'd feel like no more. Heel's fine. Just fine."

He takes it delicately and sops it in the broth. Lincoln keeps working on his side of the table but glances up at One-Two, who eats hungrily, but politely. He cradles the spoon in one hand and a piece of bread in the other and despite his size he doesn't crowd out either Lincoln or Betty. Two visitors in one day is too much. The first he didn't know existed and the second he's known all his life. Lincoln can't remember not knowing One-Two, he's always hovered on the periphery of Lincoln's world. He walks a path around the small life Lincoln and Betty have carved into the thin frame house on the corner of Third and Franklin. When the front walk ices up, One-Two comes over and chips it away. He climbs the ladder to fix and clean the sagging gutters, and shovels a pass through the mounded snow at the curb so Betty doesn't slip or fall.

One-Two's body is flush, not fat, and Lincoln sneaks looks at the smooth face skin the color of walnut, the jet-black crew cut. Strong but easy.

"We're movin," says Betty suddenly.

Both Lincoln and One-Two look up quickly, surprise etched on One-Two's face, mistrust on Lincoln's. Lincoln doesn't say anything. One-Two loads his spoon with mac.

"Cause of Simon?"

"Not no one, not even him gonna shake me outta here. Not that. Got a notice today they gonna rip her down."

"This old house? Why?"

"Make way for a gas station or some such."

One-Two chews his food thoughtfully and plays with the noodles that stick out above water level with his spoon and pushes them back down into the broth.

"When? They say?"

"Six months. A year. They ain't sure yet."

"Where you gonna go?"

"Ain't sure about that either."

One-Two sighs and pushes the empty bowl away. He chuckles to himself and takes out a package of Tops from his shirt pocket.

"Seems like they're always rippin them down. Back when I worked steel, it made me happy to see it. It just meant they'd put up a new one and I'd never be outta work."

He rolls the cigarette tight and lights it.

"Remember when you got here? They was rippin them down then, too."

"Couldn't forget that. No way."

Lincoln looks up.

"Couldn't forget what? Why didn't you tell me we're moving?"

"Don't get mopey on me. I'm supposed to ask you?" She laughs. "You go where I go."

"Come on, Betty. He can't help wantin to know."

"You stay outta this, One-Two. Out. I raised four of them and then this one's white mama come dump him on me, so I gotta do it again. Again, hear? As if the first ones weren't trouble enough."

"I was just sayin—"

"Well it don't concern you."

One-Two tips the ash carefully into the ashtray and blows out the smoke. He looks at her steadily. Her face hasn't changed much. Full lips, a stubborn jaw, and an attitude to match. Always had, even when she moved to the city with four kids and a dead husband and she was only thirty-one.

She arrived in 1960, but she did not move into the house until late spring of the next year. The house had a number, on paper anyway. The stamped metal numbers above the door had lost their black paint, corroded, and dropped off long before she carried her boxes inside during a light rain and set up window curtains. The numbers were ground right off the boards by the weather before the porch began to sag, long before Betty unboxed the kids' clothes and ordered them to make their new beds. No one in Betty's family was the letter-writing type, yet the mail—bills, collection notices, summons and subpoenas—always knew how to find her.

She moved into the no-numbered house the day the demolition workers put down their jackhammers and sledges, fired up the cranes and took the ball to the Metropolitan Insurance Building. His shoulders hunched under the pelting rain, One-Two ambled to Third and Franklin and saw her unpacking. He walked up the steps and knocked on the open door. Betty paused as she ripped open a box of clothes and looked up.

"Do I know you?" she asked.

"Not yet." He hadn't lost the GI speech swagger he had acquired in Korea.

"Something you want?"

"I just came to see if you needin help."

He looked around and even though she hadn't been there more than an hour or two there were knickknacks on the mantel and on the windowsills. Ladybug pincushions and cat figurines. It was all secondhand, rummage-sale stuff, but she placed them just so. She had a touch. He heard the children bouncing from room to room upstairs, yelling just to hear their own voices. It was an old house, but without furniture or pictures, without pans or cooking smells or cigarette smoke it felt big and new and the children shouted and laughed at their own echoes. They ran and jumped as if they could at least fill the house with sound.

"My name's One-Two. You must be Betty."

"What kinda name is that?"

"Winnebago."

The children rumbled downstairs and ran through the kitchen into the living room and out onto the porch.

"Them's my kids. Simon, Lester, and Caroline." She nodded at the corner of the room where an Indian swing was set up between the window and the sooty fireplace. A baby slept soundly in the swaddled blankets. "That one there's Irma."

"Came by to see if you need any help with liftin."

"God, don't own nothin heavy yet except Simon."

"You want to see somethin?"

"What?" Her eyes narrowed suspiciously.

"No, no. Somethin you can see only once. Never happen again. Just a few blocks from here. Kids can come too."

Betty looked out and contemplated the rain and then the box of clothes at her feet.

"Got a lotta work to do."

"Won't take that long. Come on. Give yourself a break. Rain's lettin up."

Betty looked outside again.

"Suppose those kids need a little air anyway."

She called them in and bossed them into their coats, wrapped Irma in a small quilt, and they all set off down Franklin.

When they reached the Met there was already a crowd gathered to watch the destruction, pinned like flies on flypaper to the perimeter ribbon on the other side of the street. The mood was part carnival, the rest funeral. But that was always the tenor of the city— whether they were knocking it down or building it up, whether it was jubilee or disaster. There was a quiet abandon with which the city built and rebuilt itself. But the sheer recklessness of knocking down the Met drew a crowd of hundreds into the rain under battered umbrellas, implements not often used in Minneapolis, where people went bareheaded and un-raincoated as if either daring the weather or in silent sopping agreement that they deserved whatever they got. Some people even brought wicker picnic hampers packed with lunch, as if on a summer outing. They took their children from school and bought film for their cameras.

It all seemed impossible. Even as they watched it happen, it was ludicrous that the mass of steel and glass, New Hampshire granite and Superior sandstone, that had dominated the south city skyline would be gone. They had begun in the cold-whipped month of December and wouldn't finish until early September, but everyone came out to watch the big machines get to work.

One-Two made sure the three older children followed and that Betty and Irma brought up the rear as they waded into the crowds. He didn't push or complain with his elbows but the onlookers moved out of his way. One-Two moved like a brown boulder among them until he reached the ribbon. Betty hid her satisfaction and said nothing. She hoisted Irma higher on her shoulder. For the first time in her life people moved for her, made way for her. This is what a city should be, she thought. Just walking through, no one beating us down, no one up on the kids. She smiled at the backs of their heads because she knew they could not see beyond One-Two's wide shoulders and rolling stride.

A man in a hard hat nodded when he saw One-Two and stepped up to the ribbon. They shook hands and One-Two jerked his head back toward Betty. The man looked again at the trucks that lined the curb and motioned them through. They followed One-Two around the open tailgate of a green city pickup and he stopped.

"We gotta stand up against this, okay? Good view here, but any closer'd be bad." He scanned the work zone and the crane perched ready to do damage. "We're safe here. Real safe," he said to himself.

Simon and the others were awed into silence—the looming bulk of the doomed building, the throng of white people, the workmen bustling at the perimeter like dogs around a wounded bear. The children will remember mostly the sound and the dust, the incredible soft, lazy dust. The progress of destruction itself was slow. It took a year to reduce the emptied building to rubble and to cart that away. The stone defied the wrecking balls. The great steel weights no heavier than balled tinfoil. The progress of destruction was slow. There was no sudden transformation. No eye-blink speed of difference. So the children remember the sounds of wrecking. The bone deep crunch of stone, again and again. The cranes swept their arms back as if preparing for a ponderous stiff-armed hug. And again. The stone was pinched into dust that lazed down over the now quiet street. They were awed by it, by the steady pace of defeat. Until now the building had always been treated with care, with tenderness. Simon watched with a sense of license, that in the city there were times when you could do damage, when you were encouraged to rip something apart.

After it was clear that this would continue, that architectural death, at least, was a monotonous process, they and the others drifted away and walked toward South Minneapolis, each with his or her own thoughts, distracted and alone.

Betty's house still doesn't have a number, and now it seems like no place to go either.

"Lincoln, you'd better get on to bed."

He says nothing, still careful since the morning. His head feels full, heavy with everything that has passed, so he doesn't argue. He slips the fresh copy in his folder and closes the copybook. One-Two squeezes his shoulder lightly as he fits himself past.

"You take it easy now, Delivery. If life comes at you hard, you just take it real easy."

Betty hugs him. "I'll get you breakfast in the morning. Sleep good."

Lincoln walks up the stairs, quietly glad about Betty's attempt at an apology for the morning's slap. One-Two and Betty stare at the floor. One-Two lets out an exaggerated sigh and rubs his belly. He stands and takes his plate to the sink.

"You make good bread, One-Two." She moves aside as he sets the dishes in the sink.

"Simon's out, huh?"

"Here this mornin."

"He say where he's stayin?"

"Somethin about work at the Curtis. God knows why they'd send a convict there."

"If the work's honest, that's a start. He gotta get used to the world somehow, even the dirt."

"So close. Just down the street, you can almost see it from here. Don't know if I want him that close."

"Where'd you rather?"

"It don't matter, I guess."

"He know you uprootin?"

"Naw. I didn't tell him. Barely believe it myself."

One-Two places his hand on Betty's arm. "If you—"

Betty tenses and looks up at the ceiling.

"Lincoln! If you ain't in bed I'm gonna slap you up. Again."

They hear a thump and scramble. Betty looks back at One-Two tenderly.

"Don't, One-Two. Don't."

He moves away and busies himself with collecting his tobacco from the table. He sweeps the shag into the ashtray.

"You can't keep on runnin, Betty."

"What did you say?"

"I said—"

"I know what you said. They bring me back a dead husband and I didn't run from that. My girl gets hit by a train I was the one closed the coffin. Simon kills Lincoln's dad and I took that, too. Now he's out and I ain't gonna run. Where to? Up north ain't no good. Down here ain't no better."

"I didn't mean it like that."

"The how don't matter. It's the what that counts. You're free to go."

"I meant runnin from me."

"I never asked."

"Betty."

"Go on, One-Two. Go on home."

One-Two straightens himself and brushes his hands down the front of his shirt, patting himself as if what Betty said dislodged something, his checkbook, a lottery ticket, something vital. He turns and walks from the kitchen. Betty follows him to the front door.

"One-Two?"

"Yeah?"

"Thanks for the bread. It's real good."

He leaves and for the second time that day Betty leans against the door and this time she wants it to stay closed, wants to press her back, her aching back, against it. No telling what'll come popping back through next. The broken bodies of her husband and Caroline. Lester. His sweet face crushed.

Upstairs, Lincoln slides on socked feet away from the banister and crawls across the carpet into bed without getting undressed. Outside it begins to snow.

8

Once Betty squared the house and taught the children their various routes to school—the girls to Andersen instead of Whittier, which was so cramped and dirty she wouldn't even want to board cattle there, Lester to Phillips Junior High, and Simon to South High to begin the ninth grade—she began to look for work. And kept looking for two years.

Like a blundering forgetful child, once the Bureau of Indian Affairs decided on relocation as a method for dealing with the "Indian Problem" and sent representatives to the reservations with beautiful brochures of San Diego, Chicago, and Minneapolis, it promptly forgot about the program. While the states and private corporations eyed the northern forests and western mineral deposits, as available and temporary as carnival dolls, the government forgot the Indians in the cities.

They forgot their promises of clean running water, of electricity, of sound roofing and roads, just as they would forget the Vista volunteers up north in the sixties, stranded on the reservation without any resources or much in the way of a purpose, strange white fish washed up on the shores of difference. They forgot them because America was in love. It was in love with itself, with the greedy mirror-happy love eyes of a starlet's double gaze—the outward look at the object and the inward one at what her lover might see. The only worries were of having enough to feed and urge the appetite.

The country was in love and hungry, and so the administration forgot the Indians in the cities. Forgot to tell them how to live in this new cement forest, to teach them the grammar of streets. Forgot its promises, its duty, and the government laughed at the Indians who had moved. Can't catch a bus. Can't read a street map. Don't even know what a résumé is. The government, the city, and the whites were content to map their own fears of inadequacy onto the Indians who relocated. If only Betty had known; the government decided on relocation precisely when the places they sent the Indians to were crumbling.

Betty came to the city without a job or a place of her own. Against all her motherly caution she moved to the city and slept with the children on the floor of her third cousin's Southside apartment, three to a single mattress, the apartment always damp with dish- and bathwater. When the school year was drawing to a close, without a steady job, and against her own better judgment, certain that she risked being outside come winter, she jumped at the chance to sign into the no-numbered house at the corner of Third Avenue and Franklin. She lied to Mr. Rojta, her landlord, and moved in. For the first time she laid aside the quiet shield of indifference Indians usually present to whites with power, money, or both, and out-and-out lied. Said, *Yes, I have a job*. He looked skeptical until she produced the money she had made from selling off the log cabin Jacob had built to a fisherman from Iowa, $120 in twenties, kept in Jacob's old discharge papers envelope.

Forgotten by the love-struck government, lying through her teeth and grinding down her own misgivings, she moved in, got the children settled, and looked for work. She washed clothes, scrubbed floors, cooked briefly at one of the few Indian-owned cafés on Franklin, and did whatever she could to get by. Her cousins asked her how she was doing. *Getting by*, she'd say. How? *Got some here and there, gettin a little some everywhere.* She dodged the question, because she had made rent arrangements that would have sent her dead husband into a killing rage. Out of respect for him she told no one what she did to make ends meet. Jacob *had* killed, but rage was something he had never allowed himself while alive, and because of that, she suffered in silence. Her cousin's friend, Ester, a black woman who lived on the Southside with her twin daughters, who not only liked Indians, but had married one—an Oneida who died soon after falling into the hog wires of a crane—told Betty that they were always looking for work at the hospital.

"What about the sick people? All those sick people give me the creeps."

"You don't got to look at them, honey. Not face or ass. There's lots else to do."

Betty shuddered, partly from remembering the smell of the IHS clinic and partly from the sting of the perm that Ester was giving her. The clinic always made her sick, filled with the smell of rotting flesh from diabetics and the phlegmy air of the TB ward where the sick were wheeled onto the porch to breathe clean northern air which they could neither taste nor draw properly anymore.

"I don't know," said Betty, fidgeting in the kitchen chair.

"With an attitude like that, baby, your kids gonna end up there pretty soon anyway."

"I know. I know," said Betty, bitter that she'd imagined she'd be able to do what she wanted in the city, not what she had to. That it would be a place for a black sequined purse. Jacob had been to the city before her, he had been all the way to Europe, had seen London and Paris, the Ardennes. He had described standing on the deck of a troop transport watching the lights being turned on all over London, the whole city lighting up in sequence after the war was over, when it was safe for light. He had talked of the bridges in Paris, bridges made of stone instead of iron or wood. Streets paved with stone. She shook herself out of her reverie.

"Shouldn't we rinse it out?"

"Not yet."

"It burns. I can feel it burning."

"You the one wanted curl. Wanted to look like me. I didn't tell you to do it."

"Yeah yeah."

She had wanted it. A new look, a tight curl for job hunting. Something modern, something new. Now she just wanted to rip the curlers free and rinse the ammonia from her scalp.

"My girlfriend works in the kitchen," Ester continued. "She just does the cookin. Ain't gotta stare at no bedpans or wipe any asses at six in the mornin. Could try that."

"That don't sound so bad. Cookin ain't so bad," said Betty, gritting her teeth.

With an exploding head of hair, sweaty palms, and a hot face she walked the scant blocks to the hospital. She was ashamed at the thought of asking for work, for her it was only a step above outright begging. But she got hired, had been relieved when the questions of the food service manager were over and he let her concentrate on opening the cans of beets and draining the bloodred juice away.

She worked with a determined fury and when her tasks were completed she set out to scrape the grease from the range hood and dissolve the crusted dough from the wire beater of the Hobart mixer, until her co-workers made her slow down. "Christ, girl, you gonna make all us look bad you keep workin so hard." She eased off and when her first check was waiting miraculously on the floor inside the door of her no-numbered house she stared at it, and turned it this way and that like a suspicious shopkeeper testing a twenty for counterfeit.

The transformation was sudden. She put away her work clothes and got dressed in her best hand-me-downs. She looked at the cheap wall clock and saw she had two hours before the girls would be home.

Betty practically skipped down the steps and walked briskly down Franklin toward the Chicago market. She went inside the A&P and her delight was sudden. The tomatoes, overripe and bruised, had never seemed so lovely, so full of seed and juice. She picked three of the best, almost girlishly glad for their weight, for the way they sat pregnant in her hand. For the first time she did not have to wait until after the frost to hack out a garden plot in the weak northern soil and plant the seedlings they got from the hardware store that they had had to keep alive next to the barrel stove in the thin spring. She did not have to cross her fingers and watch as they withered or grew, and wait sixty-five days for the fruit. For the first time she could simply choose which ones she wanted and have them.

She shopped with pleasure. After two years of scratching the city dirt for odd cash jobs, she had a regular income. After two years she was finally able to dig deep and plant a big meal on the table. Corn on the cob, pears, apples, stew meat, a ham, and a huge bag of potatoes. She carted the food breathlessly to the counter and put each item, one by one, on the conveyor belt. The clerk dutifully rang them up and gave her the total. She pulled the check from her handbag and presented it to him.

He looked at the check and back at her.

"This is a two-party check."

"A what?" asked Betty distractedly.

"A two-party check. From someone else to you."

"You take checks, don't you?"

"Yes. But not this kind."

"A check's a check. The hospital wouldn't pay me if it was broke."

"Hold on," said the clerk. He turned and waved to the manager, who knelt next to a display of canned pork and beans pyramided at the end of the first aisle.

"Problem?"

"Two-party."

The manager took the check and looked at Betty.

"We normally don't take these."

Even if Betty didn't understand the difference between a two-party check and other kinds, she knew what the rest meant. She knew how to read "normally" from a white man to an Indian woman, how to read the heavily lidded eyes and petty stare.

"I don't see what the problem is," she said innocently.

"You have ID?"

Betty rummaged in her bag and pulled out her enrollment card.

The manager took it and held it next to the check. He looked at Betty. "There's a two-dollar charge."

"Two dollars?"

"We normally don't do it at all."

Betty looked around at the brightly lit canned goods and the growing line of people behind her, searching the labels and faces for an ally. For someone to nod sympathetically, at least. For someone to signify that they had been in her shoes too, and had survived and brought dinner home to their children.

"Okay, okay."

The manager signed the check and sauntered back to the pork and beans display as if he had, in the dusty confines of a Western saloon, gunned down a vicious and dangerous opponent on the other side of a poker table. The bagger bagged her groceries for her while the cashier counted out her change. He wouldn't look at her, his pimply face was flushed and the coins stuck to his hands as he tried to tilt them toward Betty.

"New job?"

Betty nodded.

"Look," he said, leaning closer. "Get a bank account and you won't have to deal with that." He shot a look at the manager's doubled back.

The bag boy held the sacks impatiently. "You ready?"

"Ready for what?" asked Betty icily.

"You want me to lug these out to your car?"

"Don't got a car."

"Well?"

"Just give them to me."

He handed her the bags and the A&P breathed Betty back out onto the street.

By the time Caroline came home from school after fetching Irma from Betty's cousin on Lake Street, the groceries were piled high on the counter, the boxes and bags spilled over with colors and Betty was stirring a great pot of stew, with cubed beef instead of canned meat. The house smelled of onions and pepper. The cooking smells and riot of pot-banging covered Betty's lingering shame from the supermarket, her feeling of sudden inability. She felt better with the girls in the kitchen. This is what it's all about, she thought. It ain't about the people at the store, she told herself. It's about feeding my kids.

As for Irma and Caroline, they had never seen so much real food, raw and ready, in their house, except at funerals or giveaways. Caroline's funeral would be potlucked at the lonely Catholic church up north. As for Lester, he wouldn't have a real wake, loud with memories and offerings of food or money. His death would be awful, the coffin silent and closed. The food the stunned neighbors brought over was quiet and small, left uneaten in the kitchen, twenty-dollar bills tucked inside the pages of the Bible and the dictionary on the mantel. Simon's steel crew stood on the porch and the men talked about the job, not their absent partner, growing louder and louder the more hip-flask booze they drank until the police brought Simon and they fell silent. Betty's gathered friends from the city talked about work and the reservation up north. Anything but the present.

For now the girls, happy without knowing why, ran through the kitchen and up the stairs where Caroline changed out of her school clothes, that, while not new, were clean and without holes. Betty smiled at the sink as they tumbled back down the stairs and hugged her around the legs.

"You fold them up?"

They chattered assent. Irma stayed close to her legs, at five still hungry for physical contact, while Caroline told her about school. They fought over the Hershey's bar Betty had bought, though for once there was enough to go around. Simon and Lester arrived. Simon always hurried from the high school to the junior high to walk Lester home, even though he knew the way. Better two of us than one. Better four fists than two. When they did come home bruised and bloody they were triumphant and proud that they had held their ground. Betty was proud, too. She always made sure that her boys finished things, but didn't start them. *Your daddy wasn't a troublemaker so you better not start nothin*, she always said. When they came in after a fight she did not scold or hover. Instead she treated them like men. Gave them space to calm down, got them glasses of water, and let Simon smoke cigarettes in the house.

They dropped their books on the couch and sauntered into the kitchen where, once they were away from the juvenile eyes on the street or at school, they began tickling their sisters to make them drop the candy bar they had tried to stuff hurriedly in their mouths as soon as they heard the front door slam. Clutching the last pieces of melting chocolate, the girls jumped up squealing and ran to the back door. Simon and Lester ran after them and Betty felt a surge of contentment as she coined the carrots at the sink.

She heard screams from the back and the screen door banged shut. Betty leaned away from the sink.

"Don't play so goddamn rough! I work at a hospital. I don't run one."

The kids trooped in sweaty and flushed.

"They take your candy?" Betty asked Irma.

The girl slouched into a chair and nodded. Betty leveled her eyes at Lester.

"I took it but I gave it back."

Betty swiveled back to look at Irma with raised eyebrows. Irma looked down at the floor.

"Come here, baby. Get that chair and help me peel these here potatoes."

Irma slid her chair over and climbed on. She stood next to her mother and took the paring knife.

"You'd better eat these spuds and grow a couple inches, instead of dicing them. You ain't bigger than a sliver."

Lester and Simon pulled out the cards and the cribbage board from under the pile of newspapers and bills on the table. The pegs were lost again so they broke the heads off some blue-tip matches and put them in the holes and started dealing. Caroline sat between them on the third chair and reached across for the funny pages.

Betty kept cutting the potatoes that Irma handed her and couldn't stop laughing.

"Good God, girl. You're whittling them down to toothpicks. Just take the rough stuff off. Here, like this."

"They're hiring downtown for construction workers," said Simon.

"Good for them. No, honey. Hold the knife like this."

"Pay's good."

"Even better for them."

Lester hooted and pegged eight. Caroline crumpled the newspaper as loudly as she could to throw off Simon's counting.

"One-Two said I could probably get on. Bein so tall he said I could probably get on."

"Listen to him, and you'll probably end up livin in a flophouse and not bein able to add. Just like him."

"He can add. I need the money."

"Yeah, like that, honey. Peel them just like that. What you need money for? You're sixteen, you go to school. You come home. You go to school. What you need cash for?"

"It's good work."

"Yeah. Your daddy had good work too, and it ended him up under a tree."

Simon didn't say anything. He jammed the matchsticks down into the holes.

"Christ, bro. You gonna break them off in there."

"There's two hundred fuckin matches in the box. Don't worry about it."

Betty spun away from the sink.

"You watch your mouth around the girls."

"Yeah," said Lester, "you watch your mouth."

Betty put her hand on her hip.

"Lester, if you want your brother to kick your ass, provoke him somewhere else. Outside. This house is too small for a rumble."

Caroline snickered into her newspaper.

"And you, girlie. You'd better be laughing at the comics." Betty blew imaginary bangs from her forehead. "What do I gotta do? Hog-tie and gag all you just so I can cook your dinner in peace?"

"You don't gotta hog-tie me!" squealed Irma from the sink.

"Naw. I just gotta enroll you in peelin school." She wiped her hand on her pant leg and stroked Irma's hair and dug in the coin jar above the sink and withdrew a dime.

"Simon. Run over and call One-Two for dinner. That is if he ain't sloshed down at the CC Club already."

Simon was surprised but said nothing.

"Go get him after your game."

"You mean after he loses," boasted Lester.

"You can't even count. I'm gonna win anyway."

Simon threw his card down and extracted himself from the kitchen.

One-Two knew he wasn't invited just out of good-neighborliness, so he held his breath through dinner. He sipped his coffee cautiously as the girls cleaned up, and was quietly friendly when they jumped on his lap and demanded attention. He made polite guy talk with Lester, who urged him toward more risqué stories. One-Two kept within the bounds of what an older neighbor should encourage. He read the newspaper with resolute attention while Betty readied all the children for bed like a sergeant, though he had read it twice already, once in the morning and again up under the trusses of the Mendota Bridge, which was beginning to crumble.

After it was all done Betty took off her sweater and slumped in her chair. She steadied One-Two in her sights and he knew it was coming.

"I don't want Simon workin steel."

"You make a damn fine stew, Betty."

"I don't want him up there."

"Lotta people'd be glad to have their kids earnin money above the streets instead of stealin it on them."

"You callin Simon a crook?"

"I'm callin the city dangerous."

"You ain't his dad, One-Two," she said as she shook a cigarette from her pack.

"I seen it happen. I know this place."

"You don't know us."

One-Two sighed and drained his coffee.

"I came back from Korea. I came back here and this place was jumping. They wanted to demo half the city. Wasn't much being built but they threw new crews together all the time. Now the buildings are going up. It's the only place we can get a good wage. The only way we can get union."

"He ain't old enough. They gonna let a sixteen-year-old in the union?"

"I was shootin gooks in Korea when I was sixteen."

"I ain't gonna debate you over my son. I got him this far. Not you. I got us off the rez in one piece. Not you. I buried their daddy. Not you. I make rent on this place. Okay? I know what I'm doin."

"Okay, Betty. Okay," he said, raising his hands palm forward in submission. "All I'm doin is tryin to help."

"Then just keep your eye on him."

"I got both my eyes on all of you."

Betty tried to ignore the double meaning and earnest stare. "Don't worry about me."

"Worry ain't what it is."

Betty looked down. "Don't waste your time. I ain't got it in me."

"Everyone's got it in them."

"Not me. Not now."

"You cook a mean meal."

"Gotta be good at somethin."

"You good at a whole lot more."

"I'm tryin," she said, shivering in mock cold, to add some movement to the conversation which had gotten so still, so full and heavy with meaning.

"You cold?" asked One-Two rising to the bait.

"A bit. Just a little."

"I gotta work tomorrow. We're patchin the Mendota Bridge. Damn builders skimped on the cement and it's all flaking off."

They both stood and walked to the front door.

"You come anytime to eat. Okay? You come anytime. Watch out for my boys, but leave the decisions to me."

One-Two nodded and ducked out into the cool September air. Betty closed the door and shivered again, this time for real.

PART

TWO

9

Simon has been out of jail for three months when he sees Vera leaving a jewelry store on Washington Avenue. After three months of nosing around Southside, of searching out only those men he knew from jail, of enduring the lasting craziness of the only two he's been able to find, Split and T-Man (one without toes and the other without a brain), he is suddenly confronted with Vera.

At first he is not sure, he has to look twice. Her shoulders are more rounded, her legs like wrinkled hams under her too-short skirt. Blond, permed curls erupt away from her face. It is May and warm. The blush on her pasty skin makes her look like a doll set to life as she walks mechanically up Washington. Simon follows her, spring exploding around him like a spilled secret.

He is startled to see her. The years, perhaps. It's been eleven years since he saw her, since he sobbed against her breasts, already beginning to swell, his brother's brains sliding from the top of his skull. And all of the time in between. Her child. He moves toward her, his hand frozen in a half-wave. She doesn't look. Instead of shouting over the urban bustle, he walks on the sidewalk opposite.

Her chin is tucked in the folds of her thin raincoat, and her dress and high heels transform her stride into a metronomic click. She is twenty-eight now, he thinks, twenty-eight and she looks forty. This is what memories do: a murdered lover, an abandoned child, and her body sagging from the sheer weight of it.

This is not the way he has thought of her. Her sloe-eyed looks, legs curled underneath as she sat on the couch with his brother. She is both rounder and harder now. The years did not open her up, did not make her more of what she was then. A girl. Pretty. Unsure of herself but hungry at seventeen. But then, he is not the same either. After he takes in Vera's changed body he cannot help looking up toward the higher reaches of the city.

They sent the Indian crew skyward at noon. The other crews took the dawn and dusk shifts, when the wind was stilled in the absence of asphalt heat sent up from below like blasts from a large wing. They were allowed in the union because no one else wanted their jobs, or the shifts they kept. The Indian men were from Black River Falls, Red Cliff, Eagle Butte, Wind River, Six Nations. They were from Lac Court d'Oreilles. The names rolling off their wind-dried tongues like scattered dimes. They'd worked in Chicago on the Sears, in Saint Louis and Kansas City. They had raised this new breed of buildings from the ball-tumbled rubble of ten cities.

They went up the lift in a silent huddle. The other crews were from across Europe—Polish, Czech, German, Swedish, Irish. The rest watched as the Indians gathered and did not break into their midst with jokes or conversation. They did not disrupt the silent communion between the Indians partly because they were, after all, Indian, and partly out of respect. The Indians worked the longest shifts during the summer swelter and the winter freeze. They were assigned the most extreme parts of the frame.

The lift shimmied and rose into the noon sky stretched thin under the weight of the June heat. Twenty men, and all that muscle slabbed tight over their hands and squared at their shoulders. They birthed the skeleton of the building, but if the elevator cable snapped they would fall in a jumble of limbs. Even though they pulled the building together, they knew that what they did was more than their sum. No matter how good they were, how tightly they bolted the swinging I-beam, how carefully they set the crosses, they knew they could not argue with gravity. The earth would treat them with the same indifference as loose steel, a dropped hammer, a windblown lunch. This was the secret: the building wanted to stay standing, to grow, to sway but hold on, and so did they. The IDS Tower wanted to be noticed and admired, as did the Indian crew. Its bones of steel and skin of glass were treated roughly by the wind, heat, and ice as were their skin and bones. That was the secret they carried with them as they crammed into the steel cage that hoisted them upward. Under the watchful eyes of the ground crews and the earth itself, they were silent until they were let off to climb the last three floors with their mallets and spud wrenches dangling like extra limbs from their belts and sack lunches tucked under their shirts. Once they were alone they began slight conversation, like tinkers banging out pots, trying not to wake a sleeping family. The newer members wore harnesses until they realized they were in more danger of getting trapped and crushed by beams than of falling. Soon they went without. After a while they, too, wore moccasins to give them a better feel for their footing.

Simon was no different. When he walked down to a Gateway demo site in 1963 he was green. One-Two had told him what to say, but he was still nervous. The foreman looked him up and down. *Union?* Simon shook his head. *Permit?* Simon shrugged. *What tribe?* Ojibwe. The foreman nodded and called over the Winnebago.

"You know him?" asked the pusher.

"Yeah. Know the family." said One-Two.

"He ever work steel before?"

One-Two looked at Simon. Simon didn't say anything.

"He did some burnin. He can cut, and works like a horse." All of it lies.

"Bullshit. If he knows what to do, then why the hell he come down here instead of the hall? You know better than that."

"Work's down here. They don't know him at the hall. He'd be sittin there twiddlin his fuckin thumbs all day. Besides, all the books are on the job already, you know we're short-handed. I'll take care of him."

The pusher shook his head.

"He's your responsibility. If he goes for a dive it's your fault. If he gets someone else hurt, you're payin the widow. Go get a permit at noon."

That was that.

By the time they began work on the IDS, Simon had been working steel for seven years and had earned himself a place on one of the high steel crews. When Simon walked to the site at the corner of Eighth Street and Marquette he grew silent and walked slower, letting the businessmen rush around him. When he got to the lot, he was brooding, looming over the other workers. He joined the Indians on the lift and walked out onto six inches of metal twenty stories above the sidewalk.

After they punched out they walked into South Minneapolis together, ambling down the sidewalk, all of them marveling at the texture of the ground under their feet, shocked at the great expanse of it. It looked so smooth from above, so even and unbroken and simple.

During the summer they shuffled along until they found their way to Cressen's Bar or the CC Club. They took up two tables and let their arms creep onto the chair backs of those next to them, expansive in their weariness and pride.

After the first nine months of construction at the IDS they started building up from the ground. Nine months just for excavating and sheeting, for pouring the pilings and the substructure concrete. Then Simon and the others urged the building into the sky. As they clipped and bolted the frame together, he always looked southward while his neighborhood came into perspective. It wasn't until they had been at work for eight months, when the IDS inched over the Foshay Tower, that Simon could make out the roof of their house peeking from behind the soiled brick of Stevens Community. He paused between loads of beam and searched the stunted buildings for some recognizable part of their house, and he saw it. Each day, as they circled the building adding floors, he looked to the house and knew Vera was there with Lester. Betty was at work and the girls were at school. He was hanging high above the city. Lester and Vera were in the house alone. He was inside her, or she was biting his calf, his ear, his neck, marking him with a hidden map of their passion and time together. He thinks back, and as always, when waiting for his trial and then during ten years in prison, he rules out jealousy as a motive. He didn't want what Lester had, didn't really hunger for her young body. But maybe, maybe if he'd met her first, if he'd taken a different walk home, had reached out to her on the street, then everything would have been different.

Simon might have been walking back from the site. His legs cramped from crouching on the steel timbers, his back pinched from balancing on girders all day, his hands laced with splinters of metal that were invisible until marked with rubies of welling blood. He'd try to stand erect as he walked, strolling really, giving himself a slightly longer walk home, pacing himself on the uneven concrete. He'd light a cigarette as dusk settled down and squeezed out the remains of the day. People emerged from the portals of their working lives, hurrying for buses and taxis, cars pulled considerably to

the curb. Simon could have been among them, slower, more delib-
erate than the current of people rippling around him, and she could
have passed him on her way from Kresge's, after buying herself a
little something, a little anything to make her life more hers, to
make herself more his. She might have passed him, a pretty white
girl having just bought some lip gloss, used the test bottles of perfume, a necklace to crest her collarbones like submerged wings, on
her way to the house of the Indian boy she'd met the other day.

And it was the smell, perhaps. Her new perfume could have
brought her into his ken, to give up his bird's-eye perspective in the
steel ribs of the building where he perched like a gargoyle come to
life. The smell of her as she brushed past him. He smoked his cigarette and imagined looking after her as she walked ahead of him
down the sidewalk, her arms crossed under her breasts and her ankles slim in their sagging socks, a schoolgirl's posture. Later, after
she became a regular fixture in their house, he would try to pick her
out from the crowd—brownish hair, her birdbone wrists, the down
on her ears. Simon would try to find her on the street from the van-
tage of the building. If only he could have seen her sooner, with her
head bent from girlish shyness instead of womanly isolation. If he'd
seen her from above, or grabbed her arm, just for the smell of her as
she passed him, things might have been different. If he had done
this sooner, sooner than his brother, before she noticed the swelling
of her belly, then all of their lives would have been different. Secrets would not have been possible. But he didn't; he just smoked
and she hurried by, and then he forgot her, and finished his cigarette
as he passed over the freeway on Third Avenue, and entered the
Southside. His back and legs slowly unfolding, sloughing off the
stiffness and pain acquired from the day's work.

She crosses Third Avenue past the Milwaukee Road train shed
below the police station. She doesn't look back and so doesn't no-

tice him. Simon crosses the street behind her, on the opposite side.
The old storefronts and warehouses have been ripped down. There
is no longer any urban clutter in which Simon can hide himself, just
the wide open municipal spaces in front of new office buildings.
The streets feel naked. She stays on Washington and nothing diverts
her attention. At the corner of Broadway and Washington she turns
and walks up the overpass. I-94 runs like a moat between what is
left of downtown and the Northside. There is no escape, but he is
not ready to speak with her. He stops and watches her figure rise
into the dimmed northern sky and he turns back, not sure now
where to go.

10

One-Two knows he shouldn't, but he does. He shuts the door to the Windsor and aims his large body north on Third Avenue and begins walking toward the Curtis. It has been almost half a year since Simon was released and nothing has happened yet. There has been no resulting catastrophe, no trauma to anyone in the family. It is August. Nothing much doing. He rubs his back where the nomenclature of his spine switches from dorsal to lumbar. It is dusk, eight-thirty.

The city is beautiful, soft from the heat and cooling with the retreat of the sun. One-Two eyes Betty's house: the lights are on and he imagines she must be home.

There's not much for One-Two to do. The Windsor is ready for the fall rush of students who live on the Southside because rent is cheap, and the old buildings have nice floors and high ceilings. Across the street a red Dodge Power Ram is parked, the back crammed with cheap dressers and two mattresses standing on edge, clasped like hands.

He crosses Franklin, and he knows he shouldn't meddle, that's what Betty would call it, but he can't help himself. It's a visit, not a meddle. A drop-by. That's all.

The street hasn't changed much since he first moved into the Windsor. The dottering brick buildings of Stevens Community on the left abruptly give over to large houses that have been split into three, sometimes four, apartments. They are being bumped off their foundations by hard winters, and One-Two is surprised every spring when the old frames haven't folded. He is shocked by the endurance of the Southside. The houses stop along the overpass and he can remember when they kept stretching toward downtown. The city planners expressed regret when they were torn down, but everyone knew that they wanted I-94 as a buffer between downtown and the creeping decrepitude of South Minneapolis.

It was strange, that he'd worked on destroying the Gateway. He'd wrecked his own home but was compensated when he moved across from Betty in 1964.

It hadn't been worth much. The Gateway wasn't built to last. The flophouses flopped, the pool halls and pawnshops traded derelicts back and forth, but at least it was honest. At least it wore its sins for all to see. One-Two misses the offhand gruffness of the toughs and dealers in the old neighborhood. Then it had been an act, an attitude they put on, that they modified for shopkeepers, lovers, or their relatives. He doesn't like the modern flash, the seductivity of violence leaching into the Southside from the east.

He shakes his head and moves his hand down to his back. For what it's worth, the move pushed him closer to Betty. Not close enough. For what it's worth. Two children dead, one just out of jail, the other disappeared to San Diego, and Lincoln stuck with Betty's stubborn silence. One-Two feels that he hasn't been able to help with any of it.

He wants to tell Betty that she should tell Lincoln what happened, that knowledge can crack open the troubled child. Not break him, more like the way warmth and steam escape from a torn loaf of fresh-baked bread. He wants to tell her this but is caught, held fast on the edge of her life and unable to get closer. She could give him the final shove off the edge if he broaches the subject. The fall from the IDS wouldn't even compare to that.

They were putting in the spacing beams so the glaziers could begin to hang the skin, the mirrored glass panels that would clothe the building. It was 1971. It seemed that things were falling apart everywhere. The boys sent overseas were coming home broken. Different, at least. The news that came with them was hard to believe but impossible to refute in full color on the television. In Washington the President was denying everything.

Tucked away in the upper Midwest, Minneapolis was licking its wounds and thinking ruefully of Hubert Humphrey's lost bid, wondering how differently things might have turned out. The city looked outward from its perch on the edge of the nation and, given what it saw, everyone in the city was hurrying. One-Two, Simon, the rest of the crews, even the gnomelike architect who designed the building, were hurrying to finish it. They rushed because though the rest of the world seemed broken and unfinished, they were determined to glass the sky with the IDS Tower, a home far better than the company that bore its name deserved.

They worked quickly, the masons running ahead of the ironworkers who scampered to clear their deck before the glaziers burned at their heels. After them came the mad scramble of electricians, plumbers and the specialists who only worked on the ducting or interior walls.

They dared one another, urging speed, and every decision was weighed against the unspoken desire to make it whole in defiance of the dissolution affecting the rest of the country. They loaded the cranes with so much beam that the rear stabilizers almost left the ground. One load of beam took an hour to secure and hoist. If they piled on more, they could save days of work.

It wasn't that they were trying to stay under budget. It was too late for that. They simply *felt* it, felt it needed to be done. They rushed, pushed the equipment and men to capacity, overloaded the cranes and turned on huge arc lights so the crews could work into the night. They pulled time and a half but drank up most of it as an antidote to the tensions of night work. The bar owners ignored the one o'clock closing law so when the crews checked out they could slip in the back and slump bone-weary and body-heavy in the booths. They were tired beyond anything they'd experienced except in war, but alert, strung as tight as crane cables.

On the building the usual method of communicating by hand signals was of no use at night. So they developed their own version of Morse which they beat out on the beams with their spud wrenches. The crew spoke in a metallic staccato that cut through diesel roar and hydraulic whine, above the rip of torches and grinders.

After work, in the bars, the men still didn't talk; ordinary speech was too difficult. Instead they carried the principle of code with them. They shouted out names, buildings and dates that carried within them their own stores. *Quebec Bridge, 1907!* someone would shout and the rest nodded and drank. *Chosa! Empire State, 1931!* The bar was solemn. Then some joker yelled *Lenny Whitebird, Sakura Massage Parlor, 1969!* They all laughed until it hurt. The list of fallen expanded to include those who got the clap.

They staggered home, or, often as not, slept in the booths until the bartender woke them with eggs and coffee. They walked out to the site again, ready to climb into the sky. One-Two, as one of the oldest, didn't allow himself much excess after his shifts. His responsibility to his crew lasted until well after they left the rig. He kept them company at the bar for a while and even though high steel was solitary work, he left the bar alone and almost sober so he could walk home by himself. The darkened streets were what he imagined a decompression tank to be like—slowly giving him the ability to take full breaths and move unrestrictedly. He needed this time alone.

In the morning he retraced his steps and picked up the men who had slept at the bar and cajoled them into action. As for Simon, he kept a special eye on him. He never worried about the quality of Simon's work or if he'd show up—these were never issues for him. Rather, he tried to protect Simon for Betty's sake. Even though she hadn't opened the door for One-Two, hadn't given him much reason to hope, he hadn't talked himself out of loving her. Simon saw it plain as day.

"One-Two," he slurred though his whiskey, "she ain't gonna bend. She ain't the bendin type."

"Don't be so sure about your mom," cautioned One-Two. "She'll surprise you."

"She's always surprising. But her mind gets set and," he burped, "and that's that."

"Well, I ain't got nothin better to do. I might as well keep hopin."

"Go ahead." Simon clapped him on the back, but kept his hand there, in quiet dialogue that said, *I would't mind it one bit.*

And then there was the fall. The crane was loaded past capacity and the rear stabilizers weighted down with beam to keep it from tipping. One-Two was on the third floor signaling the load and the cable snapped.

The beam crashed straight down and the cable snaked and doubled and whipped through the corner of the third floor. It could have been worse. If the braided steel had hit One-Two directly it would have cut him in half. He'd seen it happen. Strange that metal rope, when swung fast enough, acts like a knife. One-Two turned in, as if the shelter of his shoulders could stop it, but the instinct remained, the way he saw men cringe against an onslaught of rifle fire in Korea though it did no good. The cable passed over his head and made the same sound as a gull's wings when it locked and rocketed in, making the air rip.

It passed overhead and on the way back it hit a generator and a stack of steel plate. The half-inch steel flew off the ground and slammed into One-Two's shoulder, thigh and arm. His shoulder socket was crushed, his hip shattered. The impact sent him flying off the third story. He landed in the torn sand of the construction lot, flat on his back, and he can't remember what his back hit. It could have been a lunch box or a piece of beam end, a boot, or even a small block of two-by-four left over from a foundation form. It could have been anything and he landed with his spine directly on it.

He is proud he never lost consciousness. His body was numb from the middle of his back down. His shoulder felt shredded. Simon had been on the second floor and he didn't wait for the lift or a ladder. He slid down the beam to the first floor and he jumped the rest of the way.

One-Two could talk and the foremen gathered and the site manager was there. They knew, and One-Two knew, that they'd lost the rest of the day.

You feel okay? asked the site manager, a bald man with a permanently sunburned crown. *We're gonna move you to the trailer until the ambulance gets here,* he said.

One-Two nodded to say that he understood. Simon stepped in front of him.

"Like hell you're movin him."

"We'll lose a whole day here."

"You'll lose your fuckin head if you touch him," said Simon, lifting his spud wrench from his belt. One-Two was scared: he couldn't feel his legs. He couldn't sit up, and the pain in his shoulder and arm was spreading. He looked at the site manager, framed by Simon's spread-legged stance.

"Simon, you don't understand. If we lose a day, it means we lose about ten thousand dollars."

"You ain't touchin him unless you want to fight me now and the union later," stated Simon. "That'll slow you down right quick."

That's how it went. Simon stood guard over One-Two's body until the paramedics came and strapped him on the body board and took him to the hospital. One-Two thinks back, he counts it out and is surprised: Simon was only twenty-six years old at the time.

One-Two's body was ruined. They put a steel pin in his hip, gave him a new shoulder joint and immobilized his back for six weeks to give it a chance to heal. He'd crushed two vertebrae.

After the accident the crew visited him in the hospital and when he was released Simon kept him up-to-date on construction. He talked crew politics and union position. He filled in One-Two on the gradual emergence of the building.

Neither he nor Simon was there when it was finished. Simon was in the middle of his trial and One-Two was learning to walk again, and he read about the completion of the steelwork in the papers with a mixture of pride and anger. They had put the last beam in upside down: painted white and signed by the mayor and many of the steel workers, there was so much writing on it that the placement markings were impossible to read.

While he was still in the hospital the crew took turns visiting his room, telling jokes and smoking out the window. Betty came with Lester and the girls and the men excused themselves under her fierce stare, promising not to smoke or drink in the hospital room. They gave him so much morphine he doesn't remember a lot about his time in the hospital except the melting in Betty's eyes. She wiped at them impatiently and complained about the smoke in the room, but One-Two thought maybe she was worried.

Once he healed enough to walk, he took the money the union gave him and looked for work. He couldn't get back on the crew, his body couldn't take it anymore. Instead, the manager at the

Windsor, where he had lived since 1964, offered him the maintenance job. He was able to stay near Betty, his only consolation. As
he settled into the mind-numbing work of shoring up the old building, he had only one comfort: that maybe Betty had been crying for
him.

One-Two enters the Curtis and is directed downstairs by the
pot-glazed clerk. He winds his way through the boilers and finds Simon and Dougan in the back, quietly reading *High Society*.

"Well, goddamn," says Simon, "long time no see."

One-Two can't help smiling.

"It's been a while, sonny, been a long time." He nods politely
at Dougan, who dips his head in response and stands, mock-
stretching.

"Well, boys. I think I gotta go to the can."

He steps past Simon and One-Two. They hear him humming
and tapping the rolled magazine against his thigh.

Neither One-Two nor Simon speaks. They settle down on the
crates. One-Two looks around at the rusted boilers and the plumb-
ing guts suspended from the ceiling.

"Quite the place."

Simon looks directly at him. "It's goddamn good to see you,
One-Two."

"Didn't know if I should come by."

"Should don't count for much. I'm glad you did."

One-Two is relieved. He is unused to this directness from Simon. He figured he'd have to mine him, sift past the layers of guilt
and recrimination, just to get a response.

"What you been doin?"

"Helpin out down here. Couple of friends got out of the joint
and I see them a bit."

"Stillwater?"

"Yeah."

"Guess you and Betty didn't write much when you were in, huh?" One-Two hangs his head, feeling that maybe he went too far.

Simon shakes his head. "Naw. Didn't figure she wanted to hear from me."

"You figured wrong. You should stop over, Simon. Couldn't hurt."

"Still full of advice, huh?"

"Couldn't be a bad thing to stop over. Lincoln's tryin to bend his mind around the fact he's got an uncle. Can't quite figure you out, and Betty ain't givin him anything to go on."

"You look the same. Still at the Windsor?"

"Yeah. We both in the basement now."

"Better than the doghouse."

One-Two chuckles. Sometimes laughing is easier than talking. He can tell Simon hasn't heard about Betty's move.

"You met Lincoln, then."

"Yeah," says Simon. He suddenly seems sad. "I'll be damned if he don't look just like Lester. Just like him."

"There is that," agrees One-Two.

They don't mention Vera. How she dropped Lincoln at Betty's house and left it that way. She never tried to get in touch after that. Neither man can figure that one out, they don't know how to, and the blank space where understanding should rest has been backfilled with sadness and loss.

"What you doin with yourself?" asks Simon, switching the subject.

"Little a this . . . Keepin an eye on Betty."

"Your eye's got to be gettin tired after twenty years."

This time it is One-Two's turn to be direct. "A bit, Simon. A bit," he says softly.

"Well, uncle. You never was the quittin type."

They don't know what else to say and instead pretend to listen for Dougan's return, although they know he won't be back. The boilers are silent, out of use for the summer. They will only see three more years of action, pushing the treacly steam through the radiators in the rooms above. The building is doomed, though neither Simon nor Dougan know it yet.

They sit a while before One-Two stands up. He rubs his belly with both hands and stretches. "I'd best get back."

Simon stands, too. "Come anytime, One-Two."

"Might do that. Can come our way too you know."

"I don't know."

"You can."

"Maybe.

One-Two turns and walks from the corner of the basement. "You gonna be okay, Simon?"

"If I got anything to say about it."

One-Two nods thoughtfully. I hope you do, he thinks.

When he emerges on Third Avenue it is dark, but he doesn't mind the walk. It is August and the air is cool, and he knows the way home. He can be sure of that at least.

11

On Nicollet Mall the city has been hanging wreaths and stapling holly to the lampposts. There are Yuletide banners strung between the buildings. The downtown business committee has decided to be more welcoming to its citizens in order to net their seasonal dollars, but it doesn't work, and they are at a loss. It is clear that people want to shop where they live. Since most still work downtown, those jobs, at least, haven't leaked out into the suburbs, though the last thing city workers want to do is stay downtown. This is becoming clearer as the season draws on to Christmas. No amount of bunting or carols, piped through the tinny loudspeakers mounted on the lampposts, will do the trick. The old-world cobbles don't matter to shopping feet, nor do the window displays at Dayton's draw them in. The shoppers aren't fooled, the Cities aren't New York City, they know Dayton's isn't Macy's and they drive wearily out of the city to shop at newly built suburban malls where, though they won't be surprised, at least they know what they'll get.

The abandoned storefronts and scabby discount basements between Nicollet and 94W lead like tunnels toward the Southside, where there are no banners and the Salvation Army no longer sets up on the corners; they quit asking the damned for redemption long ago.

Betty stays put. Christmas seems smaller this year, a tight season of cold and ice, far from the blistering furor of Galilee. She has only Lincoln and One-Two to buy for, but the mood of their little community is so precarious, her heart isn't really in it. Simon has been out of jail for nine months. One-Two admitted going down to the Curtis. Other than that, there has been little contact between them.

One-Two and Lincoln hang on all of Betty's moods, careful not to offend or demand, the way she sees families dance around the emotions of recovering cancer victims—reluctant to place any burden on them, but ready to read meaning into all their actions. She sees it at the hospital and feels it at home—she recognizes now the necessity of burdens. They are what keep you living. She would like to tell One-Two, Lincoln, even Simon, that they should not only depend on her a little more, they should make demands of her. But not too much. Not so much.

Betty knows they won't, and it takes all the fun out of buying their presents. She is certain One-Two will be happy with his cowboy boots and Lincoln with the new winter parka and red-swoosh Nikes he's been hinting at for months. She is confident they will like these gifts, and she is equally sure they will read the high Mexican heel and smooth nylon for her pleasure or anger.

Betty finishes wrapping. It is a gray December mid-morning. Lincoln is at school and One-Two somewhere scouring junkyards for antique sinks with which to replace the cracked porcelain in the Windsor. She ties the last bow and places the boxes under the tree One-Two has set up in the corner. She thinks maybe they are right about her gifts; since Simon's release, she has given them less of herself, and these presents, sitting like bright brutes under the tree, are her way of making up for emotional selfishness. One-Two and Lincoln's tentative analyses may be more accurate than they know.

Their first Christmases in the city were poor ones. They couldn't afford new boots or jackets, much less had time for a tree. Instead, she bundled the kids up after they came home from school and walked out among the rich shoppers downtown. They forwent the bus and, with Lester and Simon trading the girls from back to back, they walked and ran downtown where they listened to music and Betty dispensed nickels for cider and hot chocolate.

They sat on benches and chatted with strangers. Betty made faces at passing dogs, which even made Simon laugh. It wasn't just their family, maybe the times were different. People talked to one another, women nodding into each other's shopping bags and the men stood with their hands in their pockets, calling one another "buddy."

Betty and the kids didn't care that everyone around them seemed to have more, that these white people bought present after present, giddy with excess. They weren't jealous or resentful. Their family had less, that's all, and they weren't the only ones. Being poor was a fact, and at that time, not a shameful one. They had enough, and *that was enough*. No way could Betty afford twenty-five-dollar sneakers, red swoosh or no. For a kid who's just going to grow out of them anyway? She would have laughed at the idea.

Simon and Lester would start throwing snow at the girls, who shrieked and ran. They sounded scared but the looks they cast over their snowy shoulders were full of delight. They chased one another around and around the bench. Now it would be unseemly, rude, but at the time the shoppers stepped deftly out of the way and let the children have at it.

Betty sat and turned to make sure the looks and stares of the other shoppers didn't turn hard, to check that the Christmas spirit was not being overshadowed by the color of her children's skin and the mischief they were making. Whites were prepared to tolerate and even gaze fondly at a little winter fun so long as the kids were cute, were not a threat. Maybe it was the season, the good-naturedness of it, but they didn't unmask any lingering disdain, disapproval or hatred. She remembers the glow in Irma's eyes as Simon caught up to her and gloved snow in her face. Pure delight. How Lester bellowed "You leave my sister alone!" as he tackled Simon from behind. When the fight changed to man-on-man, which is very different, there was an ease, a playfulness between them, which disarmed the shoppers on the sidewalk. Thinking back on it, their rumbles seemed so harmless, so easy, the ensuing violence unreal, out of place in what she knew to be true of her sons. Simon couldn't have done what he did. Not to Lester, not to his sweet face, the face Simon had washed and wiped and soothed as much as she had. As hard as life was back then, they were always good children, good to one another. Everyone was like that. If there was trouble on the reservation or in the Indian community in the Cities, it was the kind that people brought on themselves. Destruction was always of the self, not the other. No one took out their sadness or pain or hurt on their family.

And Vera. Betty can't figure that one out. Even if life gets bad and you don't think you can do it, you manage anyway, you make it work. You don't give up your child, not that easy. I didn't do that when Jacob died, and I had four of them. Vera only had one and parents to help. Betty and the girls would have lent aid, too. She searches her mind for clues, for something about that shy white girl that seemed off, suspicious, anything that would have explained her behavior; dropping Lincoln off the way rabid fox abandon their young.

To Betty, Vera had seemed like a nice girl. If she was there when Betty came home from work, listening to the radio on the couch with Lester, she always asked *How are you?* right off and even got up to help her with grocery bags or leftover food from the hospital. She was quiet, polite, if reserved, well-dressed and clean. She blushed easily and hid her laugh behind her slim hand. Delicate maybe, but not off.

Betty remembers with shame her reaction when Vera left Lincoln with her. Vera must have borrowed her parents' car. Betty doesn't know. All the vehicles along the curb looked the same—crusted with salt and ice, the windows glazed. Vera rang the bell and stood on the porch until Betty opened the door. Betty was fatigued from work and the needs of her children. Simon had been tried and found guilty of second-degree murder. They hadn't sentenced him yet. Before Betty could stammer out a hello, or invite her in, Vera said *Here* and handed her the baby. She must have been waiting in the car with the heater on. She wasn't wearing a jacket, keeping the baby close to her breasts, one last embrace. Her face wasn't tear-streaked. She looked flushed and awkward, not distraught. *Here.* Betty held her arms out instinctively and took the baby boy. Vera turned and walked back down to the curb. She looked into the face of the baby and saw Lester's face, so brown it was almost purple, like a bruised juneberry. She knew the terror of hospital delivery, where the afterbirth is dumped into the garbage along with the umbilical cord, the rudeness of modern medicine, and she studied his face to see if he bore the effects of such impersonal attention. She looked up and saw Vera return with a piece of paper in her hand. Betty suddenly understood what was happening.

"You'll need this, too," Vera said holding out the birth certificate. Betty reached for it, her eyes glittering hard.

Vera looked around and crossed her arms, chilled and scared.

"It's blank. The name's blank," she said finally, and she turned and walked down the porch steps.

Betty yelled after her. "*Gaagokwe!* Just like a porcupine! Abandoning your boy when you get scared!" She slammed the door. Only she couldn't tell how Vera got there, didn't see the final leaving, the shifting of attention from the complexity of giving up a child to the more mundane things that demand our energy: watching for ice, wiping her hand on the inside of the windshield, getting the aging car into gear. How painful it is to make that switch. Betty still feels guilty. Maybe her words cost Lincoln some contact with his mother.

Betty folds her hands and looks at Lincoln's presents. Little does he know he has inherited his mother's indecision, her bashfulness. Betty knows he is curious, has a head full of questions. He holds her responsible because she won't talk about those times, those dark years between 1969 and 1971. He blames her because she is all he has to blame. Caroline is dead, Irma ran off, and Simon is incomprehensible.

The truth is so incomplete, so unsatisfying, not to mention painful, that she can't bring herself to tell it. She's the grandmother, after all. She's supposed to soothe. What kind of comfort is there in saying she doesn't know? I don't know why your uncle killed your father. I don't know why your mother dumped you here.

Silence and love seem the only answer. In these changed times, when people don't know how to treat one another anymore, talk about how things used to be isn't much of a solace.

Maybe the move will help. It would be a relief for Lincoln, maybe for Betty as well, to fret about the present, about a place to live, work, go to school, instead of the freight of the past. It would help if Simon let his feet work their way south to his old home. Betty had meant it when she said he should come by—for Lincoln, if not for her. She isn't comfortable with the idea of explaining everything to Lincoln. Simon would be even more reluctant, but at least he could wean Lincoln away from his lonely circuit of school and home. Maybe if Lincoln was sandwiched between One-Two's future hopes and Simon's lost ones, he could shake himself out of the solitude he has forged out of an unspoken past.

Betty looks again at the presents tucked under the tree. The expensive Nikes and new jacket are what Lincoln wants. What for? He doesn't have any friends his age, or a girl, as far as Betty can tell.

Given his head, Lincoln stays home, or, at most, tags along with One-Two as he mends the old apartment building across the way. It will be the last holiday at the no-numbered house. By the time spring rolls around, they'll be up north where Lincoln will have to make do, just as she will, without One-Two and the comfort of sameness that being in the house has afforded them.

As much as she loves Lincoln's quiet ways, she does miss the rough joy of having Lester and Simon around. In comparison, Lincoln's father and uncle seemed stronger, Lincoln more vulnerable. He is inquisitive but afraid to ask the questions. Betty is the opposite: content to let things be, but hungry for a resolution that necessitates asking the unaskable. And more important, with the passing of time, what is the sum of her life? Is she to add and subtract with each death? Jacob, Lester, Caroline. Take away with every missed opportunity? The city, work, One-Two. She subtracts continually, until what she holds is as hollow and worthless as an ant-eaten turtle shell. Complicated and brittle.

Rather than that, than the bruised boxes sitting under the tree, she would have life the way it was. Even though it was hard. Fresh snow, the felt hats of seasonal shoppers, the tumble of her children, and nothing in her hands, just the ability to catch and hold, first Irma, then Caroline, as they ran fresh-faced into her embrace, their little-girl gestures as they wiped the melting snow from their faces. Lester's voice mingling with the sidewalk sounds as he untangled himself from Simon. *I got you.* No you didn't. *I got you. I got you.*

12

It is February, and dark inside Simon's windowless room as well as out, when Simon wakes to see Split smoking his last cigarette. He puts the battered tin coffeepot on the hot plate, and plugs it into the tattered and taped extension cord that lies dead on the dank cement floor. Simon looks over at the clock. The bent hands rock beneath the scratched plastic cover and phosphor faintly in the dark. It is 4:30 A.M. Split staggers around the room hunting for clean cups and powdered creamer. Simon squints and turns away when Split pulls the light chain. The single dusty bulb moves back and forth like a censer as it throws out its pitiful light.

Simon pulls the ragged wool blanket closer, trying to dive back into the cocoon of sleep, trying to recapture his delicate silhouette of warmth.

Split stubs his feet into the slop bucket and swears. He stumbles and catches himself on the sink. Simon hears more rummaging and the clink of spoons in cups. The bed folds as Split's weight hits the middle of the sagging mattress. The enameled tin cups tumble on the floor and the spoons clang on the cement.

"Jesus," sighs Simon.

"Sorry," mumbles Split, coughing around his cigarette as he bends to retrieve the cups and spoons.

Split leans over and places them next to the hot plate on the table, whose Formica top is peeling from the particleboard like a snake shedding its skin. His weight settles back down on the bed and he sucks on the cigarette as Simon tries to ignore the weight and smell of him.

The coffee begins to perk and the bed jumps back to its usual shape as Split stands and rubs out the cigarette with the empty toe of his battered salt-split boot.

"Come on, Simon. Rise and shine."

"Go away, Split."

"But we gotta go. Coffee's ready."

Simon sits up with the blanket wrapped around his shoulders.

Split stands unsteadily in the center of the cramped room and drinks from Simon's bottle of mouthwash. He glances at Simon over the slope of the bottle and sets it down sheepishly. Simon shakes his head.

"What're you doing here? Christ, you smell worse than you did in jail."

"They made me take baths in Stillwater. Out here I'm my own man. Hurry up, we're gonna make some money."

"What?" says Simon, looking at the clock. "What are you plannin? To panhandle some hookers? Ain't no one else awake right now."

"Naw, naw. Real money. T-Man'll be over soon."

Simon shrugs the blanket closer around his shoulders and sighs. "Real money?"

"Yeah."

Split takes the coffeepot off the hot plate and pours two cups to the top and hands one to Simon. It steams and splashes and Simon holds it gingerly by the tin handle, blows and sips carefully.

"You hear about the car out on the ice down below the university? They got this car out on the ice and they're selling tickets on the radio. Whoever guesses when it'll go through gets five hundred dollars. It's not a new car, some wreck they got from the dump. Anyway, I got tickets and I know when it's gonna break through."

"You're crazy."

"I got stuff to break the ice and I got salt in case it doesn't go right away."

"You're crazy."

"Naw, man. It's sure money. No one's guarding it. Here," he says, handing Simon his pants from where they hang over the back of the single chair.

Simon sets his coffee cup on the table. He stands and slips the pants on. The jeans are stiff with dirt and cold.

They hear feet on the cement steps and the shudder of the door as T-Man leans his weight against the water-swollen wood and pops it open.

He pushes the door shut with his shoulder and stamps his feet to move the cold that sticks to his boots.

Split and Simon nod. T-Man nods back, says "Hey," and winds his way between them to the table where the coffeepot sits alone on a piece of bathroom tile that has found new life as a trivet. He pours a cup of coffee and spoons in creamer and sugar and stirs it as he sits down on the bowed bed.

"Ready to make some money?"

Simon shakes his head.

"You're crazy, too."

T-Man shrugs and drinks.

"I've heard of worse ways to scam some green."

"I got it all figured out," says Split. He tips the bottom of his cup toward the low-slung ceiling. Above, the hotel maids are already washing the yellowed sheets and pillowcases, pulling apart the stuck-together towels. "Well, we don't got all day."

"Yeah yeah yeah," says Simon as he places his cup on the table and lets the blanket fall from his now-awake body. He retrieves a crumpled shirt from a cardboard box under the bed. He pulls it on, passing his hands down the front to smooth the wrinkles and unhooks his coat from where it perches dead-winged on the corner of the iron bed rail.

"Well?" says Simon.

"All right then."

The three rise from the gloom wrapped in their jackets as tattered as winding cloth and move to the door, and out. Split picks up a piece of metal that leans in the shadow of the jamb and it scrapes across the cement floor. He folds it into his coat as they pass the row of rusted boilers and the maze of pipes that snake out into the body of the hotel. They take the steps to the dim hallway that slinks past the laundry room. Just passing shadows, they tilt darkly down the hall and out the back door into the alley. They step into the winter blackness, into the stammering heart of the city.

They set off down Third Avenue to the river, keeping to the smaller streets which in a few hours will see cars quietly lining the chipped aprons of warehouses and plants still sucking life from the Mississippi. The rest of the city averts its eyes and thinks about the cold. Downtown is still; no one is on the street, and along the straight stretch of Third the traffic lights change in succession, marking the passing of nothing, miming the flow of traffic. The buildings reach high and through the dome of orange city light the stars whisper pale and unmoved. Three blocks west the IDS Tower rises unfettered by the spare night. Dayton's storefronts are bathed in light and the mannequins sleep standing up, already surrounded by Easter fluff and rabbits wearing hats.

A taxi rolls by and T-Man and Simon watch as Split nudges a Marlboro from his pack. He holds the box out to Simon without turning his head as he fumbles in his trouser pockets for a book of matches. They light up and continue down Third Avenue behind the bobbing constellation of their cigarettes. They pass the police station with its beasts of burden parked docilely along the curb. They hurry over Fifth Street, all of them trying not to look back at the station, but not letting the others know. There are fears among men that are not shared. Third Avenue begins to rise and the gurgling of sewers and steam is replaced with the slush of the river as they near the bank. The wind blows strong over the river and the dam spins the ice-choked water in a yellow spume. It hums against the concrete banks and through the footings of the bridge. Flats of ice break free and are swept toward the violence of water and are crushed and disappear.

They retreat as far as they can into their coats and reach out with their hands only to flick the gray ash from their cigarettes.

"Where's the car?" asks Simon.

Split points downriver.

"Around the bend, before you get to the Franklin Bridge."

"Why'd we go this way, then?" asks T-Man.

"Cause it's scenic."

They cross over the river and cut along the warehouses on Main Street and the East River grain elevators. They move away from the river and follow the railroad tracks until they skirt the old stone bridge that juts out into the river like a Roman ruin, and walk under the Tenth Avenue Bridge. The wind isn't so strong by the water. The ice runs from the banks toward the center channel like the shoulders of an inhospitable and damaged road out into the night.

Split stumbles as they step over the rail and catches himself on Simon's shoulder.

"It's a bitch not having toes," he says.

He shakes his foot and sets it down carefully as they part the weeds and winter-stripped brush and step on the river's edge. Beer cans roll like tin chimes and lodge in the lee of angled chunks of ice.

Split grabs on to T-Man's sleeve as they pick their way over the frozen skin of the river.

"Don't pull so hard," says T-Man as Split's weight tips him to one side.

"You sure it's safe?" asks Simon as they venture out.

"They've got a fuckin Ford out there," he rasps. "If it can hold that, it can hold us."

Two cars putter up East River Road and onto Fourteenth Avenue.

Ahead the river deepens and the current slows. If not for the sound of the dam upstream and the loosened plates of ice in the center of the channel, they might be walking on a northern field or a mall parking lot.

The shelf of ice runs fifty feet into the center of the river and ahead the bulk of the car rests out in the open, a dark shape against the incandescent snow. Slowly, they angle away from the bank and onto the ice, approaching the car cautiously.

It is an old Fairmont, of course. The windows are broken out and two doors are missing. Inside, they see the upholstery shedding in the winter wind. The whole bulk of the car tilts crazily to one side. Both the hood and trunk lid are missing, like a broken safe. The engine has been ripped out and there are no tires: the rims have melted into the ice and frozen again, buried to the axle.

They hear a boom like a gunshot. Simon and T-Man duck. They hear an echo and low rumble across the water. A shudder runs through the ice.

Split snorts. "They ain't shootin at us. It's just the ice. It does that all the time in the spring."

"It's just the ice cracking?" asks T-Man.

"Sure."

"Then what the hell we doin out here?"

Split ignores him and limps directly up to the car.

Simon and T-Man shrug and follow behind uneasily. Split takes a bag of pickling salt from the cave of his coat pocket and sets it on top of the car. He reaches into the folds of his coat and withdraws the iron bar, a tie-rod ground down to a chisel point on one end.

"Here," he says, holding out the bag of salt away from his body without looking.

Simon takes the salt and holds it as the wind curls back the edges of brown paper.

"Sprinkle a circle around the car, maybe a foot away. Keep the line thick."

Simon and T-Man circle the car slowly, pouring the bag out in a line. The ice booms near the channel and they hear a car horn bleat across the water on the West Bank below the Law School. They move in tandem: one walking backward while the other pours. The wind is light and they shake the bag, rationing the salt into a line around the car. Split has the tie-rod in his hands and he raises it above his head and begins to sink the point into the ice, working it into flakes that spill out onto the frozen plane like crystallized sawdust. He starts near the front end of the Fairmont, shuffling back in straight lines, almost tipping over sometimes, but catching himself, and driving the metal into the ice again and again. The wind blows above the river, above the dented current and the chunky flow of water. The air is warming.

Simon and T-Man finish pouring the salt and Simon shoves the empty bag into his coat pocket, closing his ungloved hand over the rough paper. They lean up against the car as Split teeters and jams the tie-rod again and again into the ice. They scrape away the snow with their feet. The ice is dull black. The punctures made by the steel bar bleed slushy water onto the skin of river ice. Split has perforated the shelf in two long lines, from the rear doors out at angles away from the tail of the Fairmont. He turns and works his way back to the car.

He is breathing heavily as he coughs and spits. He puts the makeshift chisel down and rubs his numb hands together before he withdraws a cigarette. He hands them the pack and they each take one. Split turns into the wind and tears a match from the book, sticks it between his index and middle fingers on the palm side, strikes it and cups his hands so the pale fire crawls up the match and jumps to the cigarette. He whips it out into the snow, takes a drag, and passes the lit cigarette over to T-Man.

"Jump start," he says, giggling. "Better in the wind."

Simon and T-Man nod as they roll the cherry onto their cigarettes, inhale and pass it back to Split.

"You're a funny guy," says T-Man. "But looks aren't everything."

They all bob and nod their heads as a substitute for outright laughter, for there is a night hush, a pattern of sound that tells them a laugh would die out into the night.

"Let's go," whispers Simon, as he takes a deep pull of his cigarette.

"One last thing," says Split.

He picks up the tie-rod again and walks to the front and punches it at an angle under the right front tire. He works it back and forth, pausing to pull his jacket cuffs up over his chafed hands.

Simon and T-Man retreat into their coats and look out at Split. They hear a deep pop and seawater welling around the hole. Split grunts and moves the point six inches away. Another pop and water skates over the ice. Split lowers the bar and works it back and forth like a lever until there is a jagged line through the ice. Simon and T-Man back away from the car, lifting their feet high like dancers as the slushy water moves and channels over the blackening ice.

"Ready?" asks T-Man, watching the advance of water.

"My tickets say tomorrow and it's gonna be tomorrow," Split gasps, walking through water that is already two inches deep.

He paces around the front bumper, dragging his toeless foot behind him. He positions himself with his legs spread over the left front wheel. He raises the iron bar in both hands and aims for the ice as if offering a blood sacrifice. The ice booms again, closer this time. They hear a grating sound, like newspapers being crumpled in their ears. Another shot rings out. Water splashes up from the holes and Simon sees the front of the Fairmont shudder down into the water.

"Holy shit!" yells T-Man. He dives and scrambles away from the car. Split teeters, holding the iron bar above his head. He looks around, not sure where the sound and water are coming from.

There is another crash, and the rear of the Ford sinks to the bumper. A gout of water, black in the moonless sky, rises high above Split and crashes down. Split falls and the iron bar skids along the ice. Simon throws himself flat and tries to see Split through the water that spills and spreads in all directions. The Ford tilts front and back, sawing through the water as it begins to sink. Simon's hands are numb but he can feel the ice groaning and shimmying. He tries to scoot back farther toward shore, but the water-coated ice is too slick. He scrambles to his hands and knees and backs away, looking for a sign of Split.

The Fairmont is in the river up to the windows. The water gushes and slops over the sills and onto the floor until only the turtle-like top of the car is visible. Then that, too, is gone, and the river is calm.

"You okay?" calls T-Man.

"Yeah," says Simon.

They crawl toward each other but don't stand up. They look over the broken ice, huge triangles that bump and lift with the current where the car used to be.

"You see him?" asks T-Man. Simon shakes his head. His ears are ringing from the cold water that soaks his shoddy clothes.

"Damn," says T-Man, "he had the smokes, too."

"That's cold, man."

"Sorry. Sorry."

They hear the slabs of ice rubbing against one another, then a voice.

"You guys there? You guys there?"

It is Split.

Simon stands stooped over, as if this posture would save him if the ice gave way.

Split is kneeling on the ice across the broken expanse where the Ford used to be. He is wet all the way through, his hair shaggy and sodden down his forehead. Simon sees his teeth gleam as he grins and shakes his head, shedding water. He picks up one hand first and then the other, trying to warm them.

"We thought you drowned," says Simon, still crouching. Aware of the betrayal of geography.

"Me, too," says Split.

He pats his pockets for his cigarettes. He looks and tosses them into the slushy water.

"Wet," he says.

T-Man crawls toward Simon and stands, craning his neck to see Split.

"Sorry about the cigarette joke, man."

"What?"

"Nothin. Nothin. You gonna sit out there all day? Let's go get your money."

They see Split nod and stand. He brushes his hands off on his wool coat, takes a step, and stops.

"Fuck me," he says.

"What?" ask Simon and T-Man in unison.

"I'm floating."

He takes another step and Simon sees the ice tilt. Split's arms mill and he slips. He lands with his legs spread. The ice tilts back and forth.

"I'm floating."

Split looks around, turning his neck this way and that. Simon sees the ice tilt and Split throw himself flat on his back with his arms spread, but the motion rocks the ice farther to the side. Split hisses and rolls to his stomach, but the ice rocks and rocks. He slides and his hands and feet make shucking sounds through the iced water. His frictionless glide to the edge of the ice is slow.

"Fuck me," says Split quietly, as his legs slide into the water then his chest and arms. He vanishes from sight and the ice flips up level with the water. Simon and T-Man stand without calling, without saying his name, and hear only the lapping of water and distant car horns, and the level slick of the river as it spills past.

13

Since Split's death Simon has taken to following Vera. He has
learned her schedule, the odd hours she keeps at the jewelry store
that specializes in electroplated gold and zircon. Jewelry made to
suggest wealth but sold mostly to status-driven gangsters and businessmen who buy the fakes for their wives and the real thing for
their lovers. Their lovers have made the receipt of these gifts a sup-
plementary income. They know it is only a matter of time before
they move up or down the IDS Tower, or out to the one-level com-
plexes in the suburbs where a new boss or partner will begin with
lunch and graduate up to late nights and then to drinks, bed, sex,
guilt, and another set of earrings. Earrings are always the last choice
because they snag on sweaters and wedge in car seats like ticks to
be found at the worst times—during family picnics, high school
graduation receptions, spring cleanings, or promotion parties. So
the devious and wise stick to necklaces, bracelets and lingerie,
things that can be hidden, dismantled, but easily found.

Simon knows Vera's schedule and when he finishes his work at the Curtis he follows her a little farther each day, creeping steadily closer to where she crosses the freeway to the Northside. He is still timid in this exercise, still reluctant to follow her all the way, yet he feels he must. He has monitored her stride and carriage, her habits, but he has not seen her at rest. He has not caught her standing still or sitting, and so he cannot fully read her yet. He needs to study her stillness like a picture to accurately gauge the magnitude of her loss. He lags a full block behind in the army coat he got from the Salvation Army, with a copy of *Oui* or *High Society* he's borrowed from Dougan rolled damply in the flap pocket. Afterward he usually reads under the Third Avenue Bridge.

It is April and rainy. Killing weather, his father used to say. Killing weather, when the ducks came in low, their wings too heavy with water to sustain flight, and the deer moved slowly, feeding cautiously, released from the confines of winter. The rain hushed movement and smell as Jacob shook Simon awake before dawn and they crept out of the cabin to pole through the flooded swamps springing mallards and teal.

It is different in the city. A place of sight more than anything else. A place where Simon notices the rain, the dusty splock of water rejected by the pavement, jumped into mist that hovers above the ground. A place where certain smells register: exhaust fumes, the muddy mass of the river. But mostly it is visual. The streets of Minneapolis are too wide to box the sounds of urban life, and instead let them escape skyward like released balloons. The palette of smells from restaurants doesn't hang in the air; the greasy perfumes of pretzel stands and corner pizzerias, or the ground-hugging vapors of garlic and thyme, are absent. The buildings are either too new or too far apart, the inspectors too intent on proper venting and the commissioner of transportation overattentive to garbage, which is tucked carefully at the rear of buildings, and never collects more than a handful of bluebottles and yellow jackets.

These are the things that shield and comfort most city people, that mark the place as different from any other. This skin of noise and smell. Without it they feel exposed, naked in everyone else's line of sight. Without the apparel of the city to cloak him, Simon follows Vera a block back, hunched inside the army coat no matter the weather, banking on the drab-green martial color to hide him, a fashion craze recently taken up by anemic college students.

In the mornings Simon hurries through the tasks that Dougan sets him to in the belly of the hotel. Strange chores not so much Herculean as Sisyphean: things that have to be redone moments after. With a wire brush he scrapes the rust from outgoing steam pipes though the moisture and heat cake them with oxide again within weeks. Dougan makes him polish the pressure gauges though the dials no longer work. They are stuck and Dougan has long ago pried off the glass plates and wound the hands to the proper pressure. He says he doesn't need to look at them, says that he has a sixth sense, like Spiderman, that tells him when to vent or stoke. But the building inspectors feel better when they see the shiny dials pointing like compasses to true north, to safety. *They,* said Dougan smugly, *know nothing of the hotel's temperament.* They have not worked there for thirty years. So every day Simon has something else to do. He scrapes the lint from the air vents, mops the dusty cement floor and crawls inside the oil furnace to clean the pilots and jets and change the filters. He does it all quickly, then grabs one of Dougan's skin magazines, wolfs down lunch in the back of the kitchen and follows Vera.

The rain slows him down and as he nears Fifth Avenue he glances over the rusted train shed at the clock tower on the Milwaukee Road, though it stopped long ago. He quickens his step and lights a cigarette and holds it underneath the hood of his cupped hand so the rain won't put it out. He rushes past the jewelry store and glares in, not expecting her there. Usually the last person in the shop is the manager, a beak-nosed man with acne in wrinkle-free polyester trousers and short sleeves that expose the skin of his forearms, as pasty and pale as fish belly, studded with thick black hairs. Simon looks in quickly, and in the air trap between the doors Vera is struggling to get her arms through the sleeves of her damp plastic trench coat, like a mink caught in a leghold trap.

Simon considers jumping back into the shelter of the Mill Inn but instead ducks and breaks into a trot. Vera must have freed herself from the twisted silver plastic and the door swings open as Simon flicks the butt into the gutter and with the agility of a tailback cuts into the next door and pulls it closed with a rattling crash behind him.

He flaps the jacket open to shake off the water. He looks up into a riot of carpets in stacks and rolls and on a wall-mounted rack like posters at a head shop.

"Can I help you?" someone asks.

It takes Simon a minute to sort through the patterns and textures. A small man, no taller than five feet, hoves into view from behind a stack of rugs. He wipes his mustache with a napkin and approaches Simon with his hands on his hips, his chest thrust out even with his curved belly.

"Can I help you?" he repeats, running his hand over his bald head and searching the front of his teeth for remainders of egg salad.

"Huh?" says Simon.

"Do you need a rug?" he says, gesturing at the expanse of carpets around the store.

"Why the fuck would I need a rug?" asks Simon suspiciously, backing toward the door.

"Why do you need a *rug*, or why do you *need* a rug?" asks the salesman professionally.

"Whatever."

"Why? Because they make you feel good. That's why."

"Why would a carpet make me feel good?"

The salesman winces. "They're rugs, not carpets."

"Okay."

"They make you feel good because they are special. They are distinct. No two are the same. They make you feel good because they will last longer than you. Because," he says finally, "because they're beautiful."

"I live in a basement."

"All the more reason," he says exuberantly. "All the more reason. You'd be able to say you live in a basement with a Bokhara."

"A what?"

"Bokhara. They're from Uzbekistan."

"Where?"

"Uzbekistan. It's in the USSR. But the tribe is more important than the country."

"Where are you from?" ventures Simon.

"From India."

"So you're Indian."

"So you are too, no?"

"Yeah. I suppose. They don't mind you selling rugs from Russia?"

"The rugs are older than our countries. But I don't sell rugs. I sell beauty," he says with dignity.

"How much does it cost?"

"Beauty costs a lot."

"How much?"

"From the middle range. About five hundred."

"Jesus Christ."

"It's a lot, but it will outlast you. You can give it to your kids."

"I don't got no kids."

"Your wife."

"Don't got one a them either."

"Your parents, then. Somebody."

"I don't got anyone. And I don't got five hundred dollars to put on my goddamn basement floor," he says hotly.

"It's okay, okay," says the salesman reassuringly. "It's okay. Look at it this way. You'll have the basement. Your room, whatever, but the rug will stay with you. Become part of you. Wherever you live, it will make it better."

Simon says nothing.

"Come here. I want to show you something. You must see them."

He beckons Simon to a waist-high stack of six-by-nines. He begins flipping them back like the pages of a huge telephone book. He mutters to himself, skipping over whole countries and tribes, styles older than any structure in the Midwest.

"Not Chinese. No, not Indian. Ahhhhh," he says.

He stands back and gazes at the exposed rug tenderly. Simon looks closer, too. The red is the rust of dried blood, the brown a dark chocolate. Simon cranes his neck and the close pile takes on a sheen like liquid and the borders are both smooth and angular, a rope in red and white, twisted in on itself over and over again. Simon reaches out and touches the rug with the palm of his hand. It is soft and stiff at the same time, like deer hair.

"What's it made outta?"

"Wool."

"Really?"

"Yes."

"How'd they get the design in there?"

"It's all knots. Thousands of knots tied together. They shear off the top to make it even."

Simon keeps looking.

"How much?"

"Six hundred fifty."

Simon stands up.

"I don't got six hundred and fifty."

"Six."

"Don't got it."

"Tell you what," says the salesman, turning as if a discussion of money shouldn't take place in front of the rug. "I need someone to help me move these, unload the truck once a week. Fifteen days of work and it's yours. That's forty dollars a day. I'll set it in the back in case anyone else wants it."

"When do I get it?"

"When you're done."

"I don't know."

Simon doesn't know what to say. He can feel Vera walking farther and farther down the street. Crossing over the bridge, receding in the rain-damped air.

"I don't know."

"Tell you what. Just come back tomorrow. Think about it overnight. Come back and let me know." He pauses, letting his rush of words and proposition settle. "My name is Ashish."

"Simon," says Simon. He bundles his coat up and walks out into the rain, hurrying to catch up with Vera.

She is waiting for him under the overhang of a newly built parking ramp two blocks down. She hugs her body and shivers. When she sees Simon she stops moving and looks at him coldly. Simon is still forty feet from her when he looks up. He stops walking and squints into the rain unsure if she's seen him, to see if he has time to turn around or duck into a side street, another store, anywhere other than the open run of concrete between them—gravel, sand, water and cement mix, three-to-one, laid in, leveled with a two-by-four, troweled, and cracking under the weight of the seasons and the travel of people, the mass of their histories and emotions.

She snickers and shakes her head, toeing out the remainder of her smoldering cigarette.

Simon knows he has been discovered and he shoves his hands in his pockets and shuffles closer with his head down.

"Hey."

"Simon."

"How you been keepin?"

"What you see is what you get." She opens the clasp to her plastic purse and takes another Misty Slim from a pack and Simon scrambles in his pocket to produce a lighter.

"How long you been workin at the store?"

"You should know, tracker."

Simon hangs his head.

"I first saw you bout a month back," he lies.

"How long you been out?"

"About a year."

"They finally sprung ya, huh?"

"Yeah. Finally. They figured they incarcerated all the harm outta me."

"Well, you don't got no more brothers to bump off."

He glares down at her.

"Sorry, Simon. I didn't mean it." She looks at her cigarette and across the street and back to Simon. For the first time she seems unsure. "Since you been followin me, you might as well walk me home."

"You don't mind?"

"If I did, would you stop?"

"I'm gettin a job at the rug store next door."

"There? Shit, he's fuckin some cashier from the Rainbow Foods on Lake, right there on the rugs. Well, we gonna walk?"

"Yeah. I'd like that."

They don't talk at first. Both look at the rain-grayed buildings and construct imaginary commentary on the weather, the cold, how the city has changed or not—which buildings have been torn down, which ones are new, which have been restored to their warehouse or shipping glory but mostly sit empty, studded with boutiques and coffee shops like scattered mold.

Simon tries to match his long strides with her speedy tick, he stoops over to reduce the distance between them. He's forgotten how short she is. She'd been so slight, so small, all legs and arms, with dancer's breasts. While he was in prison he remembered her as looming, as solid, wrapped around him, holding his head against her chest, the smell of her sweet and strong. She slows and relaxes into her stride, and so, despite the rain and cold, despite his stored grief and her hoarded rage, they begin to stroll.

This was how he'd imagined prison while he waited for sentencing in Hennepin County Jail. He'd imagined slate-gray rainy days and unexpected visitors, even Vera, and a stroll in the yard tinged with remorse and delicate sadness. He had imagined himself afterward, taking slow walks like a weary zoo animal that knows the margins of steel and stone.

But no one had come to see him. His time in the yard had always been tense, spent negotiating the other islands of men. Visits took place across Plexiglas and after the public defender came to tell him there would be no appeal, no one else came. The lawyer was fresh from some second-rate law school and full of the soft enthusiasm of those who expect power to grow from privilege, and who talked with his lawyer friends about "doing some good" over Heinekens at upscale sports bars. He looked guilty and hotly ashamed when he told Simon that there would be no second chance, but banged his pink fist against the table and said that he'd fight it. Simon could see he was horrified, itchy to get free of him. Simon suspects his case was not what the lawyer had imagined. He would rather defend an innocent darkie who'd been beaten up by the police, or a single mother and her children who'd been unfairly evicted by their white landlord. He had not come back.

"You been following your mom, too?" Vera doesn't look at him.

"I dropped by."

"Feel different bein out?"

Simon shrugs. "It just feels bigger, that's all."

"You look the same," she says, looking at him now.

"Why'd you leave Lincoln at Ma's house?"

"Don't even expect me to answer you; I don't have to answer you. You," she says, her voice rising.

"I was just wondering."

"Well, don't. You lost the right to ask."

Simon fumbles with a cigarette and busies himself lighting it.

"You still live with your folks?"

"You kidding? I live down the street from the old house, but they moved out to Saint Louis Park. Up and out."

They continue up Washington, the municipal buildings petering out until the older warehouses and streetcar storefronts emerge sheepishly in their wake. The cars shoot past, sinking and rising in the sagging, potholed road. No one is on foot. Even the check-cashing stores and rental shops are hooded in the rain, neon paling from behind the besmeared windows. They cross over the freeway on Broadway. The old neighborhood is looking older, rotting away since the streetcars disappeared in the fifties. They cross Dupont and then Emerson. Neither knows what to say, so they walk on in silence until they reach an abandoned storefront on Freemont and Broadway.

"We're here."

"Upstairs?"

"Yeah. Up on top. No way in hell I'm lettin you up, though."

"I wasn't gonna ask."

"Like hell. Anyway, I suppose I'll be seein you on Washington. But if you wanna walk, ask."

"Yeah, okay."

She keys the aging Yale lock and opens the glass door. She closes it behind her, shakes the water from her jacket, and stamps her feet on the dusty industrial carpet that runs up the stairs, puffy slick stuff made for lawyers' offices and motels.

Simon turns and hunches down in his jacket and begins walking back to the Curtis. It begins to rain harder.

14

Simon boosted Lester so he could slip quietly into Vera's room before she sat up in bed, startled awake by his presence. Lester laid his finger over his pursed lips. She stared at him, still trying to shake out the last shreds of sleep and distill from the wet night real shapes from shadows. Lester danced silently around the room, tossing clothes—jeans, T-shirt, windbreaker—on the bed.

"Get dressed," he whispered, before he scampered to the sill and, like a reverse beshadowed Santa Claus, poured his long dark body back out into the night.

Vera threw her clothes on, shivering in the air that coasted in the window. She hurried. Not because of the sound. Her parents were almost deaf from working in the East Saint Paul factories. The endearments shared by most couples who had seen the worst and stuck together, usually soft, feathered words, were shouted gruffly between her parents. Their love talk sounded more like argument than testament of affection. However, her father felt the slightest draft, in any season, and the thought that a door or window was letting out the heat, releasing the small precious wages they earned, sent him stumbling around the house to find the breached dike. Vera hurried into the pants and shirt and tossed her shoes and windbreaker out the window. She didn't pause to wonder or ask what they were doing or where they were going. The few short months she'd been with Lester had conditioned her to be ready for anything, any sort of contrived adventure. She half-expected to see a circus camped on Broadway as she straddled the sill, swung her other leg out and dropped down on the dew-soaked grass. She stooped to grab her shoes and jacket, tucked a wisplet of hair behind her ear, and looked for Simon and Lester. It was late May, the azaleas and potentilla had plumped out and it wasn't until she saw a wreath of smoke rising from behind the honeysuckle that she knew where they were.

"Where we going?" she asked as she took Lester's cigarette.

"Downtown," said Simon.

"What for?"

Simon rolled his eyes. "For a class trip."

He bent down and lifted a black nylon duffel by the strap. They walked in silence until they hit Lyndale, an aging grandparent next to the emerging freeway, just then under construction. The traffic thickened and they shouted over the rumble of semis and delivery trucks. Simon reached into the duffel and pulled out a bottle of Thunderbird and passed it to Lester.

"You want me to drink this?"

"I don't notice you payin for it," said Simon with a shrug.

"Good point. Guess this'll be a real Indian party. With one Pilgrim," he said, nudging Vera.

"Very funny."

She took the bottle and drank, a little too nonchalantly.

Simon and Lester raised their eyebrows at each other but said nothing.

"So where we going?" she repeated, wiping her lips on her sleeve.

"Told you already. Class trip, to the highest point in Minneapolis. We're going up."

"Where's that?"

"Wait and see."

They kept on Lyndale to avoid the small curving streets north of Hennepin. When they neared Loring Park, Simon stashed the bottle back in the duffel after he and Lester had another long drink.

"Jesus. Slow down. The two of you got to have the longest legs I ever seen."

They all laughed and Simon and Lester slowed their pace. Vera crossed her arms and Lester held her in a one-arm embrace, liking the sweet slick of her jacket against his bare arm and the berry tartness of her breath as she smiled up at him.

"Class trip, huh? Sounds exciting."

He squeezed her closer and Simon looked away from the intimate room they had carved out of the embrace and the damp air. Loring Park was empty except for the prostrate drunks and homeless who dotted the green, here and there, next to trees and hedges. Out of the way, so they wouldn't be stepped on or singled out for ridicule, but not tucked too far from view where anything could happen to them.

They crossed the park and on either side of Grant Street the apartment buildings curved like plowed furrows around a planting disc. The buildings were solid, with wide foyers for porters and valets who were no longer needed, now piled high with phone books and rusting bicycles.

Simon walked ahead on Marquette and heard Vera and Lester share some private joke that sent Vera squealing ahead a few steps before she was pulled back tight against Lester's side. She crept under his wing, still laughing. They passed the aging Radisson, its porticoes and cornices chipped and obsolete, the name alone encouraging its clientele to brave downtown streets in lieu of the Holiday Inns and Ramadas circling the city's neck, rambling blown-up versions of ranch-style houses piled next to miniature golf courses and Country Kitchens, a whole camp for families who didn't want to stray from the interstate. It certainly wasn't the Radisson itself that lured them. Three blocks down the incomplete IDS, with its steel exposed like starched bones, took up a whole block.

"Ninety thousand," said Simon.

Lester ignored him, familiar already with the offhand awe Simon adopted in relation to the building.

"What?" asked Vera.

"Ninety thousand cubic yards of concrete for the footings and pilings."

"And?"

Lester laughed.

"And that's a lot of fucking cement. It's buried three stories deep. The supports go deeper than that even."

They walked to the chain-link Cyclone fence around the site. Vera ran her fingers over the mesh, popping them over the openings. Even that temporary thing felt more solid than she did, more present. Her head spun lightly.

There was a break in the fence, a mesh door wired to an angle-iron frame. Simon took out a key and opened the padlock.

"Can we do this?" asked Vera, taking a step backward.

"We doin it ain't we? I work here, for Christ's sake."

She looked at Lester, not trusting Simon's hard smile. Afraid of the width of his shoulders, the flat strength of his hands.

Lester smiled reassuringly and nodded over her head at Simon. He motioned them through and shut the gate behind them.

The work site was littered with cement mixers and stray two-by-fours. The trailers where the foremen and architects hassled out the logistics of the new building sat like crusted biscuit tins. Lightly rusted H-beam and steel cable were mounded here and there. The ground where the Crystal Court would be was a level of sand studded with jagged beam ends.

"Watch your step," said Simon as he took the lead again and threaded his way through the equipment to the base of the tower, just a frame of girders with only the steel subflooring riveted on the first fifteen floors. He opened the mesh door to the lift and handed out two hard hats reserved for visiting city officials. Lester took them and lowered one onto Vera's head. The plastic webbing was too large and she had to tilt her chin up to see, the same way she used to try on her mother's Old World hats. Her family didn't go to temple or observe any of the holidays. Her parents only went to weddings, funerals, bar and bat mitzvahs, her father out of neighborhood solidarity, her mother to dress up. Her father always looked stiff and uncomfortable, awkward in the unforgiving wool. He was more comfortable in his canvas overalls with his head under the sink fixing a leak or bent over someone else's car. *We are unionists,* he'd say. *We don't need religion. We don't need holidays,* he'd say with vehemence. Though he got a Christmas tree every year and gathered quietly with his friends to drink beer and toast the dead on May Day.

Lester put on the hard hat, and they all got on the shaky lift. Simon closed the door, asked *Ready?* and thumbed the switch. With a jerk they started skyward. With his legs apart and his arms crossed, rocking slightly as the lift banged its way up, Simon stood like the captain of a ship on moderate seas. Lester held on to the mesh with a clawed hand and took long pulls off the Thunderbird with the other. He grinned at Vera, who shivered between them. The mesh grate diced the view, and without perspective the city lights were just lights that blinked steadily through the metal. Lester handed her the bottle and she drank carefully, but the motion of the lift sloshed the wine and it spilled down the front of her jacket. They all laughed. The farther up they got, the more relaxed Simon appeared to be. He seemed at home in the bare structure of what was going to be the tallest building in Minneapolis, the second tallest in the Midwest.

"What do you do up here, Simon?"

"Here? Here I do everything." He turned his head to take in the girders and stamped metal subflooring that advanced and receded, the loose cables strung next to the lift. "I do everything. We'll get you on the crew, Les. When you're old enough."

"I'm happy on the ground."

"Chickenshit. You'd be happier pulling fifteen dollars an hour in the air."

"Nope," said Lester. "I like it better down there."

He held out the bottle to Simon, who took it and held it to the scant pointillist light.

"Like I said, chickenshit."

He took a long drink and tapped the stop button. The lift jerked, bobbing up and down on the cable.

"I gotta get off this thing before I puke," said Vera.

Simon motioned her back, lifted the wire door and surveyed the floor. He held Vera's cool hand and helped her out. Lester jumped out with a hop. Simon hit the kill switch so no one could call the lift back down, and grabbed the duffel. The floor was empty, just a steel surface pimpled with rivets that made them lift and plant their feet carefully. There were a few piles of rebar and H-beam, buckets of rivets, but that was all. A steel frame and floor, no walls or stairs. There were no floors above, just the unfinished structure. A cage of beams ready to keep growing. Lester and Vera followed Simon, hand in hand.

Simon walked to the edge and dropped the bag. He bent down, heedless of the open edge, and unzipped it and pulled out a tangle of nylon webbing and rope that dripped from his hand like rabbit guts. He picked through it and extracted two pieces of webbing and held them out to Lester and Vera, who attempted to appear unconcerned as they looked over the edge.

"Put these on. Like a diaper."

Lester took the seats and handed one to Vera, who turned away from him, as if pulling on her panties on the edge of the bed at midday, nervous in the unforgiving sun.

Once they had the harnesses strapped on, Simon looped a be-
lay through the safety clamps and tied it around a piece of upright
I-beam.

"Now," he said, dusting his hands off, "now we're ready to
party."

He plopped down on the edge and took the wine and a prized
bottle of Royal Canadian that ambered the scant streetlights swinging up from below. Lester and Vera walked cautiously to the edge
and sat down slowly, white-knuckling the lip of the building.

"What about you?" asked Vera.

"Me? I don't need no rope. Shit, I can fly. I can float."

"How do you know if you've never taken a dive off a here?"

"Physics. The laws of physics. I'm too light."

He uncapped the whiskey and sipped it, inspected it again, and
passed it over to Lester. Lester drank and wiped his mouth.

"How about you, baby? Can you float?"

"Don't kid, Lester." She took the bottle gingerly and drank. Her
hand shook and Simon noticed.

"You scared, Vera?"

"No."

"Come on. You're scared."

"No." She took a stronger drink.

Simon leaned forward so he could look straight down.

"Ain't nothin down there to be afraid of. Just ground. Just dirt and
concrete, just asphalt and iron. No different than when we left it."

Vera coughed.

"For Christ's sake, don't puke. That there's good stuff. We'll
make you drink it back up like cats do so as it don't go to waste."

She shook her head. "It ain't the ground," she gasped. "It's the fall."

Simon shook his head vigorously.

"It ain't that either. And it ain't the distance. It's the air."

"You're drunk."

"Nope. Not yet. It's the air, I tell you. We ain't used to it all around us, ain't used to so much so fast. You slow it down and you'll be all right. You just slow it down."

"You're high."

"Ain't that either. Though that helps with the air."

"You ain't afraid of falling?" asked Vera incredulously, looking at Simon and then at the distant earth.

"Hell, no! I ain't afraid. Why do you think they hire Indians? We're not afraid, we're better."

Lester laughed. The whiskey and wine and Vera's sleek girlish muscle pressed against him made it come out long and loose and easy. "You're so full of shit."

"Am I? Am I?"

"Does a bear shit in the woods?

Simon rose so he was standing on the edge.

"Am I? Am I?"

Lester laughed again.

"Take it easy, bro. I'm just kidding."

"Have a drink," said Vera.

Simon kept saying "Am I? Am I?" as he took off his T-shirt, his favorite one with the Rolling Stones tongue and lips.

"Am I?"

He whooped and swung the shirt over his head in a fast circle and let it go over the edge, drifting like a stricken crow over the city.

"I ain't afraid of nothin!"

He turned and grabbed the upright beam behind him. He placed his feet in the cup formed by the H-beam and started to climb.

"Get down, Si, I was just kidding."

Simon kept shimmying up, monkeylike.

"Simon, get down," pleaded Vera.

He reached the framed story above and swung his legs up until he straddled the horizontal beam. The trusses and subflooring hadn't been attached yet. There was just the skeleton of the building swaying above them. He pulled his legs under and stood. His arms hung to his sides as if he were waiting in a slow checkout line at the supermarket. A thirty-one-story fall on one side, a fourteen-foot drop to the floor on the other.

Lester and Vera stood and backed away from the edge, never taking their eyes off Simon.

"You know what this'll look like when we're done? All sided in glass, a huge lobby four stories high. The floor laid out in marble. Sixty-thousand fuckin square feet of marble. And it'll be theirs. It'll be all theirs. They'll have some black man in a uniform at the desk. And they'll tell him not to let me in. They'll tell him to ask me my business."

He spat out over the edge. Lester and Vera stood still, as if their movement were Simon's movement and if they shifted suddenly he would step over the edge, he would fall.

"You're hammered, Simon."

"I ain't even started yet!" he roared. "So up here. This," he thrust out his arms, "this is all mine. This is all mine," he repeated, turning in a slow circle on the six-inch wide girder. He took a step forward.

"God, Simon, don't."

"So am I scared?"

"Don't, Simon."

He took another step forward along the beam.

Another. Vera and Lester followed, edging sideways. Simon kept going. Vera and Lester pulled up short, tethered to the far side by their harnesses. They didn't want to take their eyes away from Simon long enough to untie themselves. Simon reached the upright and stepped out with his left foot and swung around the corner like a kid swinging on a flagpole. His muscles tensed, the long tubes of his triceps bunched under the smooth felt of his skin.

Vera squealed and grabbed Lester's hand but dropped it immediately, the flesh too warm and alive to be secure. Instead she clenched her fingers in the thin fabric of Lester's overwashed T-shirt.

"Do something. Do something," she whispered. Simon turned and walked at a right angle toward the center of the building. Lester and Vera both slumped in relief. He was still fourteen feet above the steel floor but that fall wouldn't kill him.

"Dad shoulda done this. He could do anything, Lester. You name it. He could drop a tree on a dime. Patch a canoe. Roof. Sew nets. Shit, Les, he could do anything. Too bad you don't remember nothin."

"I remember some. I remember he killed a moose once."

"Shit," said Simon scornfully, "he killed everything that moved."

"I remember. Get down."

"You don't remember nothin. I bet you can't tell me one thing he said. One word."

Simon sped up and walked at a normal pace on the beam, arms swinging. He stepped around another upright beam at ninety degrees to the other, starting on the third side of the square.

"You don't even know what happened."

"Tree fell on him."

"Bullshit. That's not what happened. You don't know."

"That's what everyone said. Everyone knows that."

Simon shook his head. He was almost trotting along the beam. "Nobody knows."

"Simon," Lester was pleading with him, "you were there."

"Yeah," he said with a hiss, "yeah, I was there." He turned back onto the front beam, the edge of the building loomed. His long flat muscles tensed and slacked to keep himself balanced, a rhythm tapped out in his flesh.

"They say Indians are better at this than blacks or Mexicans. Better than everyone. That we have a gene that makes it so we don't get afraid of heights, that lets us keep our balance."

"Is it true?" asked Vera.

"Fuck no. We just don't care if we fall."

"I care," she stammered.

"You do?" Simon laughed. "What would you do? Would it change your life? Would you do anything different? Shit, you'd feel bad, maybe. Cry a little. Fuck my brother some more. That's it."

"Asshole," hissed Lester.

"Come on, Simon, get down, just get down." Vera was crying.

Simon stopped and sat on the beam, swung his legs to one side and eased himself off so he dangled above the floor and dropped down. He dusted his hands and looked at Lester and Vera.

"See. I didn't fall."

Vera wiped her face with her jacket sleeve.

"I want to go home."

"Come on," said Simon. "We're just getting started. We're gonna do the bridge next. It's an architectural tour."

"I want to go home."

Simon sighed. "Jesus, a couple of swigs of T-bird and she starts crying."

"Leave her alone, Simon. I'll take her. I'll take her and come back."

"You, too? Shit."

"I'll come back, bro. Just hang tight. I'll come back."

"Please, Lester, please. Just take me home."

Simon turned away and picked up the whiskey and drank, great sucks at the bottle, throat clenching.

They didn't talk on the way back. Vera leaned into Lester's body for shelter and he held her without comment, watchful for trouble on the streets. He felt strangely unarmed, vulnerable without Simon's craziness to shield him and Vera from the world that poured around them. He thought he looked like an easy target, though he always got into more trouble when he was with Simon.

They reached Vera's house and walked along the back path crowded with daylilies that needed dividing. Vera always noticed those sturdy flowers and wondered at her parents' backyard bickering as to what to plant and where. Coreopsis or Jacob's Ladder? The creeping phlox here? They practically staggered home from the factory but changed into their denim gardening clothes and trundled out the metal rake and the spade to turn the compost. Vera couldn't understand their bitter enthusiasm for flowers, for something so decorative and inconsequential, for something that did not contribute, as most everything else of interest to them did, to their security or health. She mistook their civic pride for whimsy. Their botanical efforts reflected their daily wonder at the space at their disposal, so much more space and freedom than in Poland. Vera only saw it as a waste of time, not as an act of will. Her parents planted these hardy ornaments because they could, because here, at least, no one would drive a tank over them. They would not wake to find a bomb planted nosedown like a sculpture among the irises.

Lester pushed the window open and lifted Vera up by the waist. She scrambled for purchase and popped the curtain hooks from the rod before she got hold of the radiator and swung her legs inside. Lester hoisted himself quickly and shut the window. They tried to quiet their breathing and listened for other sounds. There was nothing. Vera sat on her hands, suddenly shy. She looked away from Lester.

"You not still pissed at Simon, are you?"

She shook her head.

"He didn't mean nothin. He's just drunk's all. He gets like that."

She didn't look at him or free her hands and leaned her head against his shoulder.

"Something wrong?" asked Lester.

She shook her head again. He put his arm around her. And maybe this is all we need. The gestures of others to surround us. Empty of the rush of words, the salvation of giant acts.

They lay down on the bed and undressed. Vera was matter-of-fact now. They undressed like adults, without the nervous, quivering striptease of teenagers: uncertainty and desire rolled up together so that taking off pants became a negotiation, the freeing of her breasts a promise, no matter how temporary or false. They were wise, were old, too old for their age.

Afterward, in a moment of daring, they leaned out the open window, still naked, to share a cigarette, passing it back and forth instead of conversation, letting the air dry them, laughing at the picture of her stomach, the semen dried there like invisible ink, noticed only by them, laughing in the sulfur light from the street, laughing at the delicate liquid map painted on her stomach.

Simon was where Lester had left him. He lay on his back with his head to the edge of the building, empty air touching his hair. Lester stretched out next to him.

"You remember rice camp?"

"I think I'm drunk," said Simon.

"Rice camp. In the fall. We'd lay like this in the tent."

"You was a skinny kid, Lester," slurred Simon.

"We lay there with our heads out the flaps. Mom and Dad were sleeping, the girls were just babies. We'd look up at the sky for UFOs. You remember that?"

"You were so skinny we just turned an otter skin inside out for your sleeping bag."

"Let's go home, Si. Ma's on night shift and we gotta get the girls to school."

"He got killed by a tree."

"I know."

"A fuckin tree fell on him."

"I know."

Simon raised his arms and clenched his fists. "I could lift it now. Bet I could lift that fuckin poplar off now."

"You was a kid, Simon."

"Ever lift dry poplar? Ever? There ain't nothin to it. Like cardboard."

"Let's go home."

"But wet. Wet it weighs a ton, all that water trapped there. Lester, it's so heavy when it's wet, but I know I could lift it now."

Lester helped him up and collected the empty bottles and harnesses. He held Simon around the waist until they got in the lift and closed the cage. On the street the beginnings of traffic coasted unimpeded on the broad avenues. Newspaper trucks, service vehicles, vans with ladders strapped to the roof. The sky was pink and ready to turn over. Simon pulled himself up, minus his T-shirt, and they walked home shoulder to shoulder.

Remember this. Keep the brothers walking home at dawn. Remember the curve of their backs. Simon hunched around his stomach and Lester off balance to the left, ready to catch and hold. Study their strides. Simon walks conscious of his own power, the beauty of his strength. Lester is tense, not sure if he can catch Simon if he does fall. Look at the way they move together. Lester one step behind Simon so he can react if need be.

Collect all this and hold it together and remember. Do not forget. Everyone will ask, will wonder: Could you see it, was there any echo of the violence to come? If you had been on your way home—security guard, baker, porter, desk clerk, student, or one of the countless insomniacs found in every city—would you have noticed the intent, the horrible future crouched in Simon's body, the deadly promise of his hands?

Maybe not. Perhaps not. It's been a long night. There are chores and a family waiting at home. Phone calls to make. There is only the stagger and hoarse laughter of two men trying to steady the walk home. No maps of the future. Nothing to remember.

15

Vera couldn't wait to get out of the house. The school year was almost over. She was impatient to rid herself of her books and the kitchen chores she committed like prayer next to her mother. She was anxious to shed the smells of cabbage and the fog of her father's pipe, the one bourgeois extravagance he allowed himself. She changed into pants and a sweater and brushed out her hair and when the front door banged shut behind her, the spring afternoon actually seemed lighter.

Her parents were loath to let her go. They looked perplexed at her requests to be let out with her girlfriends for a soda. Why? That's what Sundays are for. Her father turned back to the newspaper. Her mother finished whatever she was doing, washing or canning, and turned to look at Vera head-on. Vera couldn't hold her gaze and tried to sneak around the corners of it like a mouse trapped along a bare wall. Her mother looked at her. She was not stupid; she suspected that Vera's insistence was about a boy, but let her go anyway. It is different now, different times, a different place, but the same urges, so she let her go. Vera's father probably suspected the same, and together, their parental imaginations conjured up a strapping Scandinavian kid, the family recently moved in from the farm. And that was okay. *We are in America, we do what they do here,* he always said.

Vera skipped down the steps but slowed and was careful not to swing her arms. She didn't want to sweat, to feel her skin turn hot under her scratchy sweater. She slowed and turned onto Broadway and the low-slung dusk lightened a bit. The city glinted and sparkled. Everything on Broadway looked chromed in the setting sun. Bel Airs and Cadillacs coasted down the boulevard, regal and serene, sanely carrying their occupants home from work. Wives in long coats as stiff as armor lugged mesh bags from delis and corner stores, and a few carried paper sacks from the new supermarket on Sixth Avenue. There were kids dodging cars and bootblacks stepped from their stations to smoke and get fresh air on the sidewalk.

There seemed to be radios everywhere. Music and DJ-hype came from open car windows and above-shop apartments. Bridgeman's was packed with teenagers, juiced on sugar and the Rolling Stones, a throng of blushing hungry kids from north Minneapolis. The black soda jerks tried to keep up but couldn't. They didn't look at the customers, but through their lowered lashes and rapid dance of ice cream scoops and soda levers they seemed to have a language of their own that was slick and fast and beautiful anyway. No one talked about the war or the protests, some purposeful and others merely carnival, down at the University and farther away in Chicago and DC. The Democratic National Convention was a faint three-year-old echo in the upper reaches of northern hearing. They still didn't talk about it. One of their own had been there, the local boy, Hubert Humphrey, and they felt shame and sadness for him, were embarrassed.

The boys who came back from Vietnam were bitter, but the people of Minneapolis were puzzled more than alarmed. The unrest among the students and teenagers manifested itself in loud music, bad taste, and sometimes earnest dialogue. Their rebellion was treated as if it were a fad, like troubadour pants: mildly alarming but something that would ultimately pass. As for the teenagers themselves, fashion, whether material or moral, always came slowly to the north. The city seemed so new, so out of the way, devoid of monument and proclamation. It lacked memorials, or seats of power so the protestors hardly had any targets at which to direct their anger.

Vera walked past Bridgeman's and nodded to a group of her friends who nodded back solemnly, bound by a pact to cover for her, so no words were needed. They did not fully understand why she wanted to sneak away to see Lester. They hadn't officially met him but had seen him, tall and angled, waiting at the bus stop. They didn't understand why she took the risk of seeing him, were half-scared and half awestruck at both Lester and the situation. To them he looked loaded and dangerous: dark and tall, and so different. They idolized Vera because of this and guarded her secret, acting as alibi when needed.

She saw Lester ahead at the bus stop and he *did* look serious. Though she didn't know it, he wore that face out of nervousness and perceived vulnerability in a strange neighborhood, among blacks he didn't know and foreign languages he didn't understand, distrustful of what he saw as the casual wealth of the area, though it was neither casual nor all that wealthy.

He didn't see her approach. He stood and leaned against the glassed bus stop watching the procession of traffic, the angled light creeping up the brick faces of the two- and three-story buildings. She quickened her step, straightened her sweater and smoothed her pants. This is the miracle of the modern city, of modern times. All the nervous courting gestures. The bus stop lean, the approaching night, her attempts to look the way she wants to look, conscious of how she smells, hoping her perfume still has the desired effect.

These gestures are everywhere. They are familiar. The questions these lovers' signs suggest and the future they tease are ageless, though their resolution is new every time. Apprehension and delight are as old as salt. Old, too, is the fact that the young lovers think their love is a secret. They think that what they feel and want is new, freshly unpackaged and radiant, that their parents never felt the same way. They think it is a secret, though the old lady behind Vera with an umbrella and a limp can tell by the skip and clatter of Vera's step where she's going. The owner of the vacuum-cleaner store on the corner reads Lester's feigned indifference, his studied nonchalance, as a siege of will and pride against Vera's tardiness. They've seen it all, but Vera and Lester think and feel they invented it. Where do they get this confidence, like that of doctors, to believe they are making life anew?

Lester turned and caught sight of Vera over his shoulder and stood straight but didn't know what to do with his hands. She hurried to him, breathless and fresh. The Hoover dealer turned back to closing his shop, barely aware of the drama, this simple street drama of two lovers meeting at the corner, but he knew it, at some deeper level, at a lower register, so he didn't have to watch anymore. He locked the door and gently thumbed off the light as the day ended.

It dominated the trainyard. Sphinxlike, in proud ruin amid the piles of bitumen mounded at the fence edge at war with the weeds. It was king, indifferent to the rusted rails on which it sat but, as anyone could tell, led nowhere. Axles, huge dumbbells of iron, were piled carelessly, sunset colors pounded in the rigid metal.

The Twin Cities Hiawatha made its last run on January 23, 1970. The FP45 engine was harnessed to freight service, but the coaches, Superdomes and Skytop Lounges were dragged to the Milwaukee Road service yard between Lake Street and Minnehaha Avenue, destined to rust and then die.

The glass was broken out and the skylights in the dining car empty of everything except sky that saw no change, no shifting frame of landscape. Just the dark bright dark bright tunneling of the sun. The city skyline was too shallow then, too distant to offer a view.

The stuffing had been blasted from the seats by the wind, and mice and rats had nibbled through the leather. The squatters left as soon as the demo crews sauntered railside with drill and torch to begin cutting. They began at the rear and moved forward, sawing through the grooved steel and lifting the sections off the tracks to be torched by the permit workers and loaded into dump trucks. What was once proud is to be mungoed and sold as scrap. Used to motion, to making the run between Chicago and Minneapolis, the train seemed surprised by the men hammering at it and carting away its body. It was too big to move, and if it could it would have bent back and snapped at the men sparking and burning its tail. It was unused to such disrespect.

The crews didn't mind, though. They would rather have been building, but it was a job. They were committed but casual about the destruction. What was supposed to be a three-week job turned into five and then six and still they weren't done. The union office was packed with books and permits, sipping coffee there and drinking on credit at the CC Club. There wasn't much real work to be had, and with winter coming on they knew the big jobs wouldn't be starting for a while. Work on the IDS wasn't due to begin until September. They held back, trying to make the job last. What began with indifference, just another cutting job, turned into reluctance. Ripping down buildings was tough work but the need was clear. The city must grow and the older buildings were in the way or unsafe, unwanted, not turning enough profit. The Hiawatha, however, was the best, the fastest streamliner there was. Half the men who signed on to destroy her suspected they had arrived in Minneapolis on that train. They took boats from Ireland, Germany, Sweden,

Norway and Italy, and docked in Chicago, bound for the interior of
a vast land. Back then the cars were pulled by steam engines, not
with the diesels that replaced them in the 1940s. The cars had
evolved and the lounges and smoking cars improved, but it felt like
the same train nonetheless. As they cut, they figured they rode the
train to Minneapolis, carried into the dark folds of the Midwest.
Minnesota. Even the names of places felt thick on their tongues.

Lester and Vera approached from the side, out in the open. The
squatters were gone. No one wanted to be in the doomed train being ripped of its skin, its ribs and frame cut away. The eternal ad-
versaries of rail travel, the bums and bulls, had finally agreed on
something: That it was too bad. That it had been a great train, and
they were ashamed. The squatters left for the subfloors and gutted
tenements of the Gateway, and the bulls to patrol other sections of
the railyard. No one wanted to look at the train. They agreed that
destruction should be done out suddenly, catastrophically. Destruction should be mindless, not meted out by executives—a ledgered,
meticulous death. They retreated to other city haunts in shame, and
for the first time since it was launched in Minneapolis on May 29,
1935 at twelve o'clock noon, having been christened with water
from Minnehaha Falls, The Hiawatha carried no mineral or human
freight. It no longer trucked the cargo of emotion, popular myth,
shelter, or travel. For the first time, as the crews sparked the cutting
torches and rubbed their gin-reddened eyes, it was devoid of a reason for being.

So Lester and Vera approached the train unnoticed, and without fanfare, without shout or whistle-blow, the hiss of air brakes or
the scowl of flat-footed and weary conductors. They boarded the
broken steps of a sleeper car and searched for a bunk not too soiled.
They found one that had candle wax melted to the lip of the bunk
below, with soot-blackened wood paneling, and an advertisement
that shouted *Henderson's Cars! All Models!* stuck between the mattress and the wall. They lay down. They spooned, still too shy and

tender to face each other, and looked through the broken window where dogs went high-tailed and snarling through the lot grass. The errant lights of the yard bosses sprayed the side of the car, but no one approached, and, on the edge of the city, they were alone.

It became their place. Though it was doomed, eaten up by the crews car by car, as the train used to devour the alluvial landscape from the Dells to Tomah, it became theirs. They were stowaways, jumpers staying in the state cabin previously reserved for Hubert Humphrey and the mobsters who came north from Chicago out of habit, since they no longer had to boat booze across northern lakes or cart it on wagons farther west.

It became theirs, silently straining toward the past. Lester and Vera realized early on that lovers have to make their own maps of the city. They had to time their comings and goings so they didn't run into the familiar—family or friends; or the too unfamiliar—resentful strangers who read their hand-holding, brown on white, as a tragic breach of etiquette, as the worst of all possible urban outcomes.

They created their own maps, secret itineraries across the northern and southern parts of the city. Vera's house was never an option, her parents too adept at tracking them, sniffing their urgent spoor on the lace doilies and the bent blades of grass in the garden. Betty's house was easier. She blueprinted her schedule so Lester and Simon could help with the girls. Her hours at the hospital switched from day to night, split time and staggered, all of which she wrote on a note card taped next to the fridge. The girls were at school from eight until two, so they were easy to avoid. Simon's shifts, however, were unpredictable. A two-day gig might only take an afternoon, or he might skip it altogether. Sometimes he didn't come home for days at a time. After he got paid there were drinks to buy, rounds for everyone. The women perched on bar stools, who knew all the rotating pay schedules of construction workers around the city, wouldn't let him out to see the light of day until the money was gone. Other times he didn't leave the house, usually in opposition to Betty's schedule. He didn't want to be there when she was. This was more than simple avoidance and Lester knew it, so he steered clear at these times.

Betty's house was easier, but unpredictable, so they were led to the train while it lasted, to one-dollar matinees, to the far-flung parks and bridges checkering the city. Their love was urgent. They were hasty, partly because of their age—they wanted it, they needed it—but also because, as the train began to disappear, they knew they didn't have much time.

16

On the lip of a new decade that promised everything, Betty loaded up the old Chevy station wagon that on the reservation also served as a hearse, taxi, ambulance, and tow truck, and left for the city.

There was so little room. The back was packed with garbage bags filled with clothes and quilts, with boxes that promised Sunkist oranges but instead held pots and pans and a few extra shoes that walked down from oldest to youngest. The girls lay on top of the bags, nested in overwashed quilts and winter jackets. They were so small that they could stretch out all the way and watch the faster, better-tuned traffic sweep up behind them and pass in a burst of exhaust and weary loose-knuckled tourist driving, until the swamp-bordered road resumed the metered ticking of tamarack and balsam.

Lester and Simon sat in the backseat and played at fighting over seat space, but neither one really felt like it. They were too excited by the view, the reality of new surroundings. The landscape didn't awe them much. It was familiar, but its rapid passing set them straighter in their seats, made them scrutinize the vanishing reservation. This time they were not simply going south for pitched basketball games in a border town. They weren't on a mission for some exotic tool their uncles and older second and third cousins swore they needed when what they really were after was an unmonitored binge, away from their wives and girlfriends, or both. Simon and Lester were usually taken along as alibi: *Here, see? I ain't going drinking.* Usually the boys ended up sitting in the car outside small neighborhood bars until they got bored and roamed the town picking fights with stray dogs and car windshields. When they were discovered by the white kids it became a real fight. The boys held their ground and fought hard so that their bruises and bloodied clothes wouldn't destroy their uncles' excuses.

Sitting in the back of the Chevy wagon, they wondered at the passing ditches and overtilled fields and knew that this was different, more significant, and so they struggled to take in everything.

Betty sat in the passenger's seat with her hands folded over her sequined purse and her legs tucked under her seat as far as they would go, as if her funeral dress, the best she had, demanded a stiff posture, a calculated demureness.

Frederic, Boo's father, drove and offered a constant stream of talk about this place or that. How a section of ditch that looked the same as any other to Simon and Lester had cradled the crash of four (no, wasn't it five?) teenagers. Or how about that streambed where so-and-so shot two big bucks. One shot from the .308 passed through the first and lodged in the second and they both went down, but the game warden came, took both, and arrested the dead-eye for poaching.

Betty nodded but said nothing, her silent acknowledgment the extent of her participation in this memory mapping. She just clutched the envelope purse a bit tighter, nodded, lit a cigarette and ashed out of the wing window.

They crossed some tracks and Simon looked up and realized

that he had never been this far from the reservation before, had never traveled so far in all his thirteen years. They rounded a curve and the town of Spunkley crept by on both sides of the road like a skulking animal. Betty told Fred to look for a restaurant. They slowed at the Blue Ox Inn but Betty shook her head.

"I ain't goin all this way to eat shoulder to shoulder with a bunch of lumberjacks."

They cruised by and the children began studying the low brick-and-frame buildings for a suitable place to eat, though they knew they had no say in the matter, or had any idea what "suitable" might be. They passed a lone gas station and saw a sprawling frame structure made to look like a Black Forest chateau, with crossed one-by-sixes stained brown and screwed into the fake plaster siding.

A neon sign hung next to the front door that read, *John and Jen's Cozy Den and Outdoorsman's Cafe.* Betty gritted her teeth and nodded.

"*Gaawiin gosha niminwenimaasiig gaayosejig.* But, better hunters than lumberjacks."

They swung the car in and rolled to a stop, the car as heavy and wide as a barge and the children half-expected a plank to be thrown from the doors to the sidewalk. Simon and Lester were out in a flash and popped the back hatch open so Caroline could worm out. Betty lined them up and made sure their clothes were clean, checked them for face dirt and grime under their fingernails. Satisfied, she held Irma and took the lead like she was going on point. All three children were solemn and mindful, masks of obedience painted over their uncertainty. They had never eaten in a restaurant before. They weren't sure if Betty had either, but didn't dare ask.

She approached the dining room, noticed the *Seat Yourself* sign and surveyed what the restaurant had to offer. There were scattered chairs and pine-top tables and, along the window overlooking the highway, three booths. The end booth nearest the kitchen was

packed with a family of six. Four children on the inside and the two
bleary parents squeezed on the ends like corks to keep their off-
spring from spilling out into the restaurant. They were eating
French toast while clutching cigarettes in their free hands.

The middle booth held three people—a teenage boy reading a
book on motorcars, and his parents. The wife was in khakis with a
bouquet of white hair around her unwrinkled face, clouds around
an opal. The man looked slightly annoyed and sipped coffee while
trying to cross and uncross his legs under the gum-studded table.
He wore an impossibly elegant white suit. Betty arrowed for the
last booth. She knew that they were watching her, a curious wood-
land misplacement. She put the boys next to Fred and Caroline be-
side her while she held Irma on her lap.

The waitress came over and asked Betty if she wanted coffee
and handed out six menus. Betty said *Yes* and locked eyes with the
waitress, a beautiful girl of nineteen or twenty. Betty surveyed her
wide liquid eyes and kissing-thick lips and could tell she was a
mixed blood. Betty was relieved and visibly relaxed. The waitress
turned and walked back to the kitchen and Betty noticed that she
was wearing white hospital shoes and figured that she must be a
nursing student at the university down the road. Betty turned and
looked at Simon who hadn't taken his eyes off the waitress.

"*Gego ganawaabamaaken.*"

He blushed and lowered his eyes.

"Don't bother opening the menu. I'll order for all of us."

The children knew this was not an arguing point and acqui-
esced though the thrill of being in a restaurant for the first time was
dulled by being treated as if they were in the school cafeteria.

When the waitress returned, Betty ordered tomato soup and
grilled cheese sandwiches all around. What to drink? Cokes.

The waitress wrote it down and spun away, her bobbed hair
flouncing. Simon almost fainted.

Instead, he looked around the diner. Above the windows the old striped wallpaper gave way to fake wainscoting of pressed wood panel. Here and there, at various levels and poses, perched every animal that had ever walked or flown the north woods. Moose heads, deer racks, bobcats gripping driftwood. Pine martens crouched next to glazed piles of partridge feathers. There was a lynx eating a rabbit. Fisher, ermine and hawks roosted at different levels of the canopy. A dusty eagle surveyed the entire menagerie from the corner of the room. Instead of looking at the waitress and exposing himself to ridicule from his mother and brother, Simon looked at each moth-eaten creature one by one. Some appeared predatory, others simply watchful of the traffic of tourists and food below.

"I wonder what they did with their insides," Simon thought out loud.

Betty sipped her Coke.

"Why'd you think I ordered grilled cheese?"

The girls kicked their legs against the pleathered booth and let out a drawn "Ewwwwww."

The man in the suit looked at his watch and gently urged his shirt cuff down to his wrist knuckle.

"Hey, buddy. You know what time it is?" asked the man in the far booth.

The suited man looked at his wife, who checked her own watch.

"One-thirty, I believe," she said with a thick accent.

The man nodded around his French toast and squirreled the syrup-soaked bread into his cheek. His wife peeked at the woman from behind the baby she had lifted on to her lap.

"German, huh? My folks was German."

The man in the suit shifted to face her. "Was?"

"Well," She shrugged. "They died."

"I suppose," he said in a voice as thick and sharp as cranberry gravy, "I suppose German-ness is something that expires along with life itself."

"I suppose," said the woman, clearing Jell-O salad off the fore-head of the baby eating like a natural disaster in front of her.

The suited man's wife leaned in and with her hands clasped in front of her said to the other woman, "We are not German."

"Oh. Okay."

The man in the suit snorted. "Can we leave these rubicund con-vives and resume the chase?"

The man behind him overheard and nodded vigorously in agreement.

"Yep. These are good vittles."

The man in the suit hid a wide grin behind a strategic cough and stood, gently closing his son's book. They strolled to the front, paid, and left in a blue Nash with New York plates and peeled north on the highway.

Simon's neck hurt from watching out the window. He thought entering the city would be sudden—a switch from woods to the narrow margins of tall buildings, like entering a tunnel at noon on a sunny day. But it wasn't like that. The woods, at first unbroken or studded with small farms, began to fan out. Larger fields appeared gradually. The trees changed from pine to red oak and maple. These became clustered in smaller and smaller groups, around farmhouses or planted as windbreaks. The fields were vermiculate with corn and soybeans, rowed as far as he could see. Instead of everything getting larger, instead of more, the land seemed to spread; no vast-ness or vista, there was simply more space between the ordinariness of clapboard houses, silos, tilting barns.

The towns got larger. The more traffic, it seemed, the shallower and longer the faces of the cities, until they blended with one an-other and seemed endless. Simon dozed and woke when the car stopped. They were at a traffic light. The buildings were low and dirty, with a different facade on each storefront.

Fred nosed the car to the curb. Betty instructed the children to wait, and not to get out. She and Fred slammed the doors and walked down the block. Soon the car began to heat up. It was August, and the heat rolled from the asphalt in waves, crushing Simon and Lester deeper in the car. They tried to keep the backs of their legs from sticking to the black plastic seat. It seemed like forever. Waiting in a station wagon on a long stretch of Lake Avenue. Waiting in the August heat. Waiting for the next part of their lives to begin.

17

Simon arrives well before the wrecking crews, knowing they will spend two hours clearing the corner of cars and setting up orange cones that will, it is hoped, warn the traffic on Franklin and Third away from the curb.

The no-numbered house is empty. The trim, fixtures, doors and windows have been removed. It is hollow, full of echo and dust and scraps of paper, old socks, straight pins and ballpoints wedged into cracks in the floor—things you always look for suddenly exposed by the receding high water of domestic living. You always need a pen when you don't have one, a dime when you have to make a call. Now, when the sad house and its sad history are about to end, all of this stuff springs back to remind you of time lost.

Simon knows when it was built, has seen the date scratched into the screed cement on the edge of the raincap: 1906. Like most of the houses in South Minneapolis it went up fast and cheap. He can guess what the walls are filled with, old copies of *Leslie's* and *McCall's*, tamped sawdust and wood shavings. The floor joists are probably thirty inches on center instead of twenty-four or sixteen. 1906 middle-class: for warehouse supers and accountants, flour buyers and ad men for General Mills, Kellogg's, and Pillsbury.

He arrives before the wrecking crews and stands back, refusing to enter the house, minus its numbers, and now without a door to knock on or windows to climb out of.

Better that way. Better that what happened there has no cover except for the worn carpeting thrown on the floor by One-Two under Betty's red-eyed supervision. Better that the doors and windows, moldings, sinks, toilet, gas range and clanking Frigidaire were scavenged from the overpriced wreckage of their lives by the landlord, still clinging to the property after all those years, like a pilot fish swimming under the jaws of a blinded shark. It is better that what was built hastily in 1906 and had been lived down for the ensuing seventy-six years will be replaced with a cinder block Amoco gas station. Nothing important ever happens at gas stations. They are held up, people shot in the parking lot, midnight calls made through blotched mascara at the pay phone, and this station will be no different. By 1997 thirteen people will have bled to death out on the oil-soaked asphalt, but this kind of death does not leave a mark on the place, not like fratricide inside a family's home. For this reason, the replacement of the sad little sagging house is not mourned by Simon or the rest of the neighborhood, none of whom have been able to forget what happened there.

Simon had known in advance about the house's demise. One-Two had searched him out at the Curtis but had not handed him this information. Simon had been with T-Man on one of their scavenging expeditions in the Phillips neighborhood, when he saw yellow notices stapled on trees and pasted on the bus stop. They were loud and obvious to those who knew what to look for, and Simon knew. He knew what that color meant.

When he first noticed the postings he waited at the bus stop until he spied Betty trudging home from the hospital. She didn't look up until she was close, though she had seen his shape, and without really looking, had known it was Simon. Only a mother can identify her children by their gestures and posture alone.

"So you're moving."

"Who told you that?"

Simon jerked his head at the demo notice on the bus stop.

"You're moving less you plan on livin in a vacant lot."

"Rojta sold it to make a gas station."

"Asshole."

"You care about that house? Woulda thought you'd be glad to see it gone. Even before Lester. Even before all that you never did like to spend much time under that roof."

"His roof. Didn't like to spend my time under his roof."

"We made it ours, Simon."

"Not so long as we were payin him." Simon loaded the word "pay" so full with spite that Betty took a step back.

"So where you goin?" he asked.

"Figured I'd move back up north."

"There ain't nothin there no more."

"I still got it in me. I'll figure somethin out. Besides, it'll get Lincoln out of the city."

"He's comin with, then?"

"Where else he gonna go? Don't know if he'll like it. Too slow some days, too fast others."

"I seen Vera."

Betty rolled her eyes.

"How she look?"

Simon shrugged. "Looks like Vera eleven years older and thirty pounds fatter."

"She ask about Lincoln?"

Simon shook his head. "He know who she is?"

"Never told him," said Betty. "She don't wanna know him, ain't gonna keep him, then I ain't gonna make it worse. I'm the only mamma he knows."

Simon looked around, his gaze aimless. "He's a good kid, Ma."

"He'll be all right if Boo and them don't make him crazy."

"He's a good kid. I gotta go."

"You comin by?"

"Didn't know if I should."

"Too late for should. Just do it."

Simon nodded assent and she continued up the sidewalk. He watched her take the steps, and though she wasn't more than fifty-two, she pushed herself up wearily. She's old, he thought, suddenly she is struggling with steps. She's got old overnight.

He beats the crews but is late coming over. Betty already packed what she could into the back of Boo's car while he was "on the town," gave the rest away, and the next day, with Boo bloodshot but steady behind the wheel, headed north. There were no drawn out good-byes to place or people, no last ditch effort at repair between Betty and Simon. She had no regrets, as far as Simon could tell, about the promised demise of the house. Betty simply folded that moment into the next and looked hard at trying to start again on the reservation.

Simon, however, fixed the date, memorized it, and came before the appointed hour to stand at the front of the house. It was the sixteenth of April, a little over a year since his release. He takes a step toward it, then, in a hurry, mounts the porch steps and walks through the gaping doorway.

Everything is gone. The couch, the battered coffee table. The kitchen looks grungy and cramped. How, he wonders, did all of us sit in there? It is empty and grimy, tracked by dust bunnies that blow around like tumbleweeds in the chill wind that shoots through the de-glassed windows. It is not the home he remembers. There is no sense of permanence, no halo of smoke-smudge around absent pictures, no worn linoleum to mark their old habit of shedding shoes and leaving them over the kitchen vent that exhaled the fierce but ineffectual coughings of the furnace below. There is nothing to say that they'd been there, that they'd endured, and finally, finally, outlived the house. Betty's compulsive rearranging had taken care of that. There are no hidden treasures—old baseball glove, extra coat hangers, lost checks or stray change—left in closets or under the sink. Simon walks through the whole house looking. There are no rent receipts that Betty kept hidden, afraid of curious comparison between the rent demanded and the actual money paid. If there are, tucked along the baseboard or slipped down the vents, they don't show the cost, the price Betty, in her way, and Simon in his, have paid to make ends meet.

But here and there, on the wall under the now-absent phone, on the sill next to the removed bunkbed in the girls' old room, there are phone numbers hastily written in pencil, green candle wax dripped on the sill, dented plaster. In the living room Simon notices something he has never seen before: a long scratch in the sheetrock, through the paint and paper. A long score like a claw mark. Standing in the living room Simon knows what made it: a shovel blade raised overhead.

He looks down at his feet. The carpet had been put in shortly after the police led him gently to the squad car. It covers the wood floor that soaked up Lester's blood. Should have known that wood was greedy. Should have guessed that the floor, ignored most of the time, was ready to accept what they gave it.

There is a thump on the porch boards. Simon turns but does not move.

"Hey, buddy. Hey. You gotta move out."

"I moved out a long time ago. Just came to see you guys pull her down."

"A guy'd have a better view from outside."

"I'm comin."

He walks out on the porch. The city crew is already stringing orange tape around the sidewalk. Simon walks down and steps over the tape. The machines haven't arrived yet. It won't take long. Since there is so little to do until the dozer and the Cat arrive, the crew contracted to wade into the mess armed with sledges and five-foot pries huddles by the tailgate of the pickup and shares coffee from a battered Aladdin stopped with a wide cork. They are cliquish, sipping the steaming coffee and smoking, moving their heads away from the wreathed smoke to observe the traffic. Simon knows the stance. The casual gestures of men used to manipulating their environment. They are apprised of the changing shape of the city well in advance of the motorists who look from under visors and through closed car windows at the demolition site. He knows the attitude and the type of pre-job conversation grunted between sips and pulls, the oblique dig for hip flasks. The ordering of past jobs, the slow shift from job to story. The dirty brownstone job no one wanted where on the last check they found the old lady in the attic surrounded by saltines and TV dinners. They had to carry her. Though she wouldn't move, she didn't protest either when they managed her down the narrow attic stairs and into the arms of her worried relatives. They were gentle with her; they knew she was not sitting up there, her mind locked in a previous decade, out of protest. Being there had become a habit she couldn't break.

Or the other time they had to shell a house on the Northside. They emptied out all the interior walls and supports so they could fold the house in. They'd entered with sledgehammers and Sawzalls and set to work. Plastered in the wall of what must have been the old pantry they found six coffee cans full of silver dollars.

These are the other histories of the city, distant from the chartings and building codes of planners, not visible to the people on the street or driving by, all of whom are over-concerned with the skyline and right-of-way. The workers alone are aware of how the houses and tenements of the city grow around the people in them. This is the real history: the record of human dross.

Simon approaches them and asks for a cigarette. One of them grudgingly reaches into his vest and pulls out a Kool.

"Hope menthol agrees with ya."

"Shit. Smoke agrees with me. You guys on permit?"

"Hell no. We're on the roll but nothin much is goin up. Gotta take a knockdown to pay up the Xmas bills."

"Never much liked demo," Simon lies.

They all know it's a lie. They enjoy it, not because it's fun or easy, but because it is fast and they are on it from the beginning to the end, not stuck in the middle, doing the structural work after the masons and before the glaziers. In demo they are the whole show.

"Betcha liked demo pay, though."

"Yeah. Always did like that."

They hear the rumble of the Cat coming up Franklin and stub out their cigarettes.

"Let's rock and roll," says the one who gave Simon the cigarette. "You know the drill, partner. Can't have you inside the tape."

Simon nods and leans against the truck.

"I'll watch from here."

The men greet the Cat, eyeball the thin driveway and motion it through to the back.

Once it is in position they throw the clamps and lower the stabilizers and after the last inspection the driver raises the bucket and swings it sideways into the top floor, right below the dormer in Simon and Lester's old room.

Who would have thought the change would be so immediate? The timber so soft? Simon, having seen the demise of just about everything—bridges, trains, brownstone, Superior sandstone, concrete, wood trestle, frame houses, his brother's head—is shocked. The steel bucket of the Cat passes through the studs and decking like a hand through smoke. There is no resistance as the two-by-fours are scraped from the cap. The asphalt shingles bunch and break like panfish scales. Everything about it should be hard. The

Indian neighborhood demands it. Nothing that isn't hardy, whether structural or emotional, ever survives. Zoning, rent fixing, and the winters take care of that. The no-numbered house itself carried so much into their lives and resisted their contributions to such an extent, it should fight harder against those bent on knocking it down. Betty, Simon, Lester and the girls endured so much just to live there. Just to suffer the drafts and dinge, the cramp and accommodation. The house should have more grit. It doesn't, and Simon suspects their family was bought cheap.

The bucket retracts and swings back to center. It uncurls at the wrist and passes through the absent dormer and jerks through the attic to the top of the roof. Simon hears the scream of ancient nails as the joists are ripped apart.

The other men scramble underneath as the bucket passes back. They pile the debris against the base of the house. They don't need to, it can all be pushed into place with the bobcat later, but it is daredevil stuff, like soldiers jumping out of the trenches between shell bursts to taunt the enemy.

In half an hour the whole upper level has been raked down except for the front, which they plan on knocking back into the hole they have just created. Simon leans into the truck. He is surprisingly sad and angry. The crew moves the Cat toward the front of the house and throws the stabilizers again. The bucket rises and moves against the chimney. Dust billows out, a last cough, as the old brick gives. But it falls the wrong way. It topples over the bucket and caves in a section of the roof and hangs there, perilously close to the street. Simon looks at the operator, who grimaces around the Swisher Sweet clamped in his mouth. He tries again to sneak the teeth under the piece of chimney but succeeds only in driving it farther toward the front. He retracts the bucket and leans back, silently deferring to the foreman with a shrug.

The crew gathers out front and clusters on the sidewalk, studying the chimney.

"I'll be damned," says the foreman, banging dust from his gloves against his jeaned thigh. "Gonna have to monkey it."

"I ain't crawlin up there," declares one, and the rest nod their heads vigorously. They know the danger of a small job like this. The house is unstable to begin with and the damage to the upper floor could send the plaster-heavy walls down at any moment. There isn't much for footing on the damaged joists and not even time and a half will get them to risk it.

"Just cable it and pull it back."

They all turn and look at Simon. The foreman shakes his head.

"Who's gonna run it up there? You wanna do it?"

"I don't care. What the hell kind of pussy crew you runnin here anyway?"

"I can't let you up there. Union rules."

"Suit yourself. But you got yourself a pussy crew. That's for damn sure."

The whole crew turns, ready to take off their hard hats for a rumble. The foreman waves them down.

"I run a safe crew."

"Safe. Pussy. Call it what you want. I can get the cable around that chimney in ten minutes."

The foreman chews this for a few seconds. He knows he shouldn't allow it, but the insult to his crew makes him want to see Simon risk his life.

"Can't pay you."

"I know."

"We'll chip in for a twelver if you can do it."

"Don't touch the stuff no more."

The foreman shrugs. "Suit yourself."

"Gonna have to move the Cat to the back so we can pull the brick away from the road."

The foreman agrees. "Hop to it, boys."

The men move, begin to collapse the struts again, waiting for

159

the Cat to rock off the weight, pull back the stabilizers hydrauli-
cally. One hops on and checks the cable length on the come-along.
He thumbs-ups the foreman and the rest of the men hang back as
the Cat lurches in low gear to the rear of the house. They alter-
nately look at the foreman and then at Simon, who hasn't moved
from next to the pickup.

He crosses his arms and looks up at the house detachedly. He
studies the pitch of the roof, the angle of the chimney piece,
perched half in, half out, of the roof decking. He is trying to construct the lines of force, where the different parts of the system—
walls, roof, trusses, and chimney—want to go. The walls at the back
of the house want to fall outward. Without the roof to hold them
in, and with the added pressure of debris knocked inside, the walls
are aching to cave outward. The front is still solid, but the running
beams have been torn through and the whole roof could slide either forward or back, the walls inside would buckle to accommo-
date them. The chimney itself is poised. Indecisive. It could go
straight through the roof or slide through the side wall, sending the
whole front of the house into either Third or Franklin.

The Cat is ready. Simon hears the whine of the come-along, the
thrilled low-geared lisp, and walks down the driveway to the back.

"Got a lead?"

The foreman hands him the end of a piece of braided nylon
rope thick enough to hoist a car. Simon takes it and loops it double.
With a flick of his wrist he throws a bowline and settles the loop
over his head, jerking it not-too-tight around his waist.

He approaches the back door, looking out of habit for the small
patch of basil and mint Betty used to plant to the side of the steps.
He was always amazed at the rapid growth of those herbs, daring
the weather, tempting the family. They are gone, given over to dan-
delion and yarrow. The promising spears of tiger lilies that had
never bloomed and now never would. The door is missing and the
frame parallelogrammed when the walls shifted. Simon enters and

stops to map the best route for his safety and the tension of the cable. The kitchen, dining nook, and basement stairs have been filled with the broken tumble of the roof. Splintered trusses and two-by-fours, shingles, ceiling tile, drywall, and patches of dust-darkened Fiberglas insulation that Simon bought himself and installed, are strewn everywhere. Strange, that the puffy batts he laid in 1970 have lasted longer than the family. Did Irma even know that Betty had moved or that Simon was out of jail, had been for a year? Did she know that the insulation was gone? The pink rolls that made Irma sneeze while she held the trouble light for Simon, the light jerking with each sniff, Simon gasping at her to hold it steady while he tore at the batts with a utility knife—did she know that it was gone now?

Simon steps gingerly on the corner angle of a broken truss and slides his hand along the interior wall. He knows the crew is around the Cat smoking. Smoking and watching. He doesn't look back. The ceilings are eight feet high, so he needs one more solid step to reach the top of the wall. He puts his foot on a section of roof, liking the grip of his boots on the textured asphalt, the familiar catch, the hold and heft of construction surfaces. It wobbles but should be enough. He knows that if he falls it won't be fatal, just painful, pierced by nails and splinters, gashed by the newly ripped edges of stamped aluminum flashing.

He transfers his weight and the section begins to settle, the sound of wood breaking underneath. He takes it quickly, springs to a section of the stairs and gains the top of the inside wall with one foot. It is steady and without pausing he catwalks it to the front of the house. He puts his left hand on the exposed slope of the roof and vaults up and walks to the cap. Faussed in less than thirty seconds.

He reaches the chimney and unties the rope and signals the Cat operator who starts the winch. Simon begins pulling the rope up, the cable looped behind. Once it is there, Simon scrambles around the edges of the chimney piece like a referee around a wrestling match. When he sees the angle he wants, he runs the cable through the middle of the chimney, soot-black and flecked with creosote. He hitches it and steps front-side and signals the Cat again and the cable begins to tighten. It goes taut. The chimney begins to shift, cutting shingles like the prow of a clumsy ship through ice. It gets close to the back edge and the roof collapses. The chimney tumbles down harmlessly into the kitchen, where it punches through the floor and into the basement. The foreman waves Simon clear and Simon waves back and walks to the front, hops down onto the porch and swings from the gutter onto the deck.

The men are coming around the corner as he smacks the dust from his jeans.

"Christ Almighty. Good job, Spiderman."

"Easy work."

"What the hell did you do before? I thought you was gonna have to tear ass off the roof like a raped ape."

"I did that," he says, pointing at the IDS.

"You sure as hell saved us some time. You want I should get you a permit during lunch?"

"Not for me. I finished my climbing days."

"Could turn a good buck."

"Could take a dive."

"Yeah, well, could get hit by a car buyin milk at the Rainbow Foods. But have it your way."

"I plan to."

The men break to the back to move the Cat and Simon knows he doesn't want to see any more, isn't interested in seeing the end. Like a porno film he has watched too many times, he knows the mechanical posture, the false gestures, the orchestrated culmination.

It is enough to know that the house will be gone, the plot seeded with gas pumps and a low cinder block gas station. The house will be gone. This is not singular, nothing worth mentioning, it is beyond the notice of preservationists and urban historians.

What really happened there, what was sold by Betty, was forgotten anyway. Standing or being paved over, it didn't make a difference. The scars of a city never really show.

Simon turns to go and sees One-Two standing in the doorway of the Windsor, waving him over. He uses the old hand signal they developed on the high jobs to signal pulling a load of beam horizontally.

Simon crosses. They stand in silence, both turning their eyes across the street.

"Sad to see her go?" ventures Simon at last.

"Never cared much for the house. Sad to see your ma leave."

"Ain't nothin for her here. Surprised she didn't head north years ago, after Irma took off for San Diego. I probably gave her reason to get out."

"Naw, Simon. Ain't like that. Even old folk like us need change. She was just done with the city."

"How bout you?"

"What I got is all right. Makin sure these college grads slumming with jobs Uptown have heat and water." He jerks his head back at the corner apartment facing the alley. "Make sure they're nice and cozy so they can write their Great American Novels."

Simon laughs. "You ever think of movin back to the Dells?"

"No."

They stand a few more minutes and then, neither one wanting to dig any deeper or stare at the collapsing house across the street, part without saying good-bye. One-Two retreats back into the Windsor and Simon walks to the curb, where he has to step aside for a college student with a long red ponytail, a bicycle on one arm and a side bag on the other, who wants to get in the door.

He moves and walks toward the Curtis, where Dougan might share some of his stashed booze in the boiler room, where it is empty of human noise, of voices, just the thumping of machinery and the swish of water. So close to the river and they have to pump in the water from outside the city.

18

This is what happened when Simon was seventeen. He skipped school because of a girl and ended up quitting for good. The girl, with more frontage than prospects, was lost in the shuffle, her name forgotten. She is most likely married now, maybe happy, maybe not. Simon cannot remember her name, this hopeless catalyst. He remembers how he felt—how he liked that she and her friends were afraid of him, afraid of his wild difference, in awe of his strength and good looks. Simon remembers he liked it, her wide-eyed almost-fear, but he was gentle, kind in an offhand way.

It was the dead of winter and Simon skipped school to bring her to his house. They walked the twelve blocks from South High, wrapped tight in their winter coats. No one tried to recognize family or friend by face anymore. There were too many layers of clothes, scarves, hats. The whole neighborhood relied on coat color and shape.

They walked the twelve blocks home from school. Neither talked; they were more concerned with getting there.

Once inside they stripped their clothes in Simon and Lester's room, too greedy for each other's heat to unbundle at the door. He remembers little of their lovemaking, just that she was hungry and scared, hungry for him, for anything.

She left and Simon didn't want to trudge back to school. He knew he'd have to walk at least as far as the junior high to pick up Lester from the eighth grade. Instead of leaving right away he curled inside the tangle of blankets, tackling and pinning the girl's phantom warmth.

He heard the front door open and the murmur of voices. He recognized Betty's but not the man's. He was without escape. He'd have to pass them in order to get back to school. He crept to the door and listened.

They were talking, the man's voice followed by curt replies from Betty. "Here's fine," he heard the man say. There was no reply from Betty, and then Simon heard spoons clatter and a thump that sounded like a body falling.

Simon padded to the top of the stairs. He knew he couldn't step on them, the squeaks would have been too loud. He knelt and walked his hands down the lip of each stair until he was prone, and looked through the white banister slats and saw the landlord fucking his mother.

He had put her over the kitchen table. Betty endured. Simon could see one of her eyes, cool and unblinking, like a gut shot doe, alive but too weak to stand. The table wobbled on its chrome legs, but it held. So did she.

He retreated and got into bed. It was cold, the ghost of his lovemaking gone, slipped out the frost-caulked windows. He couldn't sleep, though the sounds from below had ceased soon after he turned away. The door slammed, and time sat back and crossed its arms, waiting for Simon's reaction. It was the first of February.

———

Simon at seventeen. He quit school and hired on with One-Two. He was proud of his first check, of hauling steel and doing grunt work no union man would do. He took his first check and looked up Rojta's address on the rent agreement. He snuck a look at a rent receipt and tucked the yellowed envelope behind the silverware tray in the drawer next to the sink.

It was a long bus ride to Brooklyn Park. By now it was May, and the world was creeping back open.

Rojta didn't look surprised to see Simon amble tensely up the front walk. He kept his distance, putting a low hedge of arborvitae between them. He pretended to busy himself with raking the dead leaves from the cage of exposed roots.

"How much?" asked Simon, as if every word cost him. "How much to leave off?"

Rojta didn't look up. He made Simon address the top of his skull.

"Fifty."

"Fifty," spat Simon, chewing the amount over. "Fifty bucks."

"That sounds about right."

Simon picked out two twenties and a ten. "You'll get it every month. But you leave off." He bent down and spoke as closely to Rojta's ear as he could. "You leave off or I'll break your fuckin neck."

Rojta didn't stand or shout or quake. He didn't react except to hunch his shoulders. He knew Simon could kill him. But he was wise like all moneymakers: he understood what the breaking point was, where violence would decrease profit. So he just hunched his shoulders and kept pulling leaves from the root base. Simon paid him every month and he didn't bother Betty again.

Simon at seventeen quits school and begins working high steel. He pays the landlord fifty dollars a month not to fuck his mother. At seventeen he knows his mother is worth fifty dollars a month to a white man in Brooklyn Park.

19

November, and it hasn't snowed yet. The buildings on Third Avenue rise dull and gray into the morning air. The city is huddled in on itself, and on the margins, in the Indian neighborhoods of South Minneapolis, no one is out.

It is one of those days when you look outside, at five, nine, or noon, and there is the feeling of predawn lead in the way the clouds stoop level and low over the people and buildings. No snow, but the ache of cold creeps from the cement. The cigarette butts and wrappers lie dead by the curbs. Simon leans into his coat.

Franklin is deserted as he takes the corner and crosses over 35W. The traffic butts up against itself in a slow pour into town. No one honks or passes on the right, each just follows the car ahead as if there were a first car, an initial car leading the others out of the suburbs and into the city.

On the bridge the wind pushes his chin down into his jacket. The zipper rubs his chin. He'd grow a beard if he could, but like all the Indian men in his family, he had the smooth skin of a boy, nothing to use as a disguise against the wind or the law.

At the Charities a voice from the stoop pulls him from his coat. "What up, chief?"

"Hey."

"Where you headed?"

"Hell if I know. They closed?" He stands stiff with his hands in his pockets, jerking his chin toward the door of the Catholic Charities.

"Been and gone. Been and gone. You missed breakfast. Least they could do is leave the door open."

He shakes his head. "Yeah. I suppose. You got money?"

"Naw. I'm flat, man."

"Yeah," says Simon, his eyes taking in Franklin, the cars parked as if they were waiting for orders.

"West Bank's gonna be piss-poor today. Let's head Uptown, see what's cookin over there."

"Yeah."

T-Man hops up from the steps and Simon pulls his coat tighter around, his hands still in his pockets. "Let's get the fuck off Franklin, anyway."

With that they cross over, trailing their breath behind them.

T-Man pulls out a cigarette, clears his throat and spits expertly on a dead squirrel frozen flat in the gutter. He lights his cigarette and hands one to Simon. They walk west on Franklin and cross over 35W and turn up Clinton. Since Simon met him in prison T-Man has always been this way. He has always enjoyed a casual disregard for his surroundings. Though they have both been in prison, Simon emerged more careful. Tenuously paroled, he eased into the streets, but T-Man is determined to be offhand, as if nothing can affect him.

The trees grow up over the street, a cage of thin fingers holding the low-slung clouds away from the old houses, beaten and showing ant-eaten wood through chipped paint.

They cut over on Twenty-fourth Street in front of the Institute of the Arts where leaves that haven't been squashed or washed down the gutters into the river flip and jerk over the wide, shallow steps.

"You ever try to go in those doors?" T-Man asks Simon.

Simon shakes his head and flicks the resinous cigarette butt against the steps where the cherry splits from the filter and hisses as it hits a pocket of rainwater in the stone. The butt tumbles harmlessly down the steps like a spent shell.

"Well, they're locked. They never open them. You gotta go around back. Why the fuck they put the Art Museum in the ghetto beats the shit outta me."

"I been in the back," says Simon, shoving his hands back in his pockets.

They look up at the huge wooden double doors, like castle doors, squinting against the wind that stings their eyes and against the stone building that looks so solid that it will never fall down or be razed.

Uptown is empty. The bars are closed on Hennepin. The thrift stores and prostitutes aren't showing their rags down the length of Lake Street. Simon and T-Man see a bum tottering from side to side on the concrete sidewalk, bordered by the street on one side and the battered storefronts on the other. He moves as though fixed on an invisible rail over a precipice.

T-Man snorts. "Shoot me if I start walking like that."

"Don't have a gun, T-Man."

"Well choke me or somethin."

They stare after the bum until he stops. He senses he is being watched. The bum pulls himself straight and moves his head from side to side, squinting through the postdawn gloom. Seeing that T-Man and Simon aren't cops, he pulls his ratty hat lower on his head and flicks them off with one hand while scratching at an itch on the front of his thigh with the other.

T-Man laughs and starts coughing.

"Fuck you too!" he shouts cheerfully, breaking into another cough. He wads the phlegm together with his tongue and spits the ball out, skipping it off the sidewalk.

The old man turns and walks past the Uptown Bar and Grill.

T-Man shakes his head. They hear voices down Lagoon, an argument, maybe a crowd gathering.

"You hear that?" asks T-Man.

"Yeah, yeah." Simon turns his reddening ear upwind. "Yeah I hear it."

They start walking down Lagoon to the lake, turning their heads right and left at each intersection. A couple of cars stroll glumly past, trailing bluish exhaust.

The voices grow louder. It sounds like an auction mixed with the barking of kenneled dogs.

"Jesus, we're missing some action," says T-Man. He walks ahead of Simon, craning his neck in every direction.

Simon stops. "Hey, T-Man. Those aren't people."

"No?"

"Naw. They're geese. Listen."

Sure enough, through the murmur and low city noises they hear the rubbery bark of geese mixed with the throaty chatter of ducks.

"Why didn't they fly south for the winter?"

"Why didn't we?"

"Yeah, yeah, good point. Let's go down there."

So they walk again, quickening their pace, and cross Calhoun Parkway, dead of traffic. Along the iced bank they see hundreds of geese. Some sit up on shore stabbing at the brown grass. Others pump along in the freezing surface while still more set their wings and tilt in with a splash. Mallards skitter over the water to get out of the way.

Simon and T-Man walk up to the shore. The geese part and

close in behind them. A couple jog by on the path, eyeing the geese and Simon and T-Man as they try not to step in the scattered goose shit.

"They're bigger than they look," says T-Man, squinting at a gander beating his wings against his breast and shaking them back into place again.

"Hey goose," he says. He takes a half-step toward the gander.

The goose pushes his chest out and rushes toward T-Man.

"Whoa! Whoa! Mean fuckers, too!"

The gander backs away and starts combing the ground with his beak for food invisible to Simon and T-Man.

"Yeah," says Simon, "and messy."

The shore is slicked solid with goose dung.

"You know how to cook one of these things?" asks T-Man.

"Sure," says Simon. "Rip off their feathers, throw them in an over and turn it on."

"Let's kill one," says T-Man.

"How?"

"Strangle him. Can't be that hard. Looks like they only weigh about twenty-five. You're all of two hundred."

Simon looks over the gathered geese and shivers into his collar. His feet hurt and snot drains slowly from his nose onto his upper lip. He shrugs his shoulders.

"Come on, Simon. All this food . . . just sittin here. Just reach out and grab his neck and twist his fuckin head off."

Simon looks at the feathered chaos around them; the geese strutting and fighting, shooting their beaks like bullets at the mallards, picking at food dropped by park-goers. One goose has a hot dog bun clenched in his beak and tries to hiss at the other geese who are closing in. The bun is too big and he drops it to the ground where the rest of the geese peck it to pieces.

Simon steps toward a pair off to his right. The female snakes her neck out, draws it back, and shoots it out along the ground again, glaring at Simon with one eye. The gander stands tall, opening his beak and hissing at him, his wings drumming half bent against his chest.

"Holy shit!" T-Man jumps back. "They sound like cats!"

Simon steps away from the geese. He shakes his head.

"They're too mean. Way too mean."

"Come on, Simon. It's just a bird, for Christ's sake."

Simon stamps his foot to loosen the goose shit lodged in the cracked sole of his boot. With his hands in his pockets he begins to stroll lightly in a small circle.

The geese part and sway a few feet in every direction he turns, a sea of gray feathers rolling and rolling. To the left a medium-sized goose shuffles through the collected shit and snaps its beak. He looks away and it bends it neck double and bites at the feathers in its wingpit.

Simon knows that for a moment it can't see him with its wing raised over its head. Simon pauses and jumps with his hands out in front of him.

He falls short but the ground is so slicked with shit he slides into the goose. His hands close on the scaly feet and it jumps back in surprise.

Simon scrambles to his knees holding on to the goose's feet with both hands.

It hisses and opens its wings, whipping its neck around in every direction like an unmanned fire hose. The other geese retreat nervously, calling their calls and stamping their cold webbed feet, forming a ring around Simon and the goose.

It hisses again. It flaps its wings, trying to fly away from Simon. The goose pumps the air and Simon feels the gusts in waves against his face, sees the great clenching of the goose's breast underneath the mantle of feathers and skin.

His grip is tight and the legs feel thin, no thicker than broom handles. They are cold and the skin is aubergine, scaly like the skin of a dragon. Simon feels the tendons pulling and pulling as the goose tries to take off.

T-Man is shouting. "Kill him! Kill him!"

The other geese squawk and move back. Some turn and pop up, settling down in the wintery water where they paddle back and forth like sentries or nervous witnesses.

"Kill him. Grab his fuckin neck and kill him!"

T-Man is shouting but Simon can barely hear him. All he can hear is the woosh of the wings, the snap of his wrists as the goose jerks right and left, the sharp edge of his own breathing as he tries not to fall back in the carpet of goose shit.

It quits struggling. The wings drop down and Simon staggers to his feet.

"Is it dead?" asks T-Man, looking out from behind one of the battered ornamental trees planted next to the lake.

"I don't know," says Simon.

He turns the limp goose in his hands. His knuckles are skinned and raw.

It beats its wings once and rides up above Simon's head. The sun is weak over the lake and the spread wings block it out. Simon sees the sky go dark and the world emerges as a thin light through the flexed guard feathers trailing along the edge of the goose's wing, filtered through some terrible, rearing angel.

Simon steps back and the goose dives at his head with a hiss like the breaking of water on rock. Simon tries to raise his hands to fend it off without letting go, but the wings sweep in from the sides. He raises his elbows but can't keep them high enough. The goose knocks him in the ear with its wing. His head spins and his ear feels hot. He takes another step back and the goose hits him on the other side of his head.

"Aw shit!"

He hears T-Man laughing and yelling but the words are lost on the far side of the goose's wings around his head like a violent blanket.

Simon pivots around but the wings keep beating him from the sides. The goose's neck whips this way and that. Simon tries to tuck his chin in and bring his ears below the grade of his hunched shoulders. The goose's head looms, its neck uncoiling like a cobra and he feels a sharp sting on his cheek.

He throws his head back and sees the wing coming at him level, a feathered tide sweeping across his vision. Simon tries to dodge but is too slow.

The ridge of the wing catches him on the bridge of his nose. The pain sears up and across his forehead and tears cloud his eyes.

"Damn it! Fuckin die!" he shouts as he turns and whips his arms out. With his eyes closed he steps back and swings the goose away from his body and slams it on the ground. Simon lifts his arms and swings the goose in an arc over his head and onto the ground again. He raises it up once more but his feet slip and they both go down.

Simon lands on the goose and it lets out a honk as his full weight crushes it into the grass. He rolls over and grabs it by the neck, then struggles back to his feet and swings it around and around, like a happy parent holding a child by the hands and twirling it with its body turning and turning in the fall air. Simon feels his grip slipping and sees blood on his hands. He lets his arms drop and the goose's head falls from its ragged neck. The body lands in the goose shit, rolls and stops. Simon tosses the head next to the goose's body. Its wings are broken, feathers stick out at improbable angles from its body, no longer part of the geometry of flight. Feathers float down lazily from where they hang suspended above the battlefield.

"I think he broke my nose," say Simon.

Blood drips down his chin and he tries to suck in air. It feels like splinters are being driven up his nostrils. He hacks and spits out a clot of blood. He cheeks are raw and a bruise has already formed where the goose bit him.

T-Man starts to move out from behind the tree.

"What's going on here?"

Simon and T-Man turn. Two policemen walk briskly down the path.

"Aw, shit," says T-Man.

He turns and runs back up to Lake Street.

Simon stands planted next to the goose.

The police walk stiffly along the asphalt path, pause as if trying to decide if they want to get their shoes clotted with goose dung, and walk up to Simon. They look down at the goose. One of them looks back up at Simon.

"You kill that goose?"

Simon's ears ring. He wipes the blood off his chin with his coated shoulder. "I hope so."

His voice feels small against the throaty honks of the surviving geese.

"He sure did a number on you, didn't he?"

"Yeah, I suppose."

The policemen rock in their shoes in unison as if listening to the same inaudible song.

"You know it's illegal, don't you?" The cop's voice comes out in almost a drawl.

"Really?"

"We're bringing you in."

"For this?" says Simon, looking down at the dead goose.

"Yeah, for this."

Simon looks at the cops and then back at the goose. It hasn't moved.

"But it was self-defense."

"Sure."

"It was."

"Uh-huh. Come on, let's go."

They turn and started walking to the car idling in the parking lot.

"Don't suppose I get to keep the goose?" asks Simon.

"Nope," says one cop, "don't suppose you do. It ain't dinner anymore. It's evidence."

"I was just protecting myself," says Simon.

The cop looks back over his shoulder at Simon. "Don't look like you did much of a job of it."

The other cop laughs out a puff of steam.

They reach the Caprice and open the back door and motion for Simon to enter and he does, ducking his head and sinking into the warm interior. One cop walks around to the trunk and opens it, taking out a yellow garbage bag marked *Evidence*. He starts down to the lake and over to the dead goose. He lifts it by the feet and drops it in the bag. He scrutinizes the ground for a minute before he finds the head.

He walks back to the car with the bag thrown over his shoulder and puts it in the trunk. Stepping to the passenger side, he knocks his shoes on the sill and climbs in. They pull away from the lake.

Simon looks back and sees more geese landing and swimming back and forth, talking. A society of strangers. More geese swivel in on the nose of a northern wind.

The car turns out onto the Parkway and Simon sees only the long darting necks of the geese as they close over the circle cleared for Simon's fight.

He shuts his eyes. It's been a long time since I been here, he thinks. It feels the same. Past the idle cop talk and radio static, past the hum of the tires and the gentle clawing of the heater, he hears the parting of air between the feathers of the geese as they rise and fly to some other distant place.

At the Hennepin County Jail they book him and give him a washcloth and soap to clean the blood off his face.

They lead him down the familiar halls, past still doors into the holding cell.

There are only four others in the cell. Two men play cards. Another is reading a magazine on a bunk covered in a stiff wool blanket. The fourth is curled up against the wall with his back to the others, sleeping. The door slides shut behind him. He stands and looks around the room and touches his nose with his raw index finger. He feels the bones shift but he does not wince.

The card players look up and Simon nods. The reader flips a page with one hand and scratches his chest with the other without glancing at Simon, who walks over to an empty bunk and stretches out on the rough wool.

There are rust and piss stains on the bottom of the sagging mattress above him. He crosses his booted legs and gently puts his arm over his eyes, trying not to touch his nose. He hears the slick of another magazine page and a low sniffle. After a few minutes the sound of cards sliding and snapping resume. They have been looking at him.

The jailer comes with food. The card players throw down their cards lazily and unfold themselves from the chairs.

Simon sits up slowly and makes sure that he isn't too dizzy from his broken nose and hunger to walk steadily to where the food waits on plastic trays. The reader tips the magazine down and surveys Simon and the card players and begins reading again. Simon takes a tray with a glop of stew and another lump of what looks like creamed corn. He brings it back to the bed and begins to eat. After two spoonfuls he pauses and looks up from his food at the sleeping man. He looks across to the card players.

They are watching him.

Simon swallows and gestures with his chin at the sleeping man. "He dead, or what?"

"Naw," says one of the card players around a mouthful of stew. "He just wished he was."

"Why?" asks Simon, picking at the creamed corn with the dull metal spoon.

"Got drunk, beat up his wife."

The other card player shrugs. "Won't be long before she bail him out either."

Simon looks back at the sleeping man. "You think?"

"Any woman stay mad at you for hittin her a few times?"

"Ain't ever hit a woman."

The card player with his back to Simon half-turns and pushes his chair sideways. He spoons a lump of potato into his mouth and chews. He taps the side of his nose with the greasy spoon.

"Cops do that?" he asks, looking at Simon sideways in the green light.

Simon shakes his head as he swallows the corn, wincing at the pain shooting through his nose and at the snotlike texture of the creamed corn.

The potato-chewing card player keeps looking at him. "Whatcha here for then?"

"I killed a goose."

"No shit?"

"No shit."

The other card player shakes his head.

"Who busted you up then?"

"The goose."

"No shit," he says again.

They hear the jailer cough and the squeak of his metal chair against the cement down the hall.

"They lockin you down for gettin beat up by a goose?"

"I guess so."

"That don't sound right."

The reader sets down his magazine and sits up on the bed.

"Them geese is mean fuckers."

Everyone turns to look at him except for the man sleeping off his binge in the corner bunk.

178

"They are," he repeats. "I remember back in the fall my dad would take us from the city. You know most people took vacations in the summer. Well. He'd work straight through. Even in August when it got real hot and all the other kids'd be on the lakes, some water-skiing. We'd be stuck in the city. Dad'd come home and it was too hot even to get out the barbecue. Too hot to get drunk, he'd say. So we'd sit there in the basement and he'd drink iced tea and me and my brother'd watch TV and wait for the fan to swing our way. Even our T-shirts stuck to us. It was that hot.

"So we went on vacation in the fall. By that time it was cold. No snow yet, but it'd sleet some mornings. You'd think we'd get to sleep in, but he'd wake us up at four-thirty in the morning, way before dawn.

"We'd eat hard-boiled eggs—our mother wasn't there, 'Just the guys,' Dad said—and get dressed in the dark and take the boat out. It was still dark and I had to sit up in the bow, with a big flashlight so we wouldn't ground out the boat in shallow water and burn up the prop in the weeds. Dad sat in the back with his hands on the tiller, smoking a cigarette, and my brother sat right in the middle, shivering and complaining. Though he didn't complain too loud cause Dad would get that look on his face.

"Dad had put out milk jugs on the lake, anchored to the bottom with tractor bolts so we'd know where to go. I mean it was impossible to see the shore, even with the flashlight. You could see it, but it all looked the same: just trees and more trees.

"When I saw the milk-jug buoys I'd whisper to Dad and he'd nod, his cigarette dipping in the dark, just a little red dot where his face was.

"He'd nod and angle the boat in where there was a cut in the weeds. My brother complained that it was cold, but me and my dad didn't say anything. It was cold. What could we say?

"Once it got real shallow, so I could see the bottom with the flashlight. Just green weeds and the stunned minnows, I'd whisper at him again. He got mad if we talked loud. Even though the motor was louder than we were.

"And he'd kill the motor. Pretty soon we'd stop moving. We weren't to shore yet. The weeds pulled us to a stop and Dad got out in his waders and pulled the boat closer to shore, into the cattails and we'd hand him the decoy bag and the backpack and the guns and he'd set them in the blind there in the cattails.

"Me and my brother'd climb out and put on the waders. Dad'd smoke a cigarette while we untangled lines and weights. Then he'd direct us as we threw them out, tell us how to organize the spread depending on the wind and how late it was in the season. Then we'd arrange the blind, putting our shells in reach and throw the camo deke bags over the thermos and the backpack while Dad moved the boat farther down shore so it wouldn't spook the birds. After he walked back along the shore and we settled in, we'd wait for dawn and for the first flights of birds.

"One time, it was late in the season, all the locals were gone and the northern flight hadn't come in yet, we'd set up for four days and hadn't seen a damn thing. A few singles flyin somewhere else, but that was it. Not even a coot or a mud hen, not even a grebe. The weather turned and even though it was a north wind with a little sleet, there weren't any ducks landing. We'd seen some bills come in but they'd rafted up out in the middle of the lake and didn't pay any attention to our dekes or calls.

"Anyway, it was on the fifth day and still nothing. Dad always said that just being outside was enough. But, the way he was real grumpy and smoked one cigarette after another, you could tell. Don't let anyone tell you hunting isn't a lot of work. It was getting dark. We'd been sitting there all day. We were pretty froze up and all the coffee was gone, and we heard her come in. A single. She didn't call or anything. All we heard was her wings; when it's real quiet and you're listenin and used to sittin still, you can hear a lot.

A goose's wings are about three feet from tip to tip and we heard her dip down about twenty yards out from our spread. It was just gettin dark and we saw her struttin back and forth. Dad didn't want to use the call so close cause it might startle her. So we waited and waited but she didn't pull any closer.

"So my dad says *Take it. Take the shot.* Now we were loaded up with four shot and a two to kill anything we winged. We weren't planning on seeing any geese. So . . . *Bam!* I opened up with a four and she jumped up and *Bam!* I hit her again—I could see my spread go right around her—and she settled back down. She tried to fly again but I could tell I broke one of her wings because she sat down again and just paddled out farther away from us. By now she was a good sixty yards out and even with 2-shot we wouldn't have been able to bring her in. So Dad starts down to the boat and me and my brother shucked our waders and we can see her still paddling away through the dark. Dad finally gets the boat in the water and we jump in and motor out toward her. Only, with the motor on we can't get up on her cause she starts diving so we kill it and my dad posts the oars and he and my brother started rowing. We saw her, still paddling out, her neck pumping, she was about forty yards away so I shoot again, with 2-shot, cause she's on the water and she dives. I think I got her and I say so to my dad. But she just surfaces fifteen yards farther on and he keeps rowing. I loaded up, and when we got to where she was we see her pop up thirty yards to our left.

"You wouldn't think a twenty-pound goose could dive, but let me tell you. I swing left and shoot and she goes under again. We rowed up . . . and there she was to our right this time. I shot again and she went down again. This time she didn't dive so we rowed in and got real close, maybe fifteen yards, and I raised up and *click.* I was out of shells. Totally out. Dad and my brother had left their guns in the blind and all the boxes too.

"But Dad said I'd hit her pretty hard three times and that even a goose would tire out and die so we kept closing in on her. It was almost pitch-black and every time we drew near she'd dive again. Our arms were numb from sprinting behind the oars and stopping and sprinting again. Dad's breath was coming out raspy and my brother's hands kept slipping from the oar and it fell in the water and jerked the boat around and Dad yelled at him and coughed. We kept getting closer. We moved up to about four feet away and then she'd dive but without the shells four feet could've been forty yards. I threw one of the extra paddles at her before she could dive and it hit her square on the neck but she just dove anyway and it was as dark as it'd get and we couldn't see her anymore. So we stopped and we were all breathing hard. We heard her paddling and saw some ripples. But we had to pack it in and get the decoys and we never found her."

The man scans the room: the food steaming dankly in the flickering fluorescent light, the card players, Simon, the still-sleeping drunk. He nods to himself, lies back down, and puts the magazine over his face. He starts snoring in a few minutes.

Simon eases back on his bunk, a classic holding-cell pose: his arms under his head, his eyes searching the piss-stained mattress above him. Betty and Lincoln are up north. He never visited them or the house after he got out, except to tear it down, and now, he thinks, maybe I should have. Maybe that wouldn't have been so bad. They've been gone since last May. Lincoln must be in school on the reservation. Big changes, chances everywhere to fuck it up.

After a while the rest take to their bunks and with the light still flickering, they close their eyes and go to sleep. Simon can hear, faintly, the hit of hard-soled shoes, the rasp of metal, and the jingle of keys, like bells, in the cemented distance.

The next morning at his arraignment, Simon shifts uneasily in his crumpled and bloody clothes. In the clean courtroom he can smell the goose shit on his shoes and pants, the cigarette smoke clinging to his jacket.

The judge sits leaning forward, his arms stick out from the black robes like sticks. He cocks his head when the clerk reads Simon's case from the docket. When the clerk finishes the judge remains leaning forward, looking at his clasped hands. Simon sways back and forth in his torn and bloody clothing.

"Before we jump in, you've a right to counsel, or you can waive your rights. You're being charged with poaching and disorderly conduct. You understand that?" He pushes his glasses from the crease in his nose.

"It's just a goose."

"No counsel, then?"

Simon shakes his head, but stops when the pain in his nose becomes too great.

"You killed a goose by Lake Calhoun."

Simon doesn't say anything.

"You killed a goose."

Simon squints through the court light and picks a leaf from his jacket cuff and puts it in his pocket.

"Well. Don't you have anything to say?"

"You're doin all the talkin," says Simon.

"Don't get smart. It's eight-thirty in the morning."

"Yes sir."

"Well? How do you plead? Guilty or not guilty?"

"Yeah, I killed a goose."

"So you're pleading guilty."

"I suppose."

The lights seem to pulse. Simon hears the other people waiting to be called sniffling and fidgeting on the benches behind him. The judge sighs and looks down at some papers in front of him. He takes off his glasses, pauses, and puts them on again. He looks at Simon.

"You been in jail before."

"Yes."

"In fact, you've been in prison."

"You're sending me to prison over a goose?"

"Your parole has been revoked." He looks down again at the papers in front of him. "You've been out a year and a half, but you're still on parole, remember?"

Simon is silent. He tries to speak, but looks at the judge, sitting high up in the cruel light and he averts his eyes and stares down at his bloody boots.

"Oh," he whispers.

The judge taps his hand with a pen. He looks at the paper in front of him again and back at Simon.

"Wasn't ten years enough for you?"

"Yes sir," says Simon, his voice cracking. "Yeah it was enough."

The judge sighs. "Ninety days," he says to no one in particular.

Simon hears the ruffle of papers and a new name being called off the docket by the bailiff.

A police officer comes up to Simon's side and touches him gently on the elbow. Simon pivots as if he and the officer are part of some graceful dance and the officer leads him out of the courtroom.

PART

THREE

20

Simon took the bus. He'd walked from Hennepin County Jail to the Curtis where he stuffed his clothes in a Hefty sack and okayed being gone with Dougan, who just nodded and offered him two skin magazines for the road. He was on the bus within two hours of being released. He felt that if he stopped, if he stood still for too long he would root, send down taps through the concrete into the rubble of previous versions of the city, that he would never move and that eventually trouble would find him again and he would not be able to escape.

The bus no longer served the reservation, and instead, dropped him at the town nearest the border. He had told no one of his plans, had no mail to be forwarded or anyone to explain himself to or greet him. It was three o'clock in the afternoon, late March. He had been out of jail for a day, out of prison for two years. With nothing else to do, no other options, he started walking.

It had been an easy winter. The snow was already gone, but the beaver ponds along the highway were still skimmed with ice, slushy and black, rotted from the sun and the water that flowed onto them from higher ground, from broken dams in more remote, secret swamps. The ground looked wasted, battered by the snow and palimpsested with the soggy cardboard of twelve-packs, hubcaps, and the tufted remnants of a winter's worth of roadkill racked by the wind and scavenging dogs and skunks that had begun to waddle from their burrows into the warmer air in search of food.

Cars passed him, rattling out of the distance and slapping by. No one bothered to stop. They either didn't notice him or didn't care, perhaps mistaking him for a can picker scouring the ditches for aluminum. But he knew not of the wealth that lay crusted in the ditches and passed on. He didn't try to hitch, was unwilling to endure conversation that would inevitably turn to either his past (not something he wanted to talk about) or his future (equally uncomfortable). He carried within him no surplus of small talk because he had not accumulated the requisite data about the weather or sports scores or local politics and he was too stunned by his jail time to fake it. He was like a dynamited fish that had floated to the surface and was thrown mercilessly on the bank.

The only connection he did have with the place involved the two people lost to him; his father and his brother. He couldn't help losing his father, but Lester's death weighed on him doubly because in addition to his guilt he has been deprived of his brother's company every day for twelve years. He not only took away Lester's life, he has had to do without it. Lester would have been there, would have made walking an event instead of a chore.

The sun still rode low along the skirt of the southern sky, weighted toward the horizon by the lingering cold. The wind blew warm off the fields of turned mud and just when he was getting used to the temperature, colder wind coasted in from over the lakes and large swamps screened from the road by leaf-bare poplar and tamarack.

It was, he supposed, good walking weather. Warm enough

when he was moving, brisk when he sat the seven and a half minutes it took to smoke a cigarette, perched in the ditch the way he'd
seen owls sitting on fenceposts in broad daylight, surprised and
aloof.

The sun set around seven and by his reckoning he still had at
least six miles to go. There was nothing to do but switch over to the
other side of the road, onto the shoulder of oncoming traffic, and
keep walking. He could hear the cars long before he could see
them, the lights gilding the tips of the trees and climbing down, like
fire reaching for the ground, and then snapping back toward their
source. Simon lifted his hand to shield his eyes from the lights but
kept walking, determined to make it to Boo's.

As he strode deeper into the dark, farther into the reservation,
it was as if he were approaching a foreign country. A place that was
almost familiar, as if he had stepped onto the shore of a novel. He
felt as if he should be more familiar with the road, the long sigh of
hills, the guttering of ditch water, the ganglia of service and logging
roads that swept off the highway to more remote, forbidden areas.
He felt that he should know the terrain. He had been raised here,
after all. But nothing came. There was no revelation, no recognition.

By nine o'clock he was getting tired. His feet ached and his
hand had cramped from holding the slick plastic garbage bag.
Every curve of the road, lit by six stars and a moon, looked the
same. He'd begun telling himself that town would appear around
every corner. That he was almost there. And there would be more
highway canting toward another lake or swamp, the asphalt old and
bone pale under his feet. He was out of cigarettes.

As he walked he tried to remember the layout of the reservation, where each of the villages was, the main roads, but his child-
hood memory was too shallow to contain such cartography. While
in prison he'd checked out every atlas in the library and searched
them for a detailed map of the reservation, but it always appeared
as an undifferentiated shape, mildly square, sometimes colored

gray, other times pink. He tried to remember but could not, and instead kept conjuring up two images over and over again.

One is of his father pinned under the tree: how the snow had seemed so soft, the woods respectful and still, like a loud dinner guest finally sated and retiring. His father's breath coming slower and slower, how the so-soft-snow held the blood that bubbled from his mouth. You'd expect it to burn through, to melt to the bottom and stay there, but the snow held it up. A perfect canvas.

Also he remembered that there was a trail behind their small log house that led away from the village along the lake, rutted by foot travel and later with the few dirt bikes that everyone shared. There was a bluff eroding into the lake, like sugar cakes held under the faucet, and the trees leaned out over the water. Some daredevil had climbed the trunk of one and tied on an old piece of tow rope, and the kids from the village used it to swing out above the water.

It was summer and Simon took Lester from the house for a swim. Lester was too young to swing off the rope, only five years old, but old enough to splash along the shore, old enough to *want* to swim. They took one towel and Simon dressed Lester in his underpants. They had no shoes, and punished their feet on the hot sand until they turned on the trail. Simon's feet were burning in the July sun and he hotfooted his way ahead of Lester and waited for him where the trail veered from the road. Lester scurried along and caught up, grabbing Simon's hand for guidance over the ruts and roots on the path.

When they got to the lake Lester was too scared to swim, he didn't dare climb down the tall bank with Simon and instead stood on the trail as Simon tried to cajole him into walking down the bluff. Simon blew his sweat-stuck hair from his eyes. They sat for a few minutes. Lester was content just to be with his brother. Simon eyed the water. There was no wind. He stood and unhooked the rope from the tree branch and readied himself for a swing. Lester looked serious, as if witnessing a significant act. Simon choked up on the rope, leaned back, and swung out over the lake. The wind rushed past his ears and as he swung out from the shade into the sun the water sparkled and jumped. He held on and swung back and dropped into the lake on the second pass.

He swam to the surface and shook the water out of his hair. He searched the trail for Lester and saw him standing where he had left him. Lester was crying. The towel hung forgotten from his left hand, and he was drying his tears with his right. He looked toward Simon, scared that he'd hurt himself, terrified he would not emerge. Simon yelled that he was okay, that he wasn't hurt, and half-laughed at Lester's fear.

He didn't take a second swing. Instead he climbed the grass-grown bluff and dried himself with the towel. Lester slowly quit sobbing and wouldn't let go of Simon's hand. They walked back to the cabin.

The memory isn't complete. He doesn't have a picture of the lake in his mind like a postcard, the slow tilt of water and pale blue sky, the drone of insects. He doesn't remember the rush of his swing, the feeling of perfect timing, letting go of the rope at the very apex of his swing. He doesn't recall the feel of the road sand, like sugar, between his toes, the coarse fiber of the old rope.

Instead, he remembers Lester choking back his tears, how he tried to match his steps with Simon's. How Lester wanted to hold his hand on the trail but not on the road. Simon threw the towel over his shoulder and held Lester's hand, smudged and sticky from crying. The path was wide enough for them both. He remembers looking at their feet, getting harder and harder throughout the summer, from the sun and sand, and constant walking without shoes. He remembers Lester's little feet next to his, padding along, content now that Simon was safe, content with his hand nestled in Simon's. He remembers that the trees bent over them, and the brush held back and kept from slapping their bare legs.

They turned onto the dirt road and Lester dropped his hand,

and though Simon was only eleven years old, he knew that Lester had pride. He didn't say anything as his younger brother let go of his hand, but walked close to him, his arm brushing Simon's leg, his knee hitting his calf, as if he were blind, and the casual touches kept him on the road. He said nothing as Lester dropped his hand. This is what he remembers, not the swim, nor the trees so much. Not going back home. Just Lester's hand, his studied love. His hidden admiration. His little, little hands.

21

The truck hums and whines and the fire walls have rusted through around the welds so that every ripple in the beaten dirt road cause them to rattle and jitter. The interior lights are dim and the brights are off as the road unspools through the trees. The radio is silent and the windows half down to clear the smoke of four cigarettes that drop ash, only to be cupped and borne up by the wind. Road dust sweeps in the windows and puffs through the rust-weakened floor, an offering that sticks in their hair and coats their throats.

It is April and quiet as the pickup bumps along in the dark. A human quiet. As if the recent thaw that pushes the river higher on its banks and draws the fish from the lake bottoms into the swift gravel flats chokes out human sound, voices and whispers, sounds that are far shorter and mean less than the long cough of the river and the truck.

Simon sits wedged in between the other men and lets the motion of the truck roll him into the slope of their shoulders, only to be rocked the other way along the next curve.

Boo drives in a calm that Simon reads in the low light when his cigarette lights up his face. Even though they take the sandy corners at fifty, Boo still looks as if he were on the interstate: broad and gentle, pushing cars and trucks in an even flow over the landscape. The other two almost sit on each other. Ned has the .22 magnum in his hands, the butt on the floor. They are looking for deer as they drive, scouring the narrow strip of grass between the road and the trees for the green dots of nightshine.

Even though it is April, Simon feels the temperature drop as the road dips down toward the river. Boo slows and turns into the woods and it isn't until they are ten yards down the tote road that Simon realizes they haven't gone into the ditch.

The bottom trees crowd the logging trail. Piss elm and tag alder shoulder one another in the mossy night and reach out to slap the pickup as it glides over the broken branches and dead leaves, still winter-tame and waterlogged on the ridge between the channeled ruts. Where the trees thin, the hazel brush grows like thickets of human hair for a chance at the weak northern light. Boo lifts the coffee mug that sits still somehow in the crook of his jeans and tilts it so the next bump jars the lukewarm liquid into his mouth.

Ahead Simon sees the trees open up to reveal the river skulking under the mist. The surface looks pillowed and deep. Boo turns the wheel sharply and the end of the truck swings around, shucking gravel and broken branches into the brush along the edge of the clearing. He steps on the brakes and the truck shudders into the dead grass, beer cans, and used condoms nestled in the weeds. He pops it into reverse and eases it to the river's edge. Boo leans back and blows out the last shreds of cigarette smoke from his lungs and puts the coffee cup on the dash, pushing the stiff Dairy Queen napkins, spark plugs, and a tire gauge into the seam along the windshield.

Ned and Jumbo have already popped open the passenger door and spill out into the night, stretching and walking knee-deep in river fog to the tailgate. Simon slides over the ripped vinyl seat patched with duct tape and steps into the cold. He tosses his spent cigarette into the brown grass. His breath comes out in puffs and rises away into the windless sky, away from the ground fog that hangs in a level shelf over the river. He walks to the back of the truck and stands with his hands in his pockets as Boo and Ned lift the galvanized tin washtub from the bed and walk it to the edge of the river. They set it down with a thump. The metal handles clang on the sides as they let go, sending a sliver of sound into the hush of the river's progress, banging faintly from the far shore. They walk to the truck and lift the rusted chrome door handles and the doors spring open with a pop, metallic sounds out of place in the trees and brush, at odds with the liquid surge of the river, high on its April banks. Simon stands with his hands thrust away from the chill, leaning against the rear quarter panel of the truck. The others stamp their feet and look toward Boo and Ned as they rummage in the glove box and behind the seat for flashlights.

"They runnin?" asks Jumbo as he tucks his jeans into his socks.

Boo grunts and pulls out two flashlights from the chaos of the truck cab. He stands in the lee of the open door and puts the cheap plastic flashlights in quart Ziploc bags and presses the air out as he thumbs the lips shut. Jumbo doesn't wait for an answer and jumps into the truck bed. It tilts down on its springs and Simon unleans from the quarter panel. Jumbo flips the spare tire off the waders tucked against the back wall. He takes one pair in his hands and drops the other over the side wall and leans down again, scattering empty beer cans and wood chips and comes up with two pairs of knee-high rubber boots. He whistles to get Simon's attention and tosses them toward the tailgate in a slow arc. Simon bends down and sorts through them for a set and hands the other pair to Ned. He unlaces his shoes and jumps on the tailgate. He pushes his shoes off and slips the boots on. The rubber is dry and cold on his thinly socked feet. He offers a smoke silently to Jumbo as he vaults the side of the truck with the waders in one hand. He plucks it from the pack and nods to Simon as he clenches the cigarette between his teeth, shucks his shoes and steps into the waders. He bends his head forward when Simon offers him the lit match and thumbs the suspenders over his shoulders.

"All set."

Boo hands him one of the flashlights and puts on the other waders. Jumbo flips it on while Ned bends over the tub and searches in the tangle for the anchor rope and a loose end of the net. He finds the orange nylon rope and threads it through the end of the floater line and walks it back from the river to a piss elm that juts out from the bank, its skin buckled from years of rope burn. He ties it on around the tree five feet from the ground and pulls the net closer to the tree and loops it back and ties a full hitch.

As Ned anchors the floater Boo ties the weighted line to the bottom of the tree. Once both lines are secure, they step into the water and walk out ten yards, letting the net sink and rest in the water like a submerged map. Ned steers Simon by the sleeve to the washtub where they both stand knee-deep in the water and straighten the lines. Jumbo and Boo walk out farther into the river. They pause and turn on their flashlights and nose themselves deeper and angle downstream, heading for the far shore. Jumbo walks three feet upstream from Boo, the floater line over his shoulder so the floaters and sinkers won't tangle. Slowly, with each wet step, the fog eats them from view.

Simon shakes in his coat, the river chill settling into his bones. Boo and Jumbo are gone into the dark and the net continues to slip slowly from the tin tub. Ned casually straightens and untangles it as it flows under the skin of the river. Simon hears the river bending around the rocks and then catches the wisp of Boo's chuckle and the fuzzy trajectory of their flashlights on the water. Simon jerks upright as a blue heron barks out at some other night creature or at its own feathered dream as it stands sleeping in the shallows upriver. Simon relaxes and Ned laughs and shakes his head, though he comes alert at the sound, which breaks open the night like a shell.

They relax as the sounds seek each other out and climb back into place, climbing the darkness until the night takes on its shape again. Simon looks across the river as the net stops its travel from the tub and pulls tight against the lines around the tree. The flashlights lift up from the surface of the river and rip back and forth on the far bank. Simon hears Boo and Jumbo murmuring above the slip of the river. The line pulls tighter.

Suddenly Simon and Ned hear Boo yell.

"Shit!"

They crane their necks but can't see anything.

They hear them talking again and the lights splay out on the bank. A branch snaps and Boo swears again, then laughs, so Ned and Simon ease down off their toes. Soon Simon can see Boo and Jumbo weaving out of the mist, feeling the strung net. Their breath comes out in wet puffs and they run their hands along the top line. They walk to the tree. Ned and Simon walk over as Boo slips the knots loose.

Ned and Simon hold onto the rope, leaning back over the river, the rope wrapped in their hands. The weight is incredible. The nylon rope slips on the tree bark and Ned and Simon pull back. Boo and Jumbo step into the water and grab the rope and pull it toward shore, slackening the line for Simon and Ned. Their arms are pulled straight and Simon feels the muscles between his shoulder blades stretching. He flexes his hands inside the coiled rope and grits his teeth. Jumbo does the same and smiles over at Simon.

"Heavy fuckin net, huh?"

Simon nods and pulls again, taking in another foot.

"That's all we're gonna get," says Boo and he hurries to the tree and holds the rope next to the trunk so Simon and Jumbo can walk the end up and wrap it around and tie it off.

Once that is done they all stand breathing through their nose

like spent horses. Their cigarettes appear and are lit and they stand
still. Simon realizes how much noise they've made: their stamping
and splashing, the pulling of rope and rustle of clothes, all of it
reaching out over the river. Now, as they stand still, Simon feels
small against the night. They finish their cigarettes in the hush and
flick them like tracers into the river. They turn, one following the
other, pick their shoes off the truck and shuck their waders and
boots in a pile on the dew-wet ground. When they are finished Ned
lifts them into the bed of the truck and rolls the spare tire back over
them. They get in the truck as Boo kicks it to coughing life.

They turn on the radio, though they don't talk or joke. When
they pull onto the service road Ned takes out a bottle of Jim Beam
he'd stashed under the seat and passes it along the row of silent
men like a water bucket at a brush fire. Simon drinks and passes it
on. It comes back and he drinks again. The trees fly by ranked and
filed, old Forest Service plantings. They grow straight as pool cues
and the tops are lost in the night. The men keep drinking and the
cab grows warm. Boo punches the radio dial and country music
smokes through the cab. The truck hits the highway, growls once as
Boo floors it, and flies down the darkened tar.

Back at housing they shed their outer clothing, smelling of river
fog and smoke, steaming in the glow of house lights. Chairs are
turned back in and they sit split-legged and rocking. They finish the
bottle of Beam and Boo jumps up and starts slamming cupboard
doors and rattling pans.

"Gonna make some fishin grub," he states to no one as he whips
a spoonful of bacon grease into the frying pan. The burner puffs on
and he bends over and in the fridge light he starts to hand out eggs
and bacon.

Betty shuffles out of the bedroom in a tattered blue robe. She
doesn't acknowledge the men sitting at the table. Even though she

doesn't look at him Simon balls himself up a little smaller and tries to cough in his rolled hand without a sound. She yawns and nods her head. She turns the radio on and lights a cigarette.

"Jesus," says Boo turning around from the refrigerator as he kicks it shut with his heel. "I didn't know you were up."

"I wasn't," she says through a lungful of smoke.

"Well," Boo plows on, "since you are, you hungry?"

"I ain't gonna chance it with you cooking drunk. Most likely wind up gettin my stomach pumped at IHS."

"Whatever," he says cheerfully as he holds two eggs in each hand and cracks all four into the pan.

"Where the hell you learn how to do that?" asks Ned, popping a smoke into his mouth.

"Used to be a short-order cook."

"No shit, huh?" Ned bumps his chair back and walks over to the stove.

"Show me how."

Boo grabs four more eggs.

"Okay, just sit them between your fingers. Sit them there and pop them on the counter. Don't try the edge of the pan. No edges. You catch an edge and it'll send crack lines long ways instead of sideways. See?"

He raps both hands on the counter and holds the eggs out so Ned can see the whites drip out.

"Now that they're cracked, just keep your fingers bent at the end and move your first knuckles up to the ceiling. Pretend there's a hinge on the backside of the egg."

All the eggs slide from their shells into the pan.

"Damn," whispers Ned in drunken awe, "where'd you cook at?"

"Stillwater café, right Boo?" says Betty from the couch.

"Naw, I was down in Saint Cloud. I wasn't dangerous enough for Stillwater."

"What'd you do?" asks Simon.

"I was in Duluth and drunker than hell and I got in the wrong car. Keys must have been in it cause I drove home. I drove all the way home but I went the wrong way on the highway and ended up in Wisconsin."

Everyone laughs.

"Lincoln here?" ventures Simon, looking at Betty, but quickly dropping his eyes.

"God knows where he's off to. What he's doing."

Ned, Boo and Jumbo don't look at either Simon or Betty. They avert their eyes as if something embarrassing is happening—like interrupting a lover's kiss, or seeing a parent naked after a bath.

"Probably just out gettin to know the place."

Betty scoffs. "Probably out gettin to know what the county jail looks like. He's hangin around that Burt kid, and that can't be good. He don't tell me though. Seems like bein a kid's got to be a big secret these days."

Simon doesn't know what to say, so he draws out a smoke and lights it, turning away from Betty as if to get out of the wind.

Boo hands Ned four eggs while the eggs in the pan throw off breath. The light inside the house is buttery and thick with smoke and the steam from their clothes. Betty lights another cigarette as Boo and Ned whoop and cackle over the frying pan until all the eggs in the house are gone.

Betty sits quietly, looking loosely out the window, pretending to contemplate the night. Simon has a hard time looking at her. Since he moved into the trailer on blocks behind Boo's house they are forced to see each other every day. Boo had seemed abashed about offering Simon the broken trailer, with its door that sounded like mating cats every time it was opened, the waterstained ceiling. He was nervous about putting Betty and Simon so close together, but unwilling to make Simon fend for himself. Simon was grateful for it, and shrugged off Boo's apologies. *Well,* he'd said, *I went from living next to Winnebagos in the Cities to living inside one, ain't no big switch.* Boo, Ned, and the others studiously avoided talking about the past, about the dark gossip of Simon's crime. They knew the balance between Simon and Betty was delicate, and since Lincoln was living there too they didn't want to mishandle the secret, more for his sake than anyone else's.

As for Betty and Simon, they didn't talk much. Didn't quite know how to approach each other, so they mediated their relationship through Lincoln, who would visit Simon and smoke his cigarettes. Lincoln talked to them both in complete ignorance of what Simon had done. After a while the tension grew thick and there is nothing that escapes the notice of the young, nothing they don't register. Even if they can't assemble the details, the times and places, the emotion, the rolling of blame and love, and loss, none of this is ever lost on them.

Lincoln could tell, he felt that the lines of tension, of anger and recrimination ran so thick that when he banged out the front door of Boo's house he needn't have taken the growing trail around the side to knock on Simon's door—what he didn't know, but felt, was so palpable that he could have walked it like a bridge from Betty's door to Simon's without touching the ground. He began to avoid them both, preferring to spend his time with his cousins and their friends, caught up in the novelty of their outrages.

Simon tries to relax into his chair and Jumbo pulls out the cribbage board from under the pile of pens, magazines and old newspapers nesting on top of the refrigerator. As they peg and count and the food jumps quietly on the stove, the house finds a rhythm and keeps and holds it as the night turns over and over.

They see the pregnant curve of the net even in the dark. The ropes are cutting into the tree and sing with the tension of everything that has gone up or down the river. Listening, standing there without moving, they hear the slop of fish in the current, caught fast in the net.

Boo and Jumbo wade out, stopping every few yards along the rim of the net to flick the flashlights on and hold them down to the table of water that slips past their legs. Low whispers. Soon they are lost in the river mist, tracked only by the dull flashes of their lights as they check the net on their way to the other side. Simon and Ned stand in the water and lift their booted feet against the shallow scab of mud on the bottom. They watch as the top rope pulls tighter and holds for a few seconds and then sinks back into the current.

"Shit," says Jumbo from across the river. The net pulls up again and holds.

"Not enough. Not enough," he says and the net straightens a little more. Their voices sound close.

"Just cut it close. I can't hold it here."

Ned moves to the rope and Simon follows behind.

Boo yells out, "Ready now!" and the rope bows down in the current.

Ned and Simon bend to the rope, the nylon braid cold and slick in their hands. Ned wraps the rope around his hand and digs his feet into the river bottom. Simon's hands are slippery and they slide along the wet line until his hands hit a knot.

"Pull," gasps Ned, his teeth clenched tight, but the net sags out deeper into the river, doubling in the current, a wall of weeds, fish-heavy and cold. They hear Boo and Jumbo splashing across the river. Ned's body angles away from the weight of the net, but for every pull of rope, his feet slide farther out into the current. Simon scrambles to take the slack rope behind Ned and hold it.

Ned's feet find a rock buried in the mud and he halts his skid but his body begins tilting forward. He lets his arms out in front of him to check his balance but the net keeps drifting down and pulling him slowly into deeper water.

"Simon," he says, low in his throat. Simon lets go and splashes out in front and grabs the net where the mesh meets the nylon rope just as Ned staggers, his legs chomping up and down like a workhorse. Simon grabs on and leans back, pulling his arms to his chest. His hands are numb with rope burn and iced into claws from the cold water. His back is curved and his shoulders ache. He is tipped at such an angle that the riverwater washes into his boots and they sump against his frozen feet. Behind him Ned catches his balance and finds the rope again where it dangles in the riverwater like the umbilical cord of some weedy fetus they are trying to yank feet first from the river.

They begin pulling together slowly, wreathed in the steady pulse of their breath. They can't see Boo or Jumbo. The net is still heavy against their arms, loaded and bowed out twenty yards from the tip of the island downstream, piled high with riverwashed logs and grown tall with highbush cranberries. The sagging weight pulls Simon's back out flat above his bent legs as he tries to rein it in. He starts to tip over so he brings his foot up and down ahead to check his tumble. His torso saws back and forth as the net starts to slip back into the current. The whole weight of it is steady and sluggish. Simon and Ned struggle and still the net bends toward the island, where it will be swept into the waterlogged trees and weedy branches.

Simon is desperate. If the net touches the island it will wrap completely around it and they will have nothing. His breath shoots short and wet. In the water he sees the leaded line snaking slowly toward the channel. He picks up his foot and steps on it as his hands scramble for a hold on the top line. It slides steadily under the hard heel of his rubber boots. He wraps the line around his foot and jams it as far down in the mud as he can, cigarette-stomping it deeper and deeper into the river silt.

"What the hell are you doin?" asks Ned.

Simon is about to tell him he is stopping the net when his leg is jerked out from under him and he slaps flat into the water.

Ned pulls back and Simon struggles to his feet and grabs the net again with his hands. He finds the rope and starts pulling hard.

They see Boo and Jumbo coming out of the river fog halfway to shore and Simon pulls, and Ned pulls and the body of the net slowly comes out. They see the first fish. It is a walleye, caught fast, and it flails with its jeweled tail and turns in the stuttering current, pulled sideways for the first time in its life. It twists and bulges against the spidery net. Simon sees eggs sliding from its belly with each spasm. Simon and Ned keep pulling. The net comes easier. With a low whistle Jumbo and Boo drop their end clear of the island and it trails down the current and straightens, listing like a bridal train studded with gigantic Devonian pearls. Jumbo and Boo huff through the shallows and nod at Simon and Ned, and bend to clean the fish from the net and put them in the washtub, which soon rides low and level in the river's collar.

The net is full of walleye that struggle slate-eyed and slow, along with stunned suckers kissing the air and thumping along the surface. Boo and Jumbo ease the suckers out and slide them back into their element, where they mill in the slow current around the boots of the men until they slither slowly back into the river, destined for the gravel bottom to lay their eggs. A few northern pike stare sidelong at the men and gnash their spiky mouths trying to gash either net or hand. No amount of holding will quiet them. Jumbo and Boo spread the mesh with their hands and lift the northerns up tail-first, bouncing them gently so they slide back into the river, where they still for a moment and then shoot back into the channel with a furious splash, leaving a swirl in the water and a layer of slime on the men's hands.

Soon the tub is heavy with thick-bodied walleye, nesting in a shifting heap where one, then another, will ripple and flex and then lie still, cheek plates moving in and out like the wings of scaled butterflies. The end of the net draws near and the men begin to talk

and joke as they fling away the collected weeds and sticks. Simon
and Ned ease up and only need to fold the net in.

Ned stands and straightens his back, groaning as he reaches into
his breast pocket for his cigarettes.

"Smokin now's better than smokin after sex."

"Shit," says Boo, "it's probably the smell and the teeth that remind you of it."

Ned laughs and smokes and is working up a comeback when
Jumbo pauses and says "*Wait.*"

"Wait," he repeats. They let the rope drop down in the water
and lower their arms. Jumbo swivels his head and cocks it to one
side.

They hear the river and the whisper of fish sliding slowly
against one another in the washtub. A heron barks downriver and a
beaver is gouging a ring around some doomed hardwood too close
to the riverbank. Simon shuffles his feet in the water and Boo gives
him a dark look lit by the glow from Ned's cigarette. They hear
nothing except the wind licking the trees. The river fog frays faintly
in the predawn hush, waiting to burn up and off with the sun.

"Nothin," says Ned as he catches hold of a fish that slurps along
in the water by his feet. He lifts it up and squeezes it expertly into
the tub when the night bursts open in a flood of light and a voice
cracks out over the river.

All Simon hears in the glare is "DNR!" The other three are already charging downstream along the bank, spray from their heavy
strides breaking and shimmering in the fog that holds the spotlight
like a phosphored cloud. Simon takes off after them and he hears a
motor cough up and the quick shifting of gears. He looks behind
and sees people with sun-bright flashlights pounding in the river after them. He looks ahead and sees the lights of a three-wheeler
bouncing through the brush and scattered trees of the riverbank.
Jumbo, Boo and Ned keep running straight. Simon veers off toward

the center channel and around the island where Jumbo and Boo can't go with their waders because the water is too deep. The water gets deeper and it splashes against his chest. The current is strong and he feels his feet go out from under him. His baseball cap pops off his head and bobs and drifts along the top, turning in the current until it sinks, only to be washed up limp and muddy in the cattails at the next bend where no one will ever find it.

22

Simon emerges from the forest three days later.

The water carried him downriver into the weeds, where he lay gasping, watching the headlights of the three-wheelers cross back and forth on the other bank until the game wardens shut off the motors. He imagined them dismounting; swinging their booted legs high over the plastic saddle like mounted cowboys. He could hear them swearing and talking. The sound of cigarette lighters carried across the river. Simon lay flat, his boots full of water, and pressed his body deeper into the mud as he heard the game wardens grunt and heave the washtub full of fish into their truck. He lay sucking shallow breaths and thought he was too close, so he edged himself into deeper water and began to float downstream along with the sticks and spongy logs washed away from the banks. He floated feet first and kept his head above water by moving his arms out to the side, as if boating down the river on a crucifix. It was still dark and the night sky limned the banks into a jagged border with no mark-ings except that of blackness against the near-dark sky. The river turned sharply and Simon couldn't steer himself back to the center of the channel and he washed up gently in the logs and brush along the riverbank.

He stood and grabbed the red willow that grew half-submerged in the shallows and carefully climbed the bank into the night-cast shadow of spruce and cedar, trees he knew not the name of.

The brush grew in a wild weave along the bank. Simon walked with his hands out in front of him, recoiling as every branch scooped down at his face and left a grid of dew and spiderwebs on his skin. The ground was littered with broken branches molding back into the earth. The soil itself was firm but it shuddered with each carefully set step so Simon lurched slowly, feeling the water sloshing and sucking in his rubber boots. He stopped and stood, first on one leg and then the other, and emptied his boots. It runneled like blood in the lightless night. He pulled them back on, banging them over his heels where they stuck against the wet pull of his socks, which had collapsed around his puckered ankles.

He set off again, following the river downstream, sometimes crawling under the canceled trees, beaver-chewed and random, that crossed one another on the bank and that lay where they fell stick-ing halfway in the water. He didn't know what time it was. The river fog crept steadily from the water and floated into the crum-pled earth of the banks. Simon thought he could see a change in the sky, a lighter tint against the ragged margin of trees, but he still walked arms out, with tiny steps that stuttered against the veins of tree roots half-exposed in the soul of the riverbank.

There were no sounds as he threaded the tangle. No birds, nothing nesting in the hair of the brush. Light began to bulge over the treetops on the far shore. The weeds were brittle and tense as he brushed past, crackling beneath the muzzle of mist that spun them from tan to silver in the scant light. Simon moved as if each step were a word in a sentence, a part of the answer to which way he should go. Downstream there had to be something—a bridge, a road, anything. From upriver two teal bulleted along the turns of the river, their wings doppling out of the mist until they set and tilted around the next bend.

Simon looked up at the sound and stepped out into nothing. His body pitched forward. As he hit the ground he heard his leg crack. He screamed and tried to roll to his side and grab his knee to his chest but it wouldn't come. The pain did, and he lay gasping in the leaves, his chest huffing damply and his hands on his thigh. Everything around him was a different shade of gray, outlines of true life. He turned his head from side to side, trying to see what had happened. He propped himself on his elbows and looked down.

He had stepped into an otter run, a hole through the net of roots down into the river muck below, and his leg was buried to the knee. He tried to lift his leg but couldn't get it past the teeth of roots clamped over his toe. He sat all the way up and pulled at it but still it wouldn't move.

He looked around for a stick to pry his leg out of the hole, and through the brush he saw a light moving downriver and heard the *thunk* of a paddle on an aluminum gunwale. He stood using his good leg and lifted his bad one, sliding it painfully from the wet boot without its sock as he fell on his hands and knees.

He could hear voices now from the canoe and a light frayed through the brush. Simon started to crawl, tunneling through the undergrowth, dragging his leg behind. Ten feet ahead he saw a spruce with its branches grown down into a skirt, the hem buried in the weeds. He pushed the branches aside with his head and crawled into the living cave it formed. The voices drew nearer to shore and Simon held himself tighter, knees to chest, one hand on his right ankle. Soon the voices drifted away and the paddles sploshed back in the water. Downstream the beleaguered teal piped and rose again into flight, their wing tips pocking the surface of the river until they gained a low shelf of wind and climbed higher. Simon lay in the den of leaves and fell asleep whimpering the way grown men do when they cry in their sleep.

When Simon woke up he found that he couldn't move his leg. He was stiff with cold and his neck ached from resting it on the angle of his bent arm. His hands were a lattice of cuts and scrapes, rededged and coated with grit and sap. He sat up and peeled back his pant leg to look at his ankle. It was blown up into huge blue lumps along the outside and swollen so big that his foot looked as if it had been tamped on to the end of his leg, twisted and left to harden there. Simon felt along the length of his ankle on both sides and the stiffness gave way to a warm pain that spread out from his fingers as if he had an anti-healing touch. It was still dark, not quite day. It was raining, a cold steady drizzle that squatted over the naked brush and downed timber, a steady hum with no foliage to check its fall, no leaves to break it into smaller sounds. It was steady and without remorse.

His mouth was dry from his run through the woods, and the fear that had made him crawl like a crippled baby into the arms of the spruce. A layer of scuzz coated his tongue and teeth like curd aging in some timbered vault. Without sitting up he reached into his pocket for his cigarettes and matches but everything was soaked. The matches slipped and crumbled as he tried to strike them, so he put them back in his pocket.

He lay back flat and watched the rain as it collected into large drops on the spruce boughs above to fall onto his chest and legs where they quickly seeped into his skin, already puckered and dimpled, transformed from the smooth map it had been into one of valleys and strange rubbery mountains, a map on which he could no longer trace his life. Soon he was asleep again.

When he woke up the rain had stopped and the sun was pale and weak through the trees, a bowl of slippery broth, rancid and shimmering in the blue background. He sat up, brushed the pine needles from his shirt and pants and looked down at his ankle again. There was no improvement. He shivered and rubbed his arms as the wind came cold and level off the river. His clothes were still wet and clung to his body. He looked around for something to splint his ankle with so he could move away from the water that made him both cold and thirsty.

There was nothing except the spindly shorts of broken spruce branches, matted into a thorny and rugged carpet, so he dragged himself out from under the tree with his hands. The rough ground jarred his leg. He flipped onto his back and began scooting himself up the hill away from the river, hating the calm water that kept coursing past.

His arms were sore and his ass hurt from heaving it over logs and stumps, the sharp points of beaver-shortened saplings. From the top of the hill he saw the river moving from the north and bend left into the dawning day. Simon lay back and fell asleep.

He woke up the next day curled into himself, knees up, arms in, nestled down into the leaves and grasses on the top of the small rise. The sun broke weakly through the spring-bare leaves of the poplar that crowned the low hill. He didn't feel anything in his leg—no sharp pain or crunching—so he slowly unfolded himself along the ground. His body ached and his hands had turned from brown to ash-gray. He couldn't stop shivering. He lay for a minute under the mute arms of the trees like a sacrifice and felt his stomach turn and claw beneath his bruised skin. He didn't know what time it was, nor how long he'd slept, only that his neck was stiff from the awkward bend of sleep and his head throbbed from lack of food and cigarettes. He brought his hand up to his face, raw from the wind.

Around him he saw plenty of deadfall blown from the crowns of storm-scarred poplar, so he collected some of the stronger pieces, tested them and when he found the right ones, long and straight, he broke them over his good knee and laid them to either side of his ankle. He took off his flannel shirt, scored the seams with his teeth and ripped it into strips and bound the sticks to his ankle. Then he slipped off the boot from his left foot and pulled it carefully onto his right. He winced but did not cry out. He lay back down gasping, sucking air through his teeth although the pain wasn't so bad. He moaned and sucked air because of what was to come, of what he imagined when he thought of walking out of the woods. He stood, pulling himself up with a small tree that grew next to him, trying not to bend his bad leg. He stood there tottering, mimicking the stiff sway of the trees bending on the low tongue of wind which had changed directions and blew now out of the woods and toward the river. Simon bent down and grabbed a larger branch; it held his weight so he began hobbling toward higher ground, away from the river.

The ground rose but the trees blocked out all perspective. He had no way to tell how far away he was from anything. The undergrowth crowded out his immediate vision and the swaying poplar and spruce clouded the middle distance. The ground was pocked and uneven from the craters left by windblown trees and the remnants of countless burrows partially filled with leaves and rot. With all the pain he felt Simon wanted to be buckled up in the crown of a tree. High up as when he had worked on the IDS, swaying above the city in the community of men who lived above the streets, because there the streets and parks took on a shine in the sun and the ground, no matter how rough, looked smooth and easy.

He tipped and stumbled up the incline and deeper into the woods as his stomach unwound. He kept his eyes on the earth while his body loosened. But with each step he was more lost, with each step on newer and stranger ground. The poplar gave way to jack pine. The only sound was of the naked brush sliding over his clothes, and the whisk of overhead branches slapping his creased and troubled forehead. That and the wind, steadily thrumming the branches.

Deadfalls blocked his way. The wide reach of jack pine branches were impossible to climb over. Sometimes he couldn't force his way through the hazel brush and he had to turn and walk back, punted from one trail to another. Soon he was no longer able to tell in which direction he was going. He tried to keep to the rise, always heading to higher ground. His face was a mass of welts and his hands had turned pink from the constant sting of whipping brush. He turned and limped and shouldered his way on until he reached a clearing on top of a hill. The trees shrank back and the dead grass was cut jagged from the weight of winter snow. In the middle of the clearing there was a pile of sunken and rotting tires along with a jumble of battery cases, pierced by the skeletons of milkweed stalks and goldenrod. Simon searched for a road or trail that led from the clearing but there was nothing. No ruts or tracks, and the junk offered no clues or answers to how it got there, reluctant in its rot to show the only thing that it could dare to claim: an origin. And Simon knew this and so without a sound he wept.

He woke in the night, his mouth caked with slime and again his body hurt too much to move. He lay there, the mound of tires and batteries in front of him, that in the gloom looked as if it belonged to the landscape, just a low rise of the earth. He tried to clear his mouth out but no spit came as he coughed and swished his tongue around. He had been without water for two days. He stood on his feet and swayed, his head reeling. He covered his index finger with the tattered cuff of his shirt and rubbed along the outside of his teeth. His mouth felt smoother and he smacked his tongue against his teeth. Despite his cleaning efforts it still felt dry and swollen. He shook the white cheese that had lodged in his shirt cuff free and stared into the night.

The clouds were gone and with no moon visible the stars shone clear and strong down between the treetops. There was no wind to stir his lingering breath or the mute trees. Ahead he saw an orange glow in the sky, just a tint to the purplish night that Simon figured had to be the lights of a city. He hitched up his sagging jeans, stiff with dirt and sweat, tested his bad leg inside the boot like spoiled meat left too long under plastic, and began walking slowly toward the reflection of civilization, the excess of other people's lives leaking into the sky. As he passed the tires he saw a thin section of whitewall that had been torn from the tire main. He stopped for a moment, tested it for strength and palmed the moss-eaten piece for steel belting that could possibly cut him. Finding none, he sat down, tore another long strip of cloth from the remainder of his shirt and tied the piece of tire to the bottom of his bare foot as best he could, looping the ragged cloth between his toes and around his heel. He felt foolish and looked around him in the tree-crowded dark, but there were no witnesses. He stood and tested the vulcanized sandal, and seeing that it worked, he picked up his walking stick and shuffled down the hill and disappeared into the woods.

He couldn't tell if he was walking in a straight line. It wasn't that the ground was uneven and at every step he winced as his feet sank into burrows of animals out scavenging in the night. Though this, too, made Simon curse under his breath. It wasn't these things that made Simon stop and wonder, as he craned his neck each way toward the openings in the branches above as if he were stuck in the bottom of some arboreal well. It was the succession of trees—

first jack pine, then poplar chattering uselessly in the gloom, then walls of hazel brush that he had to swim through arms first and whose fingers whipped his splotched red face. Then swamps, sudden dips where the sandy ground gave way to clumped grass and mucky pits of peat that sank him slowly to his thighs if he didn't keep moving, didn't keep jerking his feet from their grip, only to stumble on the clumps of marsh grass or stagger around the black circular pans of uprooted tamaracks that in the darkness reared like bent-fingered monsters from the murk of the swamp bottoms.

He continued. After every tree he had to skirt, or tangle of brush through which he could not pass, he paused, centered himself on the other side of the obstacle and tried to line up with the haze of city light that he could no longer see but imagined onto the night sky. He was sweating into his torn and dew-damp clothes. The night was cold but his struggle through the woods made him steam and tremble, wipe the beads from his welted forehead and continue. He was thirstier than ever, his mouth caked and filmy, his eyes stinging as if each drop of sweat was pure salt. His head spun and his stomach turned no matter whether he was moving or standing still. It was dark but he could see farther, what light there was collected in the faces of the storm-scarred birch and poplar, nested in the dew-covered underside of the bent swamp grass.

Simon passed through the woods and the light grew gray and stubborn over the land as he pushed through the net of brush and thorned bird berries into a clearing lit dimly by the approaching day. The edges were pegged with poplar saplings and the grass lay jagged and rough from the winter, broken only by clumps of waist-high brush, islands in a sea of grass. Simon moved into the open. He heard a thump and stopped. Another thud and he looked around, but nothing had changed. Then he saw it.

A deer stood ten feet to his right, its thin neck stretched high, and through the gloom Simon saw it swivel its head. Its ears flicked mechanically. He didn't move and the deer didn't move. It just tested the liquid surge of the morning air as it rolled out with the new day. Simon didn't know what to do.

Then Simon saw another rise silently from the ground like the first, its back legs tensed and one front hoof cocked daintily. It swung its head once left then right and stopped in a pose of concentration. Again, straight ahead this time, another deer climbed into sight. They kept coming, one after another, until it was as if the earth had called up one deer and then went mad making dozens of them out of nothing until Simon was surrounded. He could hear their breath, see it steaming gently from their square noses and ceiling like fog around the clearing, like the smokestacks of the city. Simon was so close he heard the musculature of their noses closing and opening. Other than that they didn't move. Not a hoof lifted, not a flank quivered, no tail flagged up from the groove of their buttocks. Simon stood frozen in mid-stride with his branch crutch supporting his crippled body. His breath loud in his own ears. They stood that way facing one another across the void of habit and genes until Simon could no longer stand still. His legs shook, the arm holding the stick wobbled and Simon slowly stepped forward through the remnants of grass and weed. The deer didn't break. Simon took another step, a small lurch of his human machinery, and still the deer didn't bolt. Simon hopped forward, a cripple among the elegant. A hunchback at a ball.

Each step Simon took sent him deeper within the company of deer, into the community of fur and animal stink and the nervous gestures of the hunted. They wouldn't get out of the way. He neared the first deer that stood in his path, its ribs heaving with the labor of breath. Its hind leg stomped to remove the phantom of a fly that had not yet been hatched out of the remiss and dawdling spring. Simon stepped to the side and moved behind the deer. He was close enough to see the grain of its hide, the sticks and burrs that had lodged there. He was three feet away and the deer swung its head to catch, perhaps, the shadow that moved in its midst, but it did not run as Simon eased around its rear. He felt as if the deer had risen bare but complete from their nests of grass and had watched and judged him and found him missing and wrong. He felt sullen and removed, as if he were the one not quite there. His foot, as it searched out the ground like a blind snake, only a half foot. The throbbing pain in his ankle a pain registered only in his own head. They let him pass unseen in their language of smells and heat. The deer decided Simon was not anything that mattered; so he passed, and with a last look while standing defeated at the line of trees on the far side of the clearing he retreated, just a small shudder in the night. Surely not something or someone from which they would run.

By midday Simon was dizzy from lack of water and food. His body gave off the odor of rotten milk under the newfound sun that heated the lowland and urged the ground moisture from the newly thawed earth. The undergrowth crackled though the liquid heat of the air ought to have cushioned it. The swamp bottoms and fire-growth jack pine greeted Simon with every dip and rise of the es-kered and morained land, which, when seen from above, rippled away in a bright scar from the river.

Simon had no hat and the droop and rasp of branches pulled his hair and stung his skin as he tried to move toward the lights he had seen the night before. As the ground slipped down again and he tore through yet another set of trees, a vast swamp sprang up in front of him. Tamaracks shorn of their waxy green needles vaulted the pale blue sky while the broken bodies of piss elm, their bark folded off their trunks, stood jagged and morose, brown and gray above the tan carpet of marsh grass. Simon stood on the edge of this dead wet hell and continued to dab at the sweat that collected on his bare head and trickled down to rest damply along his back un-der his grime-darkened T-shirt. He knew he could not ford the bog with his bad leg. He stood looking at the water pooled between the hummocks of tufted grass that had the mad look of straw-haired men buried up to their necks in water and mud. His mouth refused to unlock from lack of moisture and his tongue clacked like a slat of wood against his teeth. Not knowing what else to do, he walked to the edge of the swamp and bent on his good leg over a puddlet of water, clearing away the twigs and crackling pupae of waterbeetles. He scooped a handful of water to his lips. Then another, and more until his chapped and bleeding lips stung. He whipped the dripping water from his hand and stood. The muddy water sloshed in his stomach and he stumbled back to higher ground where he lay down in the sun and fell asleep.

When he woke the sun had escaped the net of higher trees. It shone down on Simon's shiny forehead until the brown skin flushed pink under the dirt and welts that collaged the slope of his skull. He sat up and shielded his forehead with his arm. As he rose into a splay-legged position his stomach gurgled in warning against the sudden movement. Simon lowered his arm and grabbed at his midsection with both hands and it spat again. His flesh felt spongy and strange under his own touch. He clutched his walking stick and stood as best he could. His head spun and he broke out in an immediate sweat. His stomach cramped and he bent double so that his arm and the top of the walking stick stuck out above the plane of his troubled head in a twisted bow directed at the vast swamp still sitting hunkered and solid in front of him. Simon took a step and pivoted so he faced the woods when his stomach tightened again. Two more jerky steps and another spasm doubled him over. He stumbled farther into the woods with one hand on his walking stick, the other fumbling with his crusted jeans as the pain in his stomach coursed downward. He struggled, but couldn't release his trousers in time as the first current passed through him and out into the already brown and dismal world to settle in the moist cave of his booted leg and escape in a slow stream out the cuff of the other.

"Shit," said Simon sullenly to nothing and no one as he walked farther into the woods. He stopped every few feet to let the result of his thirst take its toll on his already racked body until he stank and his pants were soaked with what moisture he had left. He didn't care anymore and kept walking in a continual fight with the sun that beat down on him in the swelter of the forest. As he passed another tangle of brush he saw a bird's nest posed in the lattice of branches and dead leaves. He approached it cautiously but there was no occupant; the only evidence of the previous tenant was a jagged piece of bright blue shell caught in the cage of open field grass. Simon plucked the nest carefully from the fingerlike branchlets and placed it on his head, running a strip of flannel over its top and tying it under his sweaty chin.

He set off again, armored now against the sun, parting the waves of spruce boughs with their jagged veins snapping against his arm and jabbing into his ribs as he turned sideways to press through a thick stand. All the while his stomach and intestines squirmed under his fevered skin. The sun scuttled up the shuttered reaches of the trees and broke meekly through the branches into little suns that watched Simon's slow progress. He was dehydrated, diarrheal, limping from the pain in his leg and cautious of his good one, the foot of which was swollen and tender from the rough ground of broken branches, rocks and stumps.

The ground sloped down and Simon dreaded the affront of yet another swamp but there was nothing else to do but follow the will of the land and gravity, so he kept damply going forward through the trees. The slope was sharp at times and he had to turn and sidestep down the hill, keeping his damaged right leg straight, pushing off with his left. The spruce and balsam grew even closer together, the undercarriage spoking maliciously from the straight boles, dead from lack of sunlight. He entered them dutifully. The branches from the evergreens were woven so tightly together he couldn't push past them; as soon as Simon pressed his body into the mesh he bounced back so he knelt down and crawled, dragging his walking stick and bad leg behind him as he tunneled under the solid rock of growth that shut out all light from above.

The ground under the pine needles was black and peaty. Here and there were pockets of black water skimmed with pine needles and water spiders, the bergs and seals of tiny oceans shut out and unknown to the rest of the world. Simon's crippled shadow loomed but he dared not threaten them because he did not know what lurked in these buckets of water set in the secret ground, eyes that reflected nothing, that gave nothing away and receded as he crawled forward.

He saw light through the branches ahead, tan and golden. With a final jerk of his body he broke free of the trees and on all fours he let out a groan as he saw the scoop of the river in front of him. On its haughty shoulder sat a hedge of marsh grass bedecked with red-winged blackbirds that scuttled from the ground into the precarious perch of the bending brown grass. Simon made no move to stand. Instead, he knelt and gawked at the foot of the river. The sun tracked its summer path and Simon wondered if he'd been gone for months. The breeze ruffled the nest on top of his head and his hair hung damp and greasy around his ears. His stomach heaved both at the river and at the microbes that gnawed at his bowels. He felt faint, and then he heard a buzz out of place in the dampened sounds of the river's syntax. It grew to a hum and then a thump. Simon tilted his head to look downstream and saw a car coast over a bridge and disappear down an unseen road. There, in the barren tangle of the river's hair, in a place Simon was convinced no one else had been, but which, in fact, had seen four generations of loggers with axes and Swede saws, power saws and skidders, there in the travel of history that all rivers have seen, Simon sighed.

The river was colder than he remembered. He eased his wasted body beneath the cover of its surface and floated feet first toward the bridge with only his mad-capped head sticking out above the water. Compared to the noisy trail in the woods, his path down the river was smooth and quiet. The water was shallow and the banks distant over the gravelly flats. He watched the bridge's iron ribs skate closer. The iron rivets came into focus and they shone like pimples on its rusted countenance. Soon its tattered geometry split the sun and Simon coasted through the brief tunnel where the swallows darted like bats from the recesses in the beams. He passed underneath and paddled with his arms to the right bank and clambered out. His clothes hugged his greasy body and he shivered. He climbed the boulder-strewn bank devoid now of grass and plants, showing only the casings of long-departed snakes, beer cans, broken bobbers, the filmy plastic of candy wrappers, and half a rubber boot that Simon wished had been left for him farther upstream. He stepped on the sun-warmed shoulder of the highway.

Cars passed Simon's sitting form, torn and disheveled, a strange bird perched on the margin of the highway, inexplicably cocking its head at the pulse of traffic. Some slowed and pulled away after surveying the ripped shirt and dirty pants, the ragged face bonneted with the tangle of the bird's nest. If Simon had looked up from his contemplation of the road he would have seen the slow swivel of heads, the shockingly white faces in the interior tint of the car as the passengers stared open-mouthed at the creature tossed up on the shore of the highway. He would have seen the mute exchanges as they exclaimed or *ooh*ed to one another and then were gone down the road, the tumble of children jumping up on their knees with their sticky tourist hands curved over the seat to stare out the back window, receding with a bump over the frost-heaved tar and then around the next curve from sight.

But Simon doesn't notice. He is still faint and incontinent, balanced on the rail, trying to stay there as opposed to the different places his head and bowels are trying to send him. He doesn't notice the semi that gears down and hisses to a stop in front of him, the diesel engine growling, until the driver slides across the seat and opens the passenger door and yells down at Simon.

"Hey! You okay?"

Simon jerks his head up and tilts it, squinting owlishly at the driver. Stunned by the sound of another human voice.

"Do I look okay?" he asks.

"Hell no. You look like a bag full of assholes."

"That's about how I feel."

"You need a ride someplace?" asks the trucker. "You sit there long enough and the State Patrol's gonna pick you up for bein crazy. The way you look, they'd pick you up for litterin."

"Yeah, well," Simon has to think out the words. His voice feels hollow. "Well, where you goin?"

"The Cities."

"Sounds good."

"Well?" says the trucker impatiently.

Simon unfolds from the rail and totters across the tar to the steel running board of the semi and grabs the solid handle mounted to the left of the door. His knee wobbles but holds as he hops up and swings the door shut. The trucker releases the brake and they begin rolling out high above the road.

It is warm inside the cab and the radio spins out music that Simon can't identify as rock or country. The CB crackles and the truck lumbers through the gears. Simon sinks back into the red upholstered seat and lets the motion of the truck rock his head back and forth. The driver stretches his arm across the cab with a pack of cigarettes held between his callused fingers and shakes it expertly so one cigarette jumps out from the ranks of others. Simon takes it gingerly and lights it when the Zippo comes across. He inhales from the Pall Mall and sighs out the smoke.

"Pepsi?" asks the driver.

Simon can barely manage a nod.

"Out in the bush there's nothin like a cold Pepsi," he says, reaching into a red and white Igloo cooler behind his seat. He hands the can to Simon and coughs and pushes against the steering wheel to unkink his back and then leans his left elbow out the truck window. Simon takes a long drink, his eyes watering from the smoke and the cold soda.

"So what you doin up here? You from here?" asks the trucker.

"Just visiting."

"You must got some rough relatives. Looks like you got hit with the wrong end of the ugly stick."

"You could say that," says Simon, tapping his ash toward the cracked window and watching it disappear as it is sucked out into the day.

"I don't want to get in your business," he shifts in his seat, "but is that a fuckin bird's nest you got tied to your head?"

"Yeah," says Simon.

"I thought so, but I didn't want to say nothin. I mean, it could be some kinda Indian thing."

"I lost my hat, that's all."

"Well, let me get straight with you. I got another hat around here somewhere. And, well, you should put it on cause I know a lot of people down these roads and it won't do much for my image if I'm drivin someone around with a fuckin bird's nest strapped to his dome."

"No problem."

He reaches out as the trucker fishes around behind the seat and produces a black baseball cap with CAT stitched on the front in yellow. Simon unties the strip of flannel holding the nest to his head and unrolls the window, tosses out the cigarette, then the damp and broken nest. It is sucked behind the truck and skitters down the tar.

Simon settles the hat, the plastic snap cool as metal on the back of his head. He leans back again and lets the truck rock him like a fifteen-ton cradle. The trucker lights another cigarette. Simon falls asleep.

When he wakes the truck isn't moving. He looks out the window. It is dark and the truck rests among others in a constellation of running lights, amber in the settled dusk. The driver appears from the sleeping compartment with a duffel bag in one hand and a plastic sack in the other. He squeezes into the front seat and slides the plastic bag over to Simon.

"Look," he says, patting the duffel for some unseen object, "I don't mind Indians. Not at all. But I do mind stink, and you stink."

"Sorry," mumbles Simon.

The driver ignores his apology.

"There's a pair of pants and an extra T-shirt in the bag. I'll give you a dollar and you can shower up inside. Hear? The shower takes quarters."

"Thanks."

"Yeah, well." He shrugs. "Well you really stink."

With that he pops open the door which swings slow and heavy like a barn door, and hops down onto the cement. Simon follows more slowly, like an old man.

As he crosses the parking lot, weaving between the parked semis, Simon hears the freeway off to the side. They clear the last of the trucks and cross the oil-stained parking lot to the truck stop, its lights blazing against the rush of night and cars. When they enter Simon tries not to look at the truckers lined up along the counter and in the booths, a society of men used to sitting, unshaven and red-eyed, their hands permanently curved from gripping their steering wheels.

"I'll be in here when you're done. I got a schedule, so don't stand around tickling your ass all night."

Simon nods and heads to the door under the sign that reads *Showers*. He strips and leaves his tattered clothes in a heap but takes the plastic bag into the shower with him. Inside the bag is a bar of anonymous hotel soap and a washcloth. He inserts a quarter and the shower gushes hot water that steams the mildewed tiles. Simon steps into its path and gasps as the water pummels his tender skin. It stings as his flesh turns red instantly but he doesn't move and begins soaping his entire body. The dirt comes off in waves and his face sheds layers of skin and grime.

He rinses and soaps again. Twigs and bark leap free from his dirt-caked neck and scalp. Once he is done he shakes off as much water as he can and puts the jeans on. He steps from the shower and dries his torso with paper towels and punches the electric dryer and turns the loose nozzle until it points up and begins blasting his hair. He puts on the white T-shirt and looks at himself in the mirror.

He is overpolished. The peeling skin hangs off his face, which shines from the hot water and the fever he carries. He has lost weight. The trucker's pants are six inches too large around the waist and ride high above his blasted ankles. He takes the belt from the splint and threads it through the loops. He still has no shoes so he carefully reties his tire sandal and slips the boot over his damaged ankle. He throws his old clothes in the wastebasket, holds the CAT hat in his hand, drops the besmeared washcloth back in the plastic bag, and leaves the washroom.

He stands in the tiled entrance to the diner scanning for the trucker and finds him hunched over a plate of corned beef hash, the snotlike yolks of his eggs churned into the greasy pile of glistening hash along with strings of undercooked hash browns. He is alone. Other truckers bend over their food like convicts and carry on conversations that Simon can barely hear over the clink of forks and coffee cups and the counterpoint of complaints between sagging waitresses and cooks through the opening to the dim and grease-pocked kitchen. Simon slides in the booth opposite the trucker.

"Well, shit," the trucker says, drawing the sounds out around his mouthful of food, "you're clean."

"Clean enough, anyway," offers Simon.

"I'll buy you breakfast, but that's it. You say you're gettin off at the Cities and you'd better, cause if not, you gonna starve. I ain't the Sal-fuckin-vation Army."

"Yeah, I got it."

With that the trucker continues eating and Simon unwedges the plastic-veneered menu from the slot in the rack of condiments, orders and sits back waiting for his food, his stomach still gurgling from the swamp water. The rush of appetite and the sullen banter under the ineffectual lighting numb Simon into a half-sleep but he fights it until the food and coffee come. He eats and they leave. They board the semi to float above the highway and gust other lesser motorists into the slow lane. Simon is carried into the faint orange sun of the city.

23

The trucker drops Simon off in the warehouse district. He waves but the trucker busies himself with his load, throwing the dead pins on the heavy steel doors of the trailer.

Simon turns, uneasy within the soiled geometry of the warehouses with their chipped cement aprons and blackened bricks. He walks painfully from Second Street to Hennepin, the breakfast still gurgling in his stomach. He stops every few yards and leans on parking meters, mercifully spaced and even. He is thankful for the sameness, the predictability of the city. His foot still throbs and he has no shoes. Only eight blocks, he thinks, only eight until I can lie down.

He turns onto Washington and from there to Third Avenue but has to stop and throw up behind a Dumpster. He sees the police station looming like a fortress up to his left. He knows he hasn't done anything. They have nothing on him this time, but it doesn't take much to look suspicious. Ill-fitting clothes, the sneer of pain on his face. The color of his skin. His injuries. Anything can be used against him. He inspects his shirt for specks of vomit. Finding none, he continues to limp forward, the parking meters stationary crutches lining his way home.

His eyes don't leave the pavement. He catches himself counting the slabs of sidewalk, counting how many sections there are between parking meters. The skyline holds no attraction for him. He emerges from underneath the skyways and linked buildings. Keeping his eyes to the ground he turns to the front door of the Curtis. Instead of the wide double doors, his fingers find only chain-link fencing. His leg hurts and his stomach has not calmed down. He looks up.

The hotel is gone. Where the Curtis used to be there is nothing but a pile of rubble on an empty lot. He sees sections of brick like puzzle pieces, bent pipe, chunks of cement with rebar sticking out like deadly thistle thorns. The debris forms a huge pyramid, atop which someone has set an old sign for the Curtis. The "C" has been half ripped away.

Simon turns around and checks the street signs, but he has never been lost in the Cities. He is sure he is in the right place. He looks back at the lot. There is nothing of value left. It is as if a bomb fell on this one building and blew out all the marble countertops, the ornamental iron, sinks, toilets, bathtubs, doorknobs and railings, leaving only great masses of brick, tamped down into rough roads that must have been used by the bulldozers. He can't quit staring at what is left of the hotel. He can't believe it.

He knows city planners and developers can push through permits as quickly or as slowly as they want. A building that took years to put up can be pulled down in days. He knows this. He has done it. But he can't bend his mind around the fact that he has no bed, his mattress buried under such a load of brick. When he closes his eyes he sees his coffee cups, his two spoons, the rusty hot plate and the few shirts he left in the box under the bed. But when he opens his eyes he is greeted by this carnage of brick.

Simon glares at it. He tries to jump and climb the fence but he can't. He jumps again and his fingers graze the top. One more time. He manages to get a hand on the bottom edge but the tying wire rips into his flesh. He swears and stands, trying to get his balance. His stomach protests and he doubles over with dry heaves.

He looks at the sign again and musters all the spit he can, pulling as much moisture from his destroyed body as possible, and spits over the fence. It lands in the center of the sign. He looks up and down the block for a break in the fence but it is newly strung. There is no give, and in keeping with the times they have trimmed the top with razor wire like lace on a dress hem. "Goddamn," he says. He thrusts his hands in his pockets and turns south, but spins to face the building again. "Fuck you," he says. Drawing out the words slowly. "Fuck. You."

Out of the corner of his eye he sees a patrol car turn onto Third Avenue from Tenth Street. Simon limps toward Franklin. The cruiser passes him and by the time he crosses I-94 it is gone.

He rests again, trying not to puke, and a car pulls up to the curb next to him. His vision is blurred from the fever and pain but he sees it is a Delta 88. He looks back down at his feet, not wanting to know more. The door opens.

"Hey, mister. Hey you, get in."

Simon looks and sees a brown car curbside. The woman driving it is leaning across the front seat. She studies him, first his one shod foot, the short jeans. She moves her eyes to the skin of his face, the strength of his hands. As always, whether at work driving the cab or studying at the hospital, she tries to assess what it would take to fix someone, whether or not he is permanently wrecked. She is curious about damage.

Simon steadies himself and returns her gaze.

"I don't always look like this."

"You'd better hope not, mister."

"I ain't got no fare."

"Just get in."

"I can't pay you."

"Just get in before the fuckin cops pick you up."

Simon staggers to the open door and falls onto the front seat. It is all he can do to shut the door.

"You drunk?"

"No."

"High?"

"I wish."

"You look like you got run over."

Simon shakes his head. "Drank some bad water." He jerks his head at the retreating lot where the Curtis used to be. "I lived there. Guess they ripped her down."

"Where you been? They ripped it down this summer."

"Away."

"Where you headed?"

"The Windsor."

"You was walkin up there?"

"Yep."

"You never woulda made it. Looks like you got a bum leg there."

"I musta broke it. I was up north."

"I guess you left your Boy Scout Manual at home."

Simon chuckles painfully, his head is spinning. "Yeah, something like that."

"Name's Irene."

"Simon."

"How'd you lose your shoe?"

"Long story."

"I bet."

She reaches across the dash for a pack of cigarettes and looks down at Simon's feet. "I'd say you did break it."

"Probably."

"Hurt much?"

Simon feels like crying. "Everything hurts, honey."

"Honey, huh?"

"Sorry," mumbles Simon.

Irene checks the rearview mirror and then the sideview as she changes lanes and turns off Third Avenue. She is expert, an engineer working the controls.

"Where you goin?" Simon asks her.

"Don't worry about it."

"Where?"

"Look here, limpy. Ain't no way you can take care of yourself. You gonna look like Lurch forever if you don't mind that foot."

"Where we goin? Don't take me to the hospital. Not to Northwestern. My mom used to work there."

"You callin me honey and now you worried where I'm takin you? That's a good one."

She turns again but Simon doesn't have the energy to lift his head to see where they are going. Simon used to pride himself on knowing how to navigate the city without looking at the streets, the corners, or the signs. Just show me the top three floors and I'll tell you what block, what street. I'll tell you when it was built. Now his vision is too blurred, his body too racked to care.

"It can't be no worse than where I've been," he says to himself.

Irene reaches out and pats his shoulder.

"Things always worse, baby."

They stop, the wide American tires crunch glass and sand in the unswept gutter. Irene gets out and walks around to Simon's door. She opens it and bends down and grabs Simon expertly behind the knees.

"I'm gonna swing these out. You lift so we don't knock your foot. You with me?"

"Yeah, yeah. I am."

Simon looks at her. Her loose shirt hangs down away from her body and he stares at her breasts that hang free, the crescent of a nipple.

"Come on. Pay attention, cowboy."

"I'm an Indian."

"Whatever. Just lift those legs."

He does and she holds him by the waist as he stands.

"Lean on me. We got some stairs, but not too many."

They walk to the steps of an old apartment building.

"Put your weight on me," she says.

She puts his arm over her shoulders and holds his hand as he hobbles alongside her.

She keys the door open and shuffles through next to Simon.

"Just a few steps to the second floor and we gonna be home free."

Simon sees the stairs and groans.

"Just use me. Put your weight on me."

He hops up each step on his good leg, his bad one held out and back like a misplaced and useless tail.

"Just use me," she whispers.

Simon feels faint, the stairs seem to tilt and fade, but they make it. She opens a door and Simon stumbles in.

The apartment is clean. The kitchen linoleum streak-free. The old wood floors waxed. There are no pictures on the Sheetrocked walls except for three medical posters. One with a human body with no skin, front and back, another with the organs exposed, and the last which shows just the skeleton. There is only one room, the kitchen hugs one corner and a door leads to the small bathroom. Irene guides Simon to the bed in the corner. She peels him off her shoulder and rolls him onto the bed. He blinks and turns his head as she walks to the bathroom. Without her touch he is suddenly disoriented, unmoored.

"Where are we?" he shouts.

"My place. Just my place. Take it easy."

"No. No. Where in the city? What street?"

"Does it matter?"

"Where? What building?"

"We're on Portland. Can't you hear the freeway?"

"I can't hear nothin."

She returns from the bathroom with a glass of water and two pills. She hands them to Simon.

"What's this?"

"Trust me. You'll like it."

He swallows them and lies back down. He closes his eyes and hears her humming. He opens them again and sees her shirt drop to the floor. She uncaps some skin lotion and rubs her arms until they glow.

"You're goddamn pretty," he says.

"No I'm not. You're just hurt."

He hears her slam a dresser drawer and she struggles into a new blouse.

"What'd you give me?" he slurs.

"Vicadin."

"We're in the Balmoral, aren't we. It was built in the teens."

"Go to sleep."

"This was the edge of the milling district. You know that after World War One Minneapolis was the artificial limb capital of the world? They needed the best white pine, no knots or weird grain. They needed that and the technology."

Irene smiles. "You gonna need one if you don't heal up." She puts her hand on his forehead.

"You smell like a flower," says Simon dreamily. "Imagine that, these huge warehouses full of feet and hands, legs, full of them."

"Go to sleep."

He nods off to the sound of the door closing and locking.

When he wakes up it is dark. Irene is next to the bed taking off her clothes.

"What time is it?"

"Shhhh."

"What time?"

"Late," she says, whispering.

She slides into bed next to him. He jumps when he feels her skin next to his.

"I ain't got no clothes on," he says in surprise.

"I took them off. They stink."

"Trucker clothes," he says, grasping groggily for an explanation. "Yours stink too?"

"Shhhh."

"I don't feel so good."

"You're sick. You got giardia."

"What?"

"Giardia. Beaver fever. From bad water."

"I don't feel good."

"Shhhh."

She moves closer and puts her arms around him as he lies on his side. He is shivering. Her skin feels cool against his, her breasts press into his back and he feels the floss of her pubic hair against his thigh.

"This is weird," he says.

"You're sick."

"That ain't what I mean."

She shushes him again and rubs his stomach and wraps her hand around his penis. Not moving, just resting it there. Cool and considerate.

"This all right?"

"Yeah."

She moves her hand slightly back and forth.

"You're sick, Simon. You got this thing inside you."

"Will I get better?"

"Your body'll get used to it. You'll feel better."

"How do you know?"

"I'm studying to be a nurse. Now be quiet. I'm tryin to get some sleep."

Her hand keeps moving and Simon tenses his legs against the sheets and she keeps touching him, moving her hand slowly.

"I can hear it."

"Shhhh."

"Portland is better than Park Avenue. Me and my brother used to call it Better Not Street, as in Better Not Park. That used to be a nice neighborhood. Rich neighborhood."

"Be quiet."

"I can hear I-94 now."

"Shhh."

"I can hear all those cars, those people. I know where we are."

24

Vera and Lester grow comfortable with each other quickly. They could be walking down the street, not talking, commentary on the sad buildings unnecessary. Not daring to ask about or discuss the future.

"My mother makes the best soup," she would say.

"Mac and cheese, stew if we're lucky."

He is in love with her strangeness. The Polish and Yiddish words so different, so unbelievably thick and consonant. When she talks about her parents, or life at home, he feels thin, his language smooth and plain. With her he feels strangely American.

It is May and they are on their way to the train. They know it is the last time. Soon it will be gone, cut up and carted away.

They hold hands.

As they turn from the street onto the service road the train-yard comes into view and their hearts quicken. They have not grown tired or casual with each other's bodies, and probably never will. Each time they fuck it is an experiment. They are young.

When they fuck they try on different emotions—anger, tenderness, pride—the way children try on their parents' clothes.

They worm through a break in the fence and look both ways for the bull, as if crossing the street. They don't see him and walk directly up to the train and climb on. There are only two cars left. By Tuesday they will be gone. Without the others, the last remaining sleeping car feels more like a boat than a train. They undress on the bunk.

The ceiling is too low and the bed too narrow for the striptease of lovemaking.

On this day, their last on the train, he is on top and her hands are locked on to the creases made by his bunched shoulder blades. He is on his hands, pushed away from her. They are making love tenuously, moving softly, more presence or pose than motion. Her hands are on his shoulder blades and she thinks to herself, *these are his wings.*

These are wings and with each crescent motion of his hips they pull together, struggle under his skin, furling and unfurling. These are his wings doubled up, but there nonetheless. Ready to come out and reach their secret proportions if needed, held in quiet reserve if not.

Afterward, they lie side by side, coffined on the narrow bed, and share a cigarette Lester filched from Simon, tapping ash into an empty Coke bottle pressed between their sweat-slick hips.

"Does Simon have a girlfriend?"

"Don't know. He dates like he works."

"How's that?"

"Hard, and whenever he can."

"He doesn't like me."

"Sure he does."

"Then he doesn't like me much."

"That ain't true either."

"Whatever." She shrugs off Lester's answer, closing it down

with a last drag on the cigarette. She uses just the muscles in her stomach to sit halfway up and drops the butt in the bottle. She leans back and snuggles into Lester as if readying for sleep, though they don't dare rest long because someone is sure to come by the train.

"Simon's throwing a party."

"Where?" she asks, mock sleep-slurred.

"The house. Ma's got night shift. Next weekend. He figures he'll get paid for this demo job."

"That an invite?"

"You don't need one. You with me."

She murmurs, pulling closer to the warmth of those words.

You with me. She sighs. You with me. Nothing beats the sound of those three words. There is nothing in this world like it. You with me.

25

Even after Simon's leg has healed and the fever was broken thanks to the pharmaceuticals Irene stole from the hospital, he did not want to move out. She didn't want him to move either. After her long shifts pacing the floors at the hospital, of hassling the big cab around the unforgiving and unforgiven streets of Minneapolis, she wants Simon around. She likes his spontaneous discourses on the city, on her building. Her work feels like wandering, aimless activity. But when she comes back to her apartment on Portland Avenue, Simon tells her the history of where she's been. He explains to her what used to stand at the corner of Grant and Fourth Avenue, when all she saw was the gray cement and two hookers in matching electric blue shoes slugging a drunk with their purses. She comes back tired and Simon explains the different histories she drove over that day, the ruined monuments. She thinks maybe he found the root of her fatigue, the cause of the numbness she tries to displace with antidepressants.

As for Simon, he has nowhere else to go. Maybe he could bunk with One-Two. He might find Dougan, but neither option sounds good.

Once his ankle heals he walks over to the Windsor to find One-Two, who is surprised to see Simon. Everyone thought that Simon had drowned. One-Two hands him a slip of paper with Dougan's new address written on it.

He goes down in search of Dougan in the basement of one of the newly refurbished warehouses along Saint Anthony. He finds him adding a poster to the inside door of the new mop closet.

"Christ, Dougan. Ain't like you got to hide those from nobody. Ain't like anyone comes down here."

"I just like them all in one place. If I start puttin them on the main wall there ain't no way I'd be able to cover it. This way, with all of them next to each other, hid away like this, makes me feel like there's hundreds of them, and they're all mine."

He secures the last corner with a strip of silver duct tape and stands back to admire his framing job. "Where you been?" he asks Simon without taking his eyes off Miss February.

"Had a bit of an accident. I'm shacked up." He looks down at his feet, guilty he hasn't told Dougan sooner.

Dougan nods thoughtfully. "Pussy's better than fist any day of the week."

"I got a job."

"You can stay with me if you need to."

"I won't."

"Don't be so sure. Thing about pussy's that fist'll always last longer." He turns back to the girls on the wall. "This here'll preserve better than both."

Simon sits down and lights a cigarette.

"Your nephew came by lookin for you."

"He's supposed to be up north."

"Yeah. He said you was supposed to be up north too."

"Naw. Didn't work out. Lincoln hanging around with that little skinny fucker? Burt?"

"Yeah. Can't say I like the looks of him. Kinda kid that's dumb enough to huff gas and smoke at the same time."

"His cousin."

"Family, huh?"

"Sorta."

Dougan rubs his beard. "You shacked up close by?"

"Close enough. I'm gonna keep the job at the rug store. Least I got that."

"I got that rug for you. They really surprised the shit outta me when they said they were gonna tear down the Curtis. They ain't even gonna build anything there."

"The Bokhara."

"Whatever. I rolled it up and put it with my stuff. Didn't want nothin to happen to it."

"Thanks, man."

"Things go down, you can always lay low here."

"I'm finished with all that. I like what I got now."

Dougan turns to look at him, to search Simon's face, to see if he believes his own words. "Yeah, you done with it. But it ain't nearly done with you."

Simon shifts uneasily.

"Can we get that rug? I wanna take it back to Irene's."

"Yeah, yeah," says Dougan wearily, "we can get it."

Simon emerges onto Main Street. As he squeezes through the black steel door in the back he realizes that for the first time, the very first time, he has something of his own to carry. A thing not rented, borrowed, or stolen. Not like his tools that were leased out from the union, that had belonged to another steelworker who took a dive. Not like the food he cooked in Stillwater, food that was owned by the state and loaned to the prisoners in exchange for work and suffering. It is his and he has a place he shares with someone. It is their roof, their kitchen. He isn't simply camped out or passing through. He doesn't owe Irene as he felt he owed his mother.

The streets are full of noon people, suited and rushing to or from lunch, secretaries with tennis shoes sticking out conspicuously from under their navy-blue stockings and short skirts, their high heels clutched in their hands, a sandwich and a can of diet soda in the other. Simon feels that they are looking at him and his strange parcel. Nobody knows, no one can see that the rug is his, purchased with his labor. The rug, rolled in on itself, might be a remnant or industrial carpeting salvaged from a Dumpster, a Chinese manufacture thrown out by an indifferent college student. No one can tell. He feels like breaking the string and unfurling the rug like a flag, to declare that this was nothing cheap or easily come by.

Back at Irene's apartment he wrestles it up the stairs and leans it in the hall while he unlocks the door and thumps it through. It falls to the floor like a body.

Irene is at work at the hospital. He sees her no-nonsense jeans and her sweatshirt on the floor. When Simon began living with her on purpose instead of by circumstance he had begged her to wear a sweatshirt, something loose, something concealing. *Who knows, you might find another derelict Indian in the gutter and I don't want him to fall in love with your tits like I did.*

He smiles at her mess, the crumpled pants. While he was still confined to bed he had gotten used to seeing her unzip her pants and relished the way they fell immediately to her ankles, not hampered by thick hips. He smiles because they still bear her impatient footprints from when she kicked them off. The sweatshirt hangs on the iron bed rail, one arm inside out. He shoves the rug all the way in and closes the door. He picks up her clothes carefully and folds them on the edge of the bed, and then sweeps the wood floors and dusts them with a damp mop. From under the sink he takes out the wax and with a soiled towel he waxes the floors.

By the time Irene sighs her way wearily into the apartment, the floors have regained the luster they once had when the brownstones and the neighborhood were new. When it was an idyllic place, barely removed from the bustle of downtown, a refuge for soy and timber merchants, where, in the twenties and thirties, piano music floated from every window in the breezed afternoons and the rudiments of big band music were exciting, startlingly unreal as they emerged from new radios. The music urged husbands from their martinis and club chairs and wives from their stations next to the fireplace. Fires were lit against the summer night chill with slats splintered from packing pallets. This new music inspired them to make love, not fuck, because business was good, the brownstones solid and new. Music had taken the place of the novel, a private world shared by the public. The radio made music common, but it was consumed alone. Everyone who could afford a radio was included and people danced, in their firelit parlors, hidden from, yet a part of, the common gaze.

Irene shuts the door and sets down her bag, looking more like a schoolgirl in her stockings and white frock than a nursing student.

"Whatcha doin? Remodeling the place?"

"Hey, baby. Just cleaning, just sprucing it up a bit."

"Looks nice," she mumbles as she sits down on the bed to untie her boxy white shoes. She gets one off and lies back, her feet, one shoed, the other cooling, over the edge of the bed.

Simon kneels and unlaces her other shoe. "See anything new?"

"This place is clean."

"Naw, anything else?"

"What is it?"

"Just look."

"I'm too tired to look."

"Look anyway."

"I'm too tired, Simon. Just tell me."

"Come on," he urges.

"You got a haircut?"

"Jesus, no. Just look around."

"Tell me."

"The rug. The fucking rug. I picked up my rug from Dougan."

She rises on her elbows and looks blearily at the Bokhara.

"Nice."

"Nice? It's beautiful."

"Yeah. It's beautiful."

"Don't you like it?"

"Sure I do, honey. Right now I wanna close my eyes. My eyelids are the best thing to look at right now."

Simon sets her shoes under the bed and crawls in next to her, wrapping his long body around her.

"You smell like lemons." He nuzzles her neck. "And medicine. Stitches in ER. Heart attack in the afternoon."

"Good nose. Quit wiggling."

"Ten city blocks and a fire at the Chinese restaurant on Nicollet."

"Mmmm. Shut up."

"You gotta work tomorrow?"

"I gotta work every day."

"Let's take a trip."

"Sure, honey. Be quiet."

"The Dells, or Duluth. We got a car. We can do it."

Irene is asleep. Simon turns on his side as her breathing takes on the regularity of traffic and the long even stretch of afternoon runs itself out as the sun leaves the carpet in shadow to sweep up over the mildewed and cracked plaster walls.

I'll do those next, he thinks. I'll spackle them and paint them. I'll level the stove that always sends the bacon grease to one side of the pan. I'll get new Formica for the counters, hinges for the water-swollen cupboard doors, and I'll shave them with a hand plane so they close good. I'll regrout the bathroom tiles. New plywood for roof decking, and tar paper and shingles for the whole building. I'll scour every brick. I'll wipe away all that time, that mess. I can fix all of that. I can lift the Balmoral and reset the stone foundations, put in copper pipe instead of lead. Insulate the crawl spaces. I can re-place the cracked bricks, put in paving stone sidewalks and sweep to the curb. I can make the whole street new. I can fix all that.

PART
FOUR

26

Lincoln finds that he has nothing to attach himself to up north. Nothing to structure himself around. There is the gas station, the grocery store that sells stale doughnuts and oversees the casual delivery of mail. The bar he has not been in, which acts like a changing room—Boo and Ned enter with their shirts half-open, their jean jackets plastered with fish guts or balsam sap and emerge hours later with studied military bearing, with perfect posture to cover their drunkenness. Lincoln has no anchor, nothing except the tremulous house he and Betty live in with Boo. Simon's vacated trailer is still out back. The coughing school bus picks up Lincoln every morning. These are the props with which he has been forced to stage his life on the reservation. He isn't sure where the time has gone. All he knows is that his time up north has been split in two: the ten months they lived there before Simon showed up, and the three months since he disappeared. Lincoln is hard-pressed to say why, but the three short months his uncle stayed in the trailer out back were important to him. Even though Simon seemed to be pained by Lincoln's presence, he knew Simon didn't hate or despise him. The conversation was always steered away from stories about the family, was kept at the safe height of skyscrapers. Simon told Lincoln building stories, the history of stone, then brick, and lastly steel, of how men worked the city up from the ground. Tales of men flying from the trusses to land on the pavement unharmed, of falling with loads of beam into the river only to break the surface without a scratch. He shared the myths of tough men, of bar fights and motorcycles. At such times his uncle relaxed and stretched out his legs, and time flew, and Lincoln finally found someone who shared his love of the impossible, the outrageous, things that could never happen out on some dusty dried-up reservation. These were city stories.

After the DNR raid they lived in stunned silence. Boo, Ned, and Jumbo all got away. Jumbo and Ned were fast enough to circle around the three-wheelers and walked back to town through the woods. Boo was too slow but had managed to hide himself in the narrow space of a tortured oak, the inside rotted out. He was squeezed inside overnight, trying not to sneeze, coughing around the punky dust like a deposed king on the run.

Lincoln finished the school year without complaint. Betty isn't working and spends the days cleaning up after Boo who groans from his hangovers or from the sudden onset of work, sporadic forays into earning money for the next round, sometimes unloading feed trucks, selling illegal walleye, and lately, staggering swollen-headed through poplar stands in search of morels, which he has heard sell for twelve dollars a pound.

No one knew what happened to Simon—whether he had drowned or was lying low. Lincoln had his own fantasies: of staged flight, showdowns with cops, shouted demands and high threat. In the short while Lincoln had known him he decided that Simon was too capable to get caught, too handy to let something as simple as the woods claim him.

When Simon first knocked on the door with a Hefty sack thrown over his shoulder, peering in the jittery windows, Lincoln had hung back, and was as nervous as Betty in Simon's presence, without knowing why. Boo had been gracious and let him stay in the mildewed trailer out back. Betty had voiced neither assent nor objection. She simply crossed her arms and smoked furiously. Boo settled Simon in and went back to bed. Lincoln lay down on the couch and tried to sleep while Betty sat in the kitchen all night lighting one cigarette off another until she was out and the sun began to burn the frost off the windows on the south side of the house.

"I'm gonna get smokes and eggs," she announced suddenly, when she thought Boo and Lincoln should be awake. She took the car keys from the finishing nail next to the door and left.

Boo woke up and shuffled in, half-blind with sleep, and started putting coffee together, squinting through his hangover.

"Delivery," he said, banging the grounds into the garbage can. "Say, Delivery? You awake?"

"Yeah."

"Go tell Simon coffee'll be ready in ten minutes."

Lincoln sat up.

"You scared of your uncle?"

"Grandma is."

Boo shook his head. "Naw. She ain't scared. She just ain't used to him yet."

"Well," ventured Lincoln, tentatively prodding the bloated body of adult relationships, "she's mad at him, then. She don't like him much."

"Wrong again, Delivery." Boo took the cigarette from his mouth. "She loves him. She loves him more than she thinks she should."

Lincoln didn't understand. "What did he do?"

"He killed a man." Lincoln didn't know what to say. Boo continued. "He killed a man, but he didn't mean to. You scared now?"

"No," lied Lincoln.

"Yeah, well. You don't got to worry."

"Why not?" he said, trying to draw Boo out, but blushing at the quaver in his voice.

"Because you're his nephew." As if that explained everything.

"How'd he do it?"

Boo looked at him hard. "You want to get red-assed? I might be hung over but I'll still spank the shit outta you." Lincoln couldn't breathe. "Some things you don't need to know. Got it? Now go fetch him."

Lincoln ran for the door. He was breathless by the time he reached the trailer.

Simon sat bent-kneed next to the fold-out card table. He was shirtless, the muscle of his forearms plainly visible as he shuffled and reshuffled a pack of cards. His shirt was spread over the other chair back above the overworked space heater.

Simon looked at Lincoln and smiled. He shuffled again. "This an eviction notice?"

Lincoln looked puzzled and Simon quickly riffled the cards as if to bury the uncertainty behind his words.

"Boo says he's got coffee."

"You gonna come in or stand out there all day? Knowing Boo, he's got the shakes so bad it'll take him three tries before he gets it right."

Lincoln stepped through and pulled the thin door shut behind him. Simon gestured at the other chair.

"That door's pretty thin," said Lincoln, grasping at any topic.

"Better than no door. Better than none, which is what I had for the last three months."

"They sent you back to prison?"

"Who told you that?"

"One-Two."

"Ahhh," said Simon. "One-Two. Well, he's got his eye on everyone. Shoulda figured he'd find out."

"What'd you do?"

"When?" asked Simon tensely.

"The second time."

"Went shoppin for Xmas dinner. Tell you somethin, Lincoln. You ever go after geese, use a gun. Use a fuckin gun," he repeated to himself. "And stand back a ways." Lincoln nodded but couldn't imagine hunting, couldn't see when he'd go after geese.

Simon stood and threw the cards on the table. He reached behind Lincoln for his shirt and Lincoln winced, startled by the swiftness of Simon's gestures, unsure of their intent. Simon shook his head.

"You don't gotta be scared of me, for Christ's sake."

Lincoln didn't know what to say. He was ashamed. He was scared.

"Nobody ever tells me nothin."

"You don't got to know everything. But know this," he said bending down to eye level with Lincoln, "you don't gotta worry about me. I'm the least of your worries." He stood, thinking that Lincoln was about ready to cry. "So," he said lightly, "how about that coffee?"

With Simon gone, either dead or lost to him, Lincoln goes out to the trailer with his cousins. The cards are still there. They play. They crib and play gin and Lincoln shuffles, trying on Simon's gestures, his finger-flourishes and card-tapping. They steal Boo's beer and think themselves sneaky, professional. They are unaware that Boo knows about their drinking, that he lets them steal a few cans here and there. His is a tough wisdom: Let them think they're drunk. Let them have a few brews instead of perfume, or mouthwash, or Nyquil. But Betty's continual vigilance drives them from the enclosure of Boo's house and the rickety trailer to the sandy streets, to the nests of older kids with rum and vodka. With speed. To more dangerous terrain.

It is summer and school is out. There is even less for Lincoln to do, and more to wonder about.

Burt is driving. Lincoln clings on behind, too conscious of their bodies, of the rules governing teenage touch. Instead of holding Burt around the waist, his hands are braced on the rear rack of the three-wheeler. Each bump in the trail sends shocks up his arms but he likes it: the danger of almost falling, the ache in the backs of his arms, the growing muscle. When he breathes in through his nose the wind feels sharp, as if it were March instead of August. He thinks maybe his nose is bleeding, but he doesn't care. He is too preoccupied with the terror of the trail. Burt yells each time the machine lifts into the air. He pushes it faster with every near-spill.

Burt's father lives in the Cities and his mother back on the reservation. He shuttles between the two of them, doing everything wrong so they decide that a change of scenery will help, will kick him from bad habits toward good ones. He moves in these different worlds, from trail to street, and imparts the wrong walk, the affectations of the city on the reservation, a wildness to his city self. Up north he saunters with a pimp-daddy limp down the highway, rolling along, certain of his cool among the ditch-driven blackbirds and marginal muskrat. Everyone thinks he's hurt himself and so they pull alongside and ask, *Are you hurt?* He shakes his head and sneers. After a month of this they start to call him Hurt. On the Southside he pisses on the sidewalk as if he were on a deer drive and lights campfires under the Cedar Avenue overpass. Lincoln suspects that he does this on purpose, has created a studied craziness for himself.

They pull the three-wheeler to the top of a rise and Burt chokes off the engine.

"Need some fuckin shock absorbers on this thing."

Lincoln agrees. Burt swings one leg over as if dismounting a horse. Lincoln does the same and shakes the cramps out of his hands.

Burt raps the gas tank with his knuckles, first at the top and then down the side until it stops ringing.

"We outta gas?"

"Naw. I'm just makin sure we got enough for transportation and refreshments." He unscrews the cap and sets it on the seat. He leans over, and with his nose a couple of inches away from the tank, inhales in short bursts. He stands and shakes his head back and forth.

Lincoln walks up to the tank and does the same. The gas is sloshing to a still and it looks black and deep through the opening, as deep as a well. He breathes in through his nose, holds it, and breathes again. Lincoln stands straight. His head feels porous, bigger than before. He exhales, as if some great truth had been casually disclosed. Burt huffs again, miming the breath-holding technique of pot-smokers, the relaxed concentration of his father and uncles.

"Mossy nose. Earthy undertones."

Lincoln giggles and takes another turn. The light hits his eyes more strongly, cutting through the trees. He squints and wipes his hands on his jeans. He thinks this is no worse than what Simon has done, though there is a sharpness to Simon, an accuracy that Lincoln knows he has not dulled by huffing.

This has become their ritual. Their daily exercise. A bumpy road out and a smooth, smooth ride back. It is the only way Lincoln can get up the nerve to venture off the road into the woods. He knows he has no purchase here. Nothing on which to pin his uncertainty. This is the only way he can mediate the possibility of finding Simon's body in the corner of some swamp. What if? What if they find him?

"Shit," says Burt. "He ain't dead. My dad saw him down on First Avenue, near the bus station."

Lincoln is stunned.

"Who cares, anyway? After what he did." Burt shakes his head and lowers his nose to the tank.

"What'd he do?"

Burt stands and wipes his nose as the mucus thins and drips out.

"You don't know? He's why you ain't got no daddy."

Lincoln starts toward him, ready to lay in. Burt waves him off.

"You don't believe me? Corral Boo or Ned. They'll tell you." He staggers off and pisses against a tree.

Lincoln huffs once more and caps the tank. He kicks the three-wheeler to life, and before Burt can zip up he turns it around and guns down the trail.

He doesn't remember the conversation. How he plied Boo with beer, made sure the spark-plug wires were loose enough so the car wouldn't start. He knew better than to ask. He knew enough just to state it. To make Boo fight the accusation. Boo wasn't up for it. Lincoln remembers squinting from the gas, though it was dim in the house. He narrowed his eyes and focused on Boo. He doesn't remember much, just Boo's fumbling words and Betty's quiet sobs coming from the corner of the couch behind him. She tried to touch him, but he evaded her. He knows. Boo apologized, stumbling in the rooms of his words, banging into corners, trying to explain why, to make Lincoln understand.

27

Getting from the reservation to the city isn't difficult. The distance is bridged by cousins or uncles visiting the VA Hospital, aunties looking for work, and everyone else heading down and back for cut glass beads, new bicycles, returning sometimes with only pocketfuls of change (all that is left after threading through the bars on Lake, Hennepin, and Franklin). Burt and Lincoln find themselves at Little Earth Housing, mostly AIMless since the seventies.

Lincoln has been gone from Minneapolis for slightly over a year and a half, but to him it feels like decades.

Once they pass Monticello he glues his eyes to the windshield. Squinting against the August glare and the coils of pot smoke that fill the car, he looks for signs of change: new buildings, the absence of old warehouses, roads pushed through crumbling neighborhoods, or abandoned lots given over to weedless lakes of asphalt. He searches the margins of the road for everything he has been told by One-Two happens in a city, the glacial pace of change quickening since his departure. But he cannot be sure what has changed, or what he is noticing for the first time.

Some of the old buildings he has never seen before look coated in at least twenty-five years of dirt. When they turn off the freeway and onto Franklin the feeling of displacement becomes more acute.

"Hey, Burt, that restaurant always been there?" he asks, pointing at a Lebanese place on the right side.

"How the fuck should I know? I thought you came here to whup up on your uncle, not for a architecture lesson." Burt speaks lazily, gesturing widely with his hands.

"Yeah, huh."

Lincoln closes his eyes, sick to his stomach from the weed and the stop-start of the car, city motions he has lost the feel for. The car is driven by a distant relative on his way to pick up an even more remote relation at the train station in Saint Paul. Lincoln closes his eyes and tried to keep them that way past Third Avenue, so he won't have to see the one thing he did know was new—the Amoco station where his house used to be. He can't manage it and opens them while they are stopped at the light. Burt lights a cigarette and Lincoln rolls down the window and stares. He'd anticipated change, but not this, not the complete removal of his old home. Not the level concrete, the lack of elevation, the cheap fence and retaining wall around the back edge that separate the gas station from the apartment building on the side and the alley in back.

He thought that maybe the driveway would still be there— with the cracked cement he used for his solitary games of marbles. He imagined that maybe, just maybe, some of the turf between the old sidewalk and the street would have been preserved. The snow used to pile up there until March or April and he watched it every day after school, looking at the buried wrappers and sticks, the crust of exhaust melting into the pile, drifting down until the grass blades poked through the pile of sand and leaves.

He searches the corner for the elm that had ignored the predictions made for it by the city park service, and managed to live, but it is gone, too. Everything is gone.

He looks over to the other side of the street. At least the Windsor is still there, and with it One-Two. Lincoln can't imagine what One-Two would be doing without Betty across the street. He is probably endlessly fixing pipes and sanding floors, clipping honeysuckle, keeping the old ship afloat, as he used to say.

Little Earth is the same, and in Lincoln's opinion, an apt name: the closer they get to it, the less green meets the eye. When they are dumped off and their ride drives away, they look at each other and start laughing; both standing by the curb with Hefty bags filled with their clothes and bedding.

"Looks like we brought our Indian carry-on luggage," says Burt.

"Shit, this place hasn't changed none."

Lincoln surveys the cement courts and the graffiti-covered fence. What had started as a mild stab at utopia has hit well below the mark.

"What you mean?" ask Burt, "we were all in the same shit before, and we're all in it together here. At least we're all still together."

"One way of looking at it," says Lincoln.

Armed with the new knowledge that his uncle had killed his father, he looks at every building differently, every corner, every Indian bar. The city is divided in four ways now. Between places his uncle had been or built, and places his presence hadn't mattered. And divided again between places he'd been before he became a murderer and places he'd visited after. These divisions put a whole new spin on Minneapolis. Lincoln knows all he needs to do is ask One-Two or the owner of the rug store for Simon's address. But he can't approach One-Two, not yet. Betty would surely have called him and told him to keep an eye out. Lincoln imagines One-Two slowly cruising the streets on foot, looking for Lincoln. He'd ask around Little Earth for sure, but Lincoln is certain he'll find Simon before that happens.

He walks during the day and stays at Little Earth at night, getting stoned with Burt and his father, listening to stories of the old AIM days. He paces Franklin from one end to the other, all the way up the numbered streets to downtown, up Washington, back down across the old rail yards along the river, through Uptown, up Lake Street and all the way on Cedar to Little Earth. His path isn't exact. There isn't much of a routine. He takes streets that, as a child, were simply impediments, distractions between the Dairy Queen or the comic-book store. Now he pays attention, to the character of the buildings, the amounts and types of traffic. He studies the city, and though he is only fourteen, he feels ancient, herding his memories within the perimeter of his footwork.

He walks his old route to school and is surprised to find out how short it really is. The city has shrunk while he was gone. He can see the changes now. How some neighborhoods are giving over to blacks, the Indians moving to the Northside, Hmong and Guatemalans fighting over Saint Paul.

He finds out quickly that the Curtis has been torn down, and once a week he walks by to look at the empty lot. It is turning toward fall when he is downtown, and after watching the rug store for Simon, goes in and asks the owner for Simon's address. Still, he doesn't use it right away. Instead he watches from across the streets, under the train shed in the old Milwaukee Road station, the iron walls covered in silver tag. He watches the rug store and learns Simon's schedule, his habits, and catches him walking to the Northside with a woman who works in the jewelry store next door.

Burt is getting bored. His father threatens to send him north again. To stave off boredom they smoke up all his father's weed and drink all his beer. They fight the other men at Little Earth, and spend hours riding Southside with whoever has a car, counting days and weeks by who got jumped when, who had fucked whom, by funerals they don't attend. These are the markers of their city.

28

Simon wakes up and walks out the front steps to get the paper. He is groggy and sweat-pantsed, fuzzily surprised to be engaged in such a domestic habit. Simon has been living with Irene for four months. This is the time of year he has always loved, the closing days of September when the heat isn't so bad, the gentle folding into fall. The ground cover is already getting brittle.

He opens the door and sees Lincoln sitting on the stoop reading the metro section. Simon looks behind him as if contemplating retreat but instead closes the door quietly, as if the noise of their meeting will climb the stairs and wake Irene. Nothing will rouse her, not the traffic, nor Simon's tossing, nothing can breach the wall of sleep that Irene erects around herself with the long hours she logs behind the wheel and on the hospital floor, and the whites she and the other nurses take to "stay positive" on the long shifts. She tries to hide it, but she comes home incoherent and in the morning emerges from the bathroom bright and bruised, like an overripe orange, sweet but wrong.

Simon sits down next to Lincoln and takes a cigarette from the pack on the step. He lights it and shivers, though the September sun is burning off the dawn fog. Lincoln looks as if he hasn't slept.

"Mornin, Simon."

"Or a late night maybe."

"Depends on how you look at it, I suppose."

Simon studies him and is amazed at Lincoln's growth in the two and a half years since he was released. At almost-fourteen his body looks twenty. Sturdy. Used to the demands of hard living, too old and too capable for his age. As if his body is impatient for some task that will tax every fiber.

"You supposed to be up north."

"Could say the same thing bout you, Uncle."

Simon shudders again, this time at the venom laced through the word *uncle*, made slick and heavy with dangerous knowledge.

"Well. It didn't suit me."

"Me either."

"You supposed to be in school. I ain't."

Lincoln looks at him hard, his eyes limned in red, his cheeks taut.

"I don't think," he says slowly, "I don't think you got any right to tell me what to do."

"Watch your tongue, sonny. I ain't your dad, but I am your uncle."

"If it weren't for you, my dad would be here right now."

Simon looks away. "You know."

"Yeah. I know."

"Who told you?"

"Boo."

"Goddamn him."

"After you took off in the woods no one figured they'd see you again. So they talked."

"Well, shit, Lincoln. Knew you'd figure it out someday. What you here for then?" He faces Lincoln, as if readying himself for a blow. "You might as well give up tryin to make me feel bad. I've felt worse than anything that can happen now."

"I need some money to get back up north. Grandma's gonna declare me a runaway if I don't hightail it back."

"Are you?"

"Am I what? A runaway?"

"If I give you the dough are you gonna use it to go back?"

"Yeah."

"We don't got much. Maybe enough for the bus."

"Who? You and that white bitch that works next door to you?"

"Her? Vera? Naw, my old lady's name's Irene. What'd you do? Follow me?"

"I knew where you worked. Your boss told me where you live."

"Hold on."

Simon stubs his cigarette out and flicks the butt onto the sidewalk. He stands and goes into the building. He comes back with eighteen dollars.

"Where's your partner in crime?"

"Burt? Over at Little Earth."

"Don't give none of this to him. Just head over to First and get on the bus."

Lincoln turns to go.

"Hey, Lincoln. You might as well know. That white bitch is your mother."

"What? Her?"

"Vera."

"Her?"

"She's all right."

"You gotta be kiddin me."

"She's all right."

"Give me a fuckin break. Why'd you tell me?"

"Thought you might want to know who you was callin bitch."

"Why'd you have to tell me?" He retreats down the steps with the unfolded bills in his hand, backing away from this new knowledge.

"Lincoln."

"Her?"

"Lincoln. It don't matter. You're here, okay. You're here. It don't matter."

Lincoln laughs.

"Lincoln."

"This takes the fuckin cake."

"Lincoln."

"This takes the goddamn fuckin cake."

He turns and begins walking up Portland, shaking his head.

"Lincoln."

But he does not turn. Lost in knowing.

Simon stands with one leg on the next step down, poised to run after him but lacking a reason, knowing Lincoln will not listen.

Simon walks to work. All the time his eyes search the garbage-blackened alleys and porticoed nooks of old buildings for Lincoln, places where those watching would stand, close enough to be ready, but out of the main channel of the downtown human current, eddies where the cops wouldn't bother to look. He doesn't see him anywhere. He passes the rug store and walks down to the bus station to see if, by chance, Lincoln has actually decided to leave. He opens the spit-stained double doors and wrinkles his nose at the smell of sweat and diesel exhaust that pours out. He searches the bathrooms and the bus docks but no one is there except for a migrained bus driver leaning on a bollard, luggage resting carelessly on the oil-soaked asphalt. Inside, people wait for their buses like murderers for verdicts, hands clasped, their faces filled with apprehension and resignation.

An Indian walks in and sits next to a blushing priest and Simon starts forward, but wait, the hair is too long, and he is too tall to be Lincoln.

Simon leaves and hurries back to the rug store.

"You're late," says Ashish from behind a crumbling croissant, as Simon strides to the back room to deposit his coat.

"Hope we didn't lose any business in that half-hour," he says over his shoulder.

"Getting smart, too."

Simon ignores him and hangs his jacket on the office chair as Ashish combs his mustache for crumbs.

"We got a load of kilims we need to put out front. And those Persians need to be rotated," he says, nodding at the pile of eight-by-tens near the door that Simon had just moved the day before.

"Jesus. Anything else?" He knows the rearrangement is Ashish's way of feeling that business is crisp.

"Want some coffee?"

"Yeah."

"We must move the rugs. We must move them. Our customers come in two, maybe three times before they buy. They walk past our store every day on their way to work. Not like Americans buy cars. Buying rugs makes them nervous. When we move the carpets, always showing new ones, they think they must buy soon, buy quick."

Simon nods and sips the weak coffee, aware of Ashish's attempts at reconciliation but groaning inwardly at the amount of work his selling philosophy necessitates.

"You give some guy my address?"

"He said he was your nephew."

"He is."

"Well then, he is family."

"Just warn me next time."

"You cannot escape family. Your family can always find you."

"I ain't hidin."

"Yes. But you are not waving at them either."

"Yeah, yeah." He drains the coffee and throws the styrofoam cup in the garbage. "I don't see none of your family workin here."

"Never hire a relative. Sell to them, but never hire them."

Simon begins lifting.

Despite his intricate, modern, tried-and-true selling philosophy, Ashish does not believe in air-conditioning. *I moved to Minnesota so I would not need it*, he explained to Simon when he first complained. *In India we were too poor to afford it and the heat drove us crazy, so I moved here.*

Simon regrets it as he flips and rolls the carpets and hugs them standing and shuffles them to the side. His arms begin to itch and are rubbed red by the wool fiber. He carries the rolled kilims from the loading dock, one on each shoulder, and starts to sweat. He feels the sweat roll down his back. When he unrolls them and slaps them down into position, the dust rises and settles in his nose. The whole while he thinks about Lincoln and hurries to be done so he can warn Vera and T-Man and anyone else who might recognize him. And then what? What kind of refuge or embrace can he offer?

When he is half finished the electric doorbell sounds. Simon, expecting Lincoln, jerks his head up and sees a blond girl, no older than twenty, with stirrup pants, a puffy sweater and violent hair, standing in the entryway.

Simon scrapes the sweat from his forehead. "Can I help you?"

She looks around nervously.

"You wanna buy a rug?"

"Ummm."

"You come here for a rug?"

"You Ashish?"

"No. Can I help you?"

"No, mister. I'm here to help him."

"Really?"

Ashish suddenly appears from the back, weaving between the stacked rugs, amazingly able to keep his upper body straight and gracious, the hips of a salsa dancer.

"You must be Candy."

The girl nods.

"Please. This way. I'll show you to the back."

The girl clicks along on her too-high heels and wafts past Simon as she follows Ashish. He turns to look at Simon. "That's enough for the day."

Simon looks down at Ashish. "Candy?"

"All kinds of people buy rugs."

"Not people named Candy."

"No?"

"No. People named Candy just like to fuck on them."

Ashish opens his clasped hands in either supplication or explication. "Simon. I am a businessman. I know the price of what I want."

"Sure, boss."

"Do you want to finish later? Please? I will pay you for a full day."

"Sure. Sure."

Simon lays the carpet down and dusts his hands. He walks to the back room where Candy is leaning against the office chair.

"Excuse me," he says.

"You, too?"

"What?"

"You, too? It'll cost extra."

"You're leaning on my jacket."

She looks over her shoulder and sees that her ass is pressed warmly against his coat, doubled over on the chair back.

"You sure?"

"Sure I want my jacket?"

"Sure you gonna leave."

267

"I got what I want."

"Really," she drawls, "I imagine if you did you wouldn't be workin for him," she says, tilting her head, the hairs on which do not budge, toward the main door.

"I know I don't want you."

"Suit yourself."

"I aim to," he says and he slides his coat out from under her. She moves just enough for it to pass, letting it brush against her tight pants.

Simon walks to the front where Ashish is waiting by the door. He holds it open for Simon.

"Knock yourself out, boss."

"I aim to," he says with a mustached grin.

He shuts the door behind Simon and throws the bolt. Simon looks over in time to see Ashish's hand, with thick dark hairs on the back, flip the *Yes We're Open!* sign to *Sorry, We're Closed* and then the hand retreats and the lights go off.

"What the fuck ever," Simon says to himself under his breath as he squares his shoulders and turns into the jewelry store.

Jerry is at the counter aimlessly sizing all the rings and placing them back in their nests of mock velvet. His pasty skin—like that of a high school sophomore unaccustomed to either light or kind attention but used to the illicit fluorescence of habitual ferocious Princeton plain-sewing—is showing from the short sleeves of his dress shirt and his black pencil tie is shiny and specked with ketchup. A cheap jeweler imitating an accountant, imitating a second-rate jazzman.

"Well, if it isn't the blues brother."

"Hi, Simon." Jerry is afraid of Simon. He does not know what he did, but he has a habitual distrust of stronger men, of men who work with their hands.

"Vera here?"

"She's in the back."

Jerry steps away from the counter, afraid of Simon's broad strength. Arrogant because he knows the color of his skin places the rules on his side, like a nervous high schooler facing down a bully outside the teacher's lounge.

"Is she busy?"

"She's working."

"Don't mean she's busy."

Jerry backs farther away. "Vera," he squeaks. "Vera!"

Vera comes out and looks in surprise at Simon. Her hands are gray from polishing silver and she shakes them as if to dislodge the grime.

"What's up, Simon?"

Simon looks at Jerry and back at Vera.

"What's up? You need your flatware polished?"

"It ain't even close to flat."

"Simon!" She glances at Jerry. "Let's take a smoke break."

Simon nods and follows Vera next door to the Mill Inn.

"You seen Lincoln?"

Vera shakes her head.

"He ain't been by here?"

Vera seems embarrassed. "Don't quite know what he'd look like. I figure fourteen years old. Tall. Good-looking."

Simon laughs. "And pissed off and on the run and you about got it."

"I gotta worry?"

"Can't say. If he comes by give a holler next door and I'll take care of it." Finally it is his turn to smooth her worry. "I gotta check one more place."

He turns and starts for the door. She calls after him.

"Hey, Simon. Does he look like Lester?"

Simon doesn't stop but turns and speaks softly over the bar talk, his words William-Telling into her ear.

"Spitting image, Vera."

Simon is out of breath, huffing by the time he reaches the West River Parkway. He steps off the sidewalk and pushes the tangle of blackberry and sumac out of his way. There is a slight path that skirts the thicker brush and half-submerged tires, packing crates, kerosene tins, stoves and refrigerators skretching off their blasted enamel to the weather and moldy growth of the riverbank.

He smells wood smoke and there's a veneer of burning rubber that hangs around the high bank like a bored borderline ghost unsure as to the stygian direction. Simon takes the last few steps down the path and breaks into a small clearing hacked from the brush and stacked with every conceivable reject or second. T-Man sits on a five-gallon tar pail next to a stuttering fire roasting something on a spit that doesn't so much cook as release grease that runs down the ashed flesh in rivulets to drop into the fire.

"T-Man. Is that a possum?"

"I sure as hell hope so. Simon, at last. You drop by."

"Shit, T-Man. Haven't seen you since I got picked up for chokin that goose. You got quite the place here."

"Works for me. Sit down. How you been keepin?"

"Little of this, a little of that."

"From what I hear you been gettin a lot of this," he says, placing his hands on imaginary hips and humping the empty air.

"It's honest work."

T-Man laughs. "Ain't ever been anything honest about it."

Simon nods and looks around. The slope of the bank is arrested by a retaining wall built from old tires, a terrace of vulcanized rubber that juts over the slope of hardy weeds and rusted tin. Behind T-Man Simon sees an opening dug into the hillside framed with old timbers and rough packing pallets. A blanket hangs in lieu of a door.

"Nice digs."

"I'm homesteading. Another five years and I get forty acres and a mule."

"You seen my nephew?"

"That skinny one?"

"Ain't but one. You know."

"I don't get any visitors except the ones I want."

T-Man's hair is matted with leaves and grease. He hasn't shaved or changed in weeks.

"But you get out. You hear things."

"I'd tell ya, Si. I ain't heard nothin."

"I don't hear much anymore."

"That's what pussy'll do to ya. Deafen you right up."

"You look like shit, T-Man. You look like a fuckin bum."

T-Man snorts and pats his hair.

"I *am* a fuckin bum. But," he gestures at the clearing and the fire and the damp mouth of his cave, "I'm makin it on my own. I ain't no burden."

"No. You right about that."

"I can see everything from here. The lawyers jogging across the river in the morning, students out for romantic walks. Everything passes down there," he says, gesturing toward the river with his eyes. "You know how many times a week those Southsiders dangle someone off the bridge? I can give you the figures. Your old neighborhood's changing. Big time. My kind's kickin out yours. Won't be long and Franklin won't be the rez anymore. It'll be the hood."

"Back in Nam." He shifts on the pail and turns the possum. "Back in Nam we woulda given just about everything for a command like this. Three-hundred-degree field of vision. Height of land. Troop movements. From here I could call in any kind of strike I want. Watch the ordnance come in nose first."

"You ain't seen or heard nothin?"

"How long's he been down here?"

"Month or two."

"He got a place?"

"He's down at Little Earth."

"They hold tight down there."

Simon hears something behind him and looks over his shoulder at the blanket-hung doorway. He sees the spunky cloth move and a girl steps out. She isn't older than twelve. She is wearing a grimy Vikings T-shirt that reaches to her knees and nothing else, her legs are streaked and her hair tangled. She scratches her leg and Simon can see she is barely flossed between her coltish legs and she looks at Simon from under her hair like a kickaway dog. She leans into the makeshift door frame for protection and whimpers.

"For fuck's sake, T-Man. Didn't know you had company."

T-Man looks at her and then back at the fire.

"Go back to bed. I'll be there in a second."

"What the fuck are you doin?" asks Simon.

T-Man shrugs.

"It's already been done. Too much antifreeze and not enough Wheaties. I'm just stayin warm before it's over."

"I gotta go."

"You gonna eat?"

Simon stands and zips his coat.

"I'll tell you if I hear anything, Si. I'll find you."

Simon nods but can't say anything. He fights his way up the trail until he emerges slapped and gasping on the narrow sidewalk that runs skinny but true on the high shoulder of the street.

29

Christmas has come and gone and Vera thinks she is seeing ghosts. She catches sight of a figure out of the corner of her eye, next to the iron fence around the old train shed, the Ceresota grain elevator in the background, then it turns out of sight, like a bird that launches so quickly it looks as if it has vanished.

Her heart quickens. She takes three rapid steps, her arm stretched in front, the way mothers call children to their side from across the room. She stops, thinking it is absurd. Lester is dead, after all. Why does this always have to happen in the winter, when the cold locks you down so hard, your legs stiff, nothing about you or your life prepared for action?

She pulls her jacket tighter and strides toward home. The sounds of traffic, of people frantic to escape the downtown and the dreariness of work, mix with the rush of the river. She crosses the street and can't help herself, cannot stop from looking down Washington to see if he is still there, pressed flat like a TV criminal against a wall. No one. She is not the kind of person who sees things.

This has been her private curse. She is unable to substitute history with memory, her mind cannot conjure, knows no sleight of hand. She has no versions of the truth with which to stack the deck. Her parents remain in her mind stuck at the various stages of their own development. Tired at the fringes of their youth from factory work, weary and gray at middle age. Locked into the cells of their own habits, their whole lives spent dancing around each other. When they found out she was pregnant they never once broke character. There were no fights, no tearful reconciliations. Nothing like that. They stepped around it and were equally unruffled when she gave the baby to Betty.

Vera's memory is fearfully exact. There is no way she saw Lester leaning against the corner of the train shed to disappear like a startled brush bird. She had seen him dead.

She had seen his skull smashed in, his smooth face cracked and angled, the shell underneath ruined forever. She remembers clearly how his legs jerked, how he smelled when his muscles relaxed, the delicate rattle of beer cans as his legs flailed them over. She remembers with shame how her first thought was that if he spilled the beer, then Betty would know they had had a party.

It wasn't a real party, not one with a haze of smoke, strangers clogging the kitchen or sorting through the slippery stack of forty-fives, anxious to put on the next groove, anxious to keep the tempo of mindlessness cranked up. It was just the three of them. The steel work on the IDS was almost finished. Since only a few of the workers were invited for the topping out ceremony, and the only salute the IDS corporation saw fit to give the workers was to spin the spotlight on Labor Day, Simon decided to have a ceremony of his own.

He bought the whiskey and the beer and arranged it on the coffee table. He was wild that night, as he uncapped the bottle, drank and passed it to Lester. Vera remembers how loud his voice was, how tight his posture. Lester tried to keep up, but the amount of liquor and the secret he intended to share with Simon were too heavy and he couldn't pace Simon.

Simon was in it alone. "Come on kids! It's on the house!"

She cannot forget this. Every time she sees a movie and a character makes the same oath—*It's on the house!*—she has to turn away. She cannot watch because as soon as she hears *on the house!* instead of seeing friends and barflies crowding the bartender, she sees Simon with a bottle in each hand, towering over her and Lester as they sit on the couch.

Even then the party seemed endless. All she wanted was to sneak away with Lester to his room where they could talk and touch each other. But they were chained to Simon, and had to rise with his exuberance, fall with his hidden sorrows.

All this is mercilessly fresh. Finally, after helping Simon with half a bottle, Lester told him Vera was pregnant.

How Simon had roared when he found out. He kept yelling— *You fuck everything up! You fuck it all up!*

"Easy, Si," said Lester. "Easy, man. It ain't the end of the world."

Simon's body tensed. "You don't know shit. Who takes care of you? Who takes care of all a you?"

"We'll figure it out."

"You're too dumb to figure it out."

He seemed to calm down as he grabbed the shovel standing inside the door. He leaned on it like a crutch. Lester breathed and tried to joke the tension out of Simon. "Whatcha gonna do? Brain me with a shovel?"

Simon picked it up and took one step toward Lester.

"That's what I'm gonna do!" he said. The steel and skull and "that's" all met at the same time. Lester fell.

"That's what!" Again.

"That's what!" For the last time, the shovel raised so far above his head it scraped the ceiling. And he was done, and they saw Lester's face was gone and his legs were jerking and then he was dead.

Vera held Simon until the police came. He sobbed into the breasts she had shown to Lester before the party started. "See," she'd said, "they're bigger." She held him against those breasts, so firm and perfect and ready to help. She held Simon as he cried.

"What happened? What happened?" he kept mumbling.

She remembers saying, but can't imagine how she did it, "You killed your brother, Simon."

"Did I?"

"You killed him, Simon."

She said it softly, as if reassuring him. Soothing him with the fact that the worst had come to pass. All the while, she stroked his hair and wondered how a shovel got into the house in the summer.

So it couldn't have been Lester on the street. She takes one last look as she nears the top of the overpass. Nothing. The water is choked with ice. Deadheads collect in the wire mesh of the docks at Saint Anthony. She crosses over to the Northside.

She doesn't want to admit the other possibility: that she has seen her son. The son she took to Betty's and left there because it hurt too much to look at him every day. The son she dropped at Betty's while she was still nursing so that her breasts grew, stretched tight and ached every moment until she went to the hospital and demanded they give her a shot to dry them up.

She did dry up. Her breasts shrank and the memory of Lincoln remained as small as his wet, brown body had been, just a collection of gestures—the way he looked as if he was kissing someone in his sleep, how he sucked in his bottom lip, let it out, and in again, breathing through a single gill—her body as well as her mind was empty.

She knows it was Lincoln on the corner. It would be just her luck to give birth to a son who looks exactly like his dead father. His ghost had taken the only form available to it.

She doesn't think she could stand a reunion. What would he say? What would she? The feelings they both have are so predictable. His anger. Her guilt. Their sadness. She knows what happened, had seen the shovel sledge into Lester's face, had caught the look of subsiding rage, disbelief, and panic on Simon's. She relinquished him to the police who were gentle, but who carried an air of judgment within their dismay.

Lincoln would want to know why. Simon was sad, ashamed, ruined, but Lincoln would want to know why Vera had taken the next step and given him up. What the connection was.

It made sense to her at the time and when it no longer seemed like the right thing, the only thing, to do, he was already two, then four years old, then six, nine, and it was too late. It was too late from the beginning, and no explanation could ever take the place of those years. It would weigh in like feathers against lead. She would have nothing to say to Lincoln, nothing to offer.

She would have wanted to say, *I just did. It just happened.* That, too, would have been less than enough, so she is glad that Lincoln didn't step beyond the corner, that all she got was a glimpse, the whorl of his jacket in the city air like a disappearing bird.

She opens the door, her face and hands chilled, her feet cramped and sore from being spooned into her pumps and left there all day to rise like dough. There is no mail. The apartment is cold, and she kicks off her shoes and gets into bed.

After she gave Lincoln away to Betty, the pain in her breasts had been worse than this. Had been worse than anything she'd felt, including the birth. At least then something new was happening, the dull ache and wet spots on her shirt meant that she was left with less than before. She was sixteen and trying to do what was right. Her father had urged her to see the doctor, but she refused. *I did what was right. I know.* For her, to go back to the hospital was to admit she had been wrong. Her parents kept vigil, sitting in the living room with the lights off. Her father with his pipe and paper, her mother pushing off the floor to send the rocking chair into motion. After a while, after checking in her room, they would go to bed.

Vera would throw the covers off and pull up her shirt, trying to touch her breasts back into stillness. In the dark, nearing Christmas, she took them, one at a time, and tried to get the milk out herself, sucking first on one and then the other. The snow brightened the city and the moonlight bounced around until it poured into her room. And Vera sat up and nursed herself, surprised at how warm it was.

30

Simon isn't there when the overwrought man—no one knows who he is or why he does it—takes the elevator to the twenty-third floor of the IDS, throws a five-pound weight out the window, then calmly steps out the newly appeared hole. Simon is walking when this happens. Ashish doesn't want him in the store to interrupt while he drills yet another impossibly young hooker. Irene's apartment is becoming less and less of an attractive option. He has fixed everything that was broken: improved the water pressure, laid in new linoleum, lined the cupboards with freezer paper, scraped and repainted the windowsills and attached new rope and counter-weights to the sashes so now they slide open easily. He is done with all of that and is left with nothing to do. He cannot fix her.

Irene comes home and is either climbing up with Dexedrine or settling down with Demerol. Her moods, the drugs she gets too eas-ily from the hospital, begin to feel like vacation spots, ridiculous tourist traps you can't avoid: Percodan, Illinois. East Demerol, Arkansas. Morphine, Indiana. He watches her head tilt, her throat

279

clench the pills down, and she gives him that look. He doesn't bother asking how she gets them. There are doctors lined up, all of them too willing to give her pills. All of them too willing to fuck her silly in the supply closet.

Simon is out walking but he doesn't see the man jump. Misses it when he hits the pavement. He sees the police lines and a gathered crowd. He notices the way everyone looks up, and he doesn't need to be told. The bystander, to whom the man gave five dollars to clear the sidewalk, has been questioned by the police and wanders inside the yellow tape, holding the bill in front of him, not sure what to do with it. He keeps asking: *Can I spend it? Is that okay?*

People refuse to leave the scene, even though the police have constructed hasty curtains around the unfortunate's pulped body. They cluster expectantly as if there will be an encore, some kind of instant replay. This kind of aerial act only happens once, but the public needs to see more, wants to see the melancholy and terror that lurk in the dusty corners of their lives. They need a public display of their private worries and so hope for a sequel. Death has become an art, but not an original one.

Twenty-three stories, three hundred twenty-two feet, eleven seconds of freefall, give or take a few seconds for wind resistance and body position. This is a painting he can only do once, so the man, out of consideration for his audience, made sure the canvas was clear. No one, after all, wants to be killed by art. He gave a man in the Crystal Court five dollars to clear the area below and took the elevator to the twenty-third floor and circled through the perimeter offices—lawyers, accountants, actuaries and secretaries, all leaping to their feet—until he found the right side of the building, and though the police had been notified, there wasn't enough time to stop him.

The weight shattered the safety glass perfectly, sending a prelude of shards waterfalling to the concrete below. He didn't scream or jump or fly or act in any way that requires some hasty verb. He simply walked out into the city-thick air.

The few who witnessed the impact won't forget the performance, how the body actually *bounced*. How the skin wasn't even compromised.

Sadly, the artist wasn't very original—as usual, people from New York are well ahead of the Midwest when it comes to performance art; though the audience wasn't as cynical as East Coast viewers, they didn't make jokes about yuppie doom. They were from the upper Midwest. They didn't laugh or ooh, or cry. In the days afterward, there were no cartoons that linked his behavior to market or seasonal trends. It was April. Instead, they wondered how embarrassing it must be for him. It lacked propriety. People felt bad, certainly. But with all the space, the trackless forest, they wondered if a city setting was really such a good idea. I mean, think of the children. What would they say if they had seen it happen?

In this way, as people ate away their federally allotted fifteen-minute break and returned to work, and then motored home, the tragedy became the artist's fault. People can be so selfish, you know? Maybe a woman has gotten off work, and then made her way home and is standing in her kitchen, careful not to touch anything or bump against the cupboards because she is still in her business suit. Her husband returns and shucks his Bass shoes at the door. People can be so selfish. She shakes her head, perhaps. She certainly didn't want to see it. Her husband has already heard the news on the radio during the drive home.

This tsking propriety can be heard all over the city—how times have changed, how people have no consideration, do not take other people's feelings into account anymore.

Just goes to show. As children are dropped unceremoniously at day care and shipped north to camps in the summer, while family life sits splay-legged on the point of the decade, the man, his potential reasons and flawed rationale forgotten, steps into thin air and falls at their feet.

Even so, when they go to bed, after the lights are out and the children are asleep, the parents dream their own dreams. They sleep as a remedy for the future, because all they can be sure of is that they will be tired, that much is certain. Living has become a demand, something that uses up time they could spend on something else. Eventually they go to sleep and dream.

Over and over again, they see the man's free fall. It is visually persuasive but predictable. They see the body spinning, turning gently through the atmosphere. They see the concrete below him littered with fragments of safety glass. The body jumps off the ground at impact. The body bounces, and just when it will come to rest—a bag of blood and viscera and unknown reasons—the dream repeats. The body walks out the empty window and spins for a long eleven seconds . . . it hits the ground and bounces and the dream begins again at the twenty-third floor. Over and over again. This time they think maybe he waved at them. Or was it simply a reflex as he stepped out into nothing? An unconscious jerk of his hand as the body tumbled? Don't worry, here we have all night.

The dream eye begins to pick out details: how his scuffed wingtip turned on the sill, his windbreaker flag-snapped in the breeze generated by his fall. When he bounces the blue nylon catches the spangles of glass and throws them up like confetti. The details are vivid. His face is serene until it hits the pavement and in the split second of the bounce it loses all shape, becomes, for a moment, a cartoon face, or like a magician's sagging cane; the structure underneath going from rigid to elastic as the head is crushed. The skin does not break.

After a while the dreamers notice the coffee cup on the desk next to the window, how his step from the sill draws the eyes to the cup in the foreground so that they can read the cheery office motto: *A job done right!* The dreamers reflect on how pretty the blue enamel is, almost cobalt. A color they haven't thought of since an art-survey course in college, how the cobalt is mirrored in the glass and then, *poof!* Gone, set against the sky, which doesn't come close to matching the cheap mug in beauty or intensity. They collect these details—half-wave, the whipping windbreaker, collapsing head, the glass, the cobalt mug—and hold them together like a bouquet as the dream repeats, adding the slate of the concrete and off to the top of the frame, the pink contrail of a jet.

There is too much to hold, but the dream repeats. Like it or not, the man winks. You're sure of it. He steps, brown wing-tip on the gray carpet, his hand in a half-wave that draws your eyes to the cobalt coffee mug, and when you look back his head is disappearing, but you swear, as it dips below the windowsill, you swear that he winks at you.

This is doubly selfish, but there is no helping it. It is unfair for him to jump to his death in front of you and then he waves and winks, and the colors are so beautiful, but you can't ask him whether or not he really winked, and who placed the mug there. He is dead now, and you can't ask him.

It repeats. You know you could have turned away earlier, that you needn't have watched and now the price is being paid—you are chained to the dream and cannot stop it.

So selfish. The first beautiful day in April and he has to go and ruin it. You want to lift the yellow tape and step close to the body. The man with the five-dollar bill is still wandering nearby and you ignore him, give him the cold shoulder. He, after all, could have asked the jumper why. Why will you jump? So you ignore him and you want to walk up to the body which is leaking blood onto the bubble gum tessera set into the concrete. The body has not moved and when the medics do lift him they will have to use long plastic boards like shovels to keep his body from slipping away like a feed sack. You want to ask, did you really mean it? Did you really mean to do it? But you refrain. It is, after all, a stupid question. He stepped, waved and winked. Rather, would he do it again? But you know the answer to that, too. If he could. If he could stand up and brush off his clothes and bow to the crowd, he would take the elevator and step out again. He would fall and fall. Each time adding a new twist, milling arms maybe. A swan dive, a backward leap. He would do it. You know that. He would jump, and will jump, as long as you close your eyes.

31

Betty is surprised at how slowly spring comes up north. She'd forgotten to notice the turn in the city, left behind memories of how
the seasons graded into one another, just as she'd left her old life to
start a new one. It is almost May and she inspects the poplars. The
leaves haven't begun to bud yet. She is taken aback and quickly
checks the ditches to see if the cattails have risen, and scans the
fields and sure enough, no green to be seen anywhere.

She sits in Boo's kitchen and gauges the changes outside the
window. Boo tries to fight her melancholy with suggestions he
knows she has already thought of and dismissed.

"Maybe you need to go back to work. Maybe that'd help. You
get a job at the school or the clinic, no problem."

She turns from the window and fixes him with a stare.

"Just cause you feel bad for telling Lincoln the truth don't
mean you gotta try and get me off my ass."

Boo shakes his head. "Look, Auntie, it ain't your fault either, so
don't be flickin me shit." He says it without anger, without blame.

He leaves, walking slowly up the road toward town with a garbage bag over his shoulder, hoping to collect enough cans to sell for a six-pack of beer.

She could get a job at the school, the clinic. She knows it. But it would only make things worse. It's already spring, and Lincoln is nowhere to be found. The clinic, on the other hand, would only bring back more memories of the city, of having to identify Lester's body. Better she perch by the window and mark the earth's slow orbit around the sun by the poplar buds, getting riper by the day. This is safer. Boo had remarked on that, too.

"Old ladies are like birds, we need good perches."

"Yeah, sure," he responded in a rare moment of lucid sarcasm, "but they need the worm every now and then." Referring to One-Two.

"Oh, really? Well, this eagle needs more than that inchworm, that's for sure."

"Whatever," he'd said, his back to her as he attempted to clean the pilot light on the oven with his splayed toothbrush.

Now she isn't so sure. One-Two could fix the stove just by looking at it and he could find Lincoln if she asked him. Could check in on Simon, would do things for her if she asked. But . . . He's there and I'm here, and here ain't no place. Just room enough for one set of claws on this branch.

She does worry about them. She frets that both One-Two and Lincoln are too dreamy, Lincoln about the past and One-Two regarding the future, to face up to the demands of the city. She fears they aren't prepared for the price of living and that she failed all her children and One-Two. She, at least, is clear about how to survive.

It was so bad, her immobile worrying, that Boo got frustrated with her.

"It ain't that complicated. Burt ain't the sharpest knife in the drawer. He and Lincoln are probably at Little Earth, and if you can't find them there, look around the nearest gas pump."

"What do you mean?"

"They been sniffin, Auntie."

"You're fine one to talk."

"Hey, I get plowed, sure. But I don't flood the engine," he said, tapping his temple.

"No, I guess not. You just busy blowin your tranny."

She doesn't want to believe it, though she knows it to be true. Her experience of Simon, Lester and Vera should have taught her that children are capable of anything. Not that hers were devious. Rather, they shielded her from their true selves, protected her from the fact that they were less than she'd hoped they'd be: Simon more violent, Lester willing to make bad choices, and Lincoln slaved to the past so much it excluded a future. To her they would remain trapped in her constructions of them: Simon sober and responsible, even at age ten acting like a father to his siblings; Lester shy and soft; Lincoln dreamy, isolated, turned in just like his feet as he walked to school. As for the girls, they are fading fast, becoming more distant every day.

She wonders out the window. Maybe she was wrong all along. She never protected them, never mothered them. She was wrong: children protect their parents, not the other way around.

Better to sit, then. Much better to hold the view of budding leaves, the dust-brittle brush creeping closer to the road. The one thing she is sure of is that things can always get worse, and though people usually won't surprise you, at least they are always true to form. The scabby fields and cut-over woods, however, well that *will* surprise you. Surprised Jacob. He of all people should have known how to avoid the tree, to fend off the floral rage he was tampering with.

One-Two should have known better when he was up on the building. She hadn't known him all that well when the accident happened. When Simon came home, gray and shaking, finally able to let his fear and concern come out once One-Two had been brought to the hospital, he sat down heavily in the kitchen and told her about the accident. Her heart skipped, but she handed Simon water and finished cooking dinner for the children, and after the dishes were put away she took the leftovers in a pie tin and wrapped them in a towel and calmly walked to the hospital. Visiting hours were over but she knew the hospital staff wouldn't kick out his crew or her.

She could tell by the cloud of cigarette smoke that the men were in there and once she had shooed them out, she thought maybe One-Two was grateful for her company, for the home-cooked food. He ate, and told her that Simon had saved him, saved his legs at least.

"That's Simon," she said. "Stubborn."

She'd wanted to say, *No, not you, too. You have to stay safe. For me.* But she couldn't, afraid if she made that demand he would follow Jacob's example and die, and after Lester was killed, and Caroline was smashed by the train, it cemented in her the idea that she couldn't place any demands on him, that her needs were dangerous to those around her. So, by his bedside, opening the window to let out the smoke, she kept him company, fearful that he would die and leave her alone.

She needs him now, as she wonders what has become of Lincoln, afraid he might commit some grand stupidity in the city. Boo is right, One-Two is only a call away. A moment from making her worry disappear. She can't do it.

She ponders the view and racks her brain, testing her memory for which plant or tree will bud and blossom first. Birch maybe. Or was it the uneventful hazel brush? Maybe, she thinks, with some shred of hope, maybe the maples will be next. And the maples, as we all know, they give us everything.

32

Simon sees them pass the rug store, their hunched and purpose-heavy postures leaking through the glass. He has seen it too many times not to know—seen it on the corner, in prison, on the block and in the cafeteria—the jerky try-not-to-be-noticed stride of men who will act. Will club or kill, or shoot, who have launched plans and are nearing their target.

His hand is on the door when he hears the first shot and he is in the jewelry store by the time he hears the second and third. He sees Jerry's feet sticking out from behind the counter. His Rock-ported feet are jerking and crossing and uncrossing. There is blood on the wall behind him. Burt's body is crumpled just inside the store, one leg folded back, the arm with the gun outstretched and the other raised above what is left of his head in an exaggerated salute. He is laid out angel-like, painted to fly on the floor. Except there is a hole the size of Simon's thumb in his face and the skull looks as if it is resting too close to the floor. The entire back of his head is missing.

Lincoln is in the corner, fetused and shaking. Vera is crouched in the door to the back. She is saying, "Son? Is that you? Lincoln? Son? Son?"

Simon takes three steps and he is across the room, kneeling over Lincoln. Lincoln is racking, trying to keep his insides in. With every gurgle and shudder, Vera keeps saying *Son? Son?*

Simon puts his hand on Lincoln's arm. "Close the store. Turn the sign," he tells Vera. "Turn it."

She barely moves. "Son?"

Simon rises and flips the sign and turns the deadbolt and switches off the lights.

He rushes back to Lincoln. He is quiet, shuddering into himself, rocking around the hole in his stomach. Simon takes off his flannel shirt and with one hand lifts Lincoln off the floor by the collar and shoves his shirt underneath him. There is no blood on the floor, but there is a hole in the back of Lincoln's Bull's jacket. Blood seeps out around the edges but not much. Vera is kneeling now.

Simon looks up and sees a hole in the wall with a piece of flesh no bigger than a kernel of rice next to it. He looks back down at Lincoln and presses his knee on Lincoln's chest and the other on his thighs, as if he were holding open a trap that could spring shut. With his hands he pulls Lincoln's shirt up and sees the entry wound down and to the left. The blood is dark and seeps out steadily.

There is no stately hush, no paced action, no tragic silence. Death is not a steady march, it is a mad scramble. Lincoln is screaming and Vera has her hand on his forehead.

Everything is happening at once.

"I had a name for you."

"Vera." Simon feels he is losing time.

"I had a name. I didn't use it, but I had one."

"Vera."

Lincoln is coughing and Simon looks away from Vera's strained face. He studies Lincoln's lips. They are chalked with dried spit but there is no blood.

"Me and your dad, we planned stuff, you know? You weren't part of the plan, but that was okay."

"Vera."

"I got pregnant on that old train. Can you beat that? An old train."

"Vera. He's bleeding. We gotta get him outta here."

"Honey," she is crooning softly. "I never meant for things to happen like this."

Simon steadies Lincoln with one hand and with the other jabs Vera viciously in the chest, above her breasts. She gasps and falls back against the display case.

He pins her with his eyes.

"We have to move him to the back so he don't bleed on the carpet. Then you gonna find something to hide that hole, see?" He points at the bullet hole on the back wall. He rocks his knees off Lincoln's body and stands up. They each grab an arm and a leg and half-slide, half-carry him to the back room. Lincoln sucks in great mouthfuls of air, he tries not to cry out.

"Lincoln, you hear me?"

He nods.

"We're gettin you outta here. We're gettin you outta here and you ain't gonna go to jail."

"No?" he says, the short word packed with hope.

"No."

He raises Lincoln's shirt and grabs his finger. He locates the entrance hole and jabs Lincoln's finger in the hole to stop the bleeding. He makes Vera hold his hand in place and stands. He hears something in the front room.

The door rattles and Simon lunges out and sees Jerry on his knees trying to turn the bolt. Simon grabs him by the hair and throws him on the floor. There is blood all over the front of his shirt and he is gurgling and shouting. Simon looks at the .357 on the floor. He picks it up but knows he cannot afford to shoot.

He pops the cylinder and sets it on an empty chamber and eases the hammer down. He switches it from left to right and grabs it by the barrel and kneels on Jerry's chest. Jerry screams and tries to buck Simon off, but he is too weak. Simon raises the revolver and brings it down on Jerry's head. Jerry stiffens and a welt appears on his forehead. Again. On the same spot.

He raises the gun and with his shoulder behind it he hammers on Jerry's head. Jerry begins to shake and the skin on his forehead splits to the bone. Simon grunts with each stroke and never takes his eyes off the spot on Jerry's head. Again. And again.

Jerry grabs for the carpet, for Simon's arm, but gets nothing. Simon is rasping and he pauses. He hears a gasp and turns to see Vera standing on the other side of the counter.

"Go in the back."

He doesn't look after her, just adjusts his grip on the barrel and resumes as if pounding rivets, the motion practiced and smooth.

Simon grimaces as the butt slips off the mark and he hears Jerry's nose crack, and then the cheekbone.

It takes longer than he thought it would. Longer than with Lester. One. Two. Three.

Finally it gives and a section of his forehead the size of an orange caves and the fluid that slips out is pink and shiny, like cake frosting. Jerry doesn't move. Simon is winded, and staggers to the back room and runs his hand and the gun under the tap.

The jewelry store is quiet. Lincoln is groaning lightly but his eyes are open and he blinks. Vera is crouched in the corner. She tsks and shakes her head.

"Why'd you have to go and do that?" she asks, as if Simon had kicked a stray dog or yelled at a crying child.

Simon shoves the gun in the top of his pants. He takes Jerry's windbreaker from the back of the door.

"Don't you get it? Lincoln ain't going to prison. Understand? He ain't ever gonna go there."

Simon walks over and kneels down next to her.

"I'm gonna get a car. Don't do nothin, okay? Just wait here and find something to cover him up with. I'll be back in fifteen minutes."

Vera nods but doesn't move.

Simon opens the back door and once in the alley, breaks into a dead run. It is cool, fifty degrees. Five blocks to Irene's apartment.

He takes the stairs two at a time and flings the door open.

Irene is asleep on the bed, her arm flung out as if waiting for a transfusion. He sorts through her clothes and then sees her purse on the table. He finds the keys and shakes the purse until four white tabs spill out.

He fills a glass and eases down on the bed. She stirs.

"Hey. Hey. Take these." She opens her hand and pops them in her mouth.

"Why?" she asks around the water.

"You're sick. Real sick, you need them."

This seems to make sense and she collapses back on the pillow.

He pulls into the alley and rushes in the back of the jewelry store. Vera has put her jacket over Lincoln and is stroking his hair.

Simon bends and picks Lincoln up. Except for the blood, he could just be a sleeping child, dream heavy and ready for bed. The body is light and Lincoln puts his arms around Simon's neck and rests his head against his chest. Vera moves ahead and opens the door and then opens the back door of the Caprice.

"I'm sorry, Simon. I'm sorry. I'm sorry."

Simon shakes his head. "No, no. It ain't your fault. It ain't you. You'll be all right."

"I just wanted to pay her back. I didn't mean for nothin to happen."

"Nothin's gonna happen. You'll be all right."

He puts Lincoln in the back, his body tightens and he winces. Simon shuts the door and opens the front.

Vera's arms are crossed and she is shivering. Simon looks at her but doesn't know what to say.

"Call the police after we leave," he says finally.

"Jacob."

Simon looks at her thoughtfully. "Junior."

"Yeah. We was gonna name him Jacob. Junior."

"I'll tell him."

"He gonna be all right?"

"I'll tell him when he's better."

Vera shivers her arms tighter around herself. "What do I tell the police?"

"Tell them it was me. It was me. It was me and Burt."

He slams the door and backs out of the alley. Vera pulls the steel door shut behind her.

33

Simon doesn't waste time. He turns left on Washington and onto 94 West and begins what is to be his last crawl out of the city. He knows he can never go back.

As he passes the last of the warehouses and the small homes which were zoned as commercial property and dutifully added cheap plateglass and storefronts, he realizes he has never known this place, never seen it for what it truly is.

As a child, to him every building had been a present, a mystery. The uses of each old packing plant, warehouse, storeroom, office building, factory, rail station, firehouse, or stable, had been a guessing game of utility he never tired of. With Lincoln moaning and bleeding in the backseat he realizes that the signs and billboards, placards, street names, even the cornerstones on the more important sites, never told him much of anything. The IDS itself would never be known as the place that changed his life, that almost took One-Two's. Vera's jewelry store was a no-place in the scheme of the city, just a small store that was needed to keep up income but wasn't expected to do much business. He realizes, as he chauffeurs Lincoln's bleeding body around, that the city was designed to be like this: it functioned around ignorance, yet he and everyone else who lived there yearned, not so much for notoriety, but simply to be noticed. Even so, his contributions would go uncataloged. There will be no plaque for him, no brass-stamped sign commending Lincoln's confused little life. In the city it isn't enough just to have lived, to hold certain places, specific moments, close to one's private heart. It makes you want everyone to notice, to see how your life was different.

When Simon started school at South High in 1960, all of the kids were still trying to brag about The Mall. They told one another extravagant lies about how their clothes were purchased at The Mall. Anyone with one eye should have noticed that the shoes were old, the too-loose jeans cinched tight with cracked leather belts, the T-shirts and button-downs washed into antique softness; that, to them, none of it was new.

Built in 1956, the Southdale Mall was the first modern shopping mall in the country, and therefore, in the world. Strip malls abounded, based loosely on the Palearctic concept of the arcade: open-air shops protected from the worst of the elements. The Southdale Mall, however, was supported by anchor stores, completely roofed in, climate-controlled, excessively lit. Like Noah's ark, it contained not one, but two, of everything, but unlike his, it was the first of its kind, not the first and last.

The mayors of Saint Paul and Minneapolis were there along with the aldermen from Edina. For the first time the Cities could boast about something they had created, not simply that they were kings of lumber, grain, and taconite—raw materials bound for other ports, to be made into something mentionable in other places. For the first time the Cities were creating something unseen elsewhere in the world. In later years it could do this with ease, bragging about 3M or Honeywell, about Control Data, even the IDS, designed by

Philip Johnson. And they did, patting themselves on the back, congratulating themselves on progress and development.

The Mall opened in 1956, when procession was still synonymous with progress. The city officials sat regally on their folding chairs underneath bunting, in front of two-hundred lucky shoppers who had won the right to buy products they had been buying for years elsewhere. There were speeches and accolades, music played by nervous, poorly taught high school students. In the center of the mall, next to the food court stood a wooden statue of an Indian, a benediction for the shoppers, turning consumption into something noble. The civic pride, the carnival of excess spoke to two desires held by leaders and shoppers alike: to prove their Americanness and hence not their European roots, and to vault the area from being a mere mercantile center to one of genuine modern commerce. Their desires were universal, their realization of them ridiculously parochial.

As the ribbon was cut accompanied by fanfare and confetti, the women threw back the veils on the front of their hats (abandoned elsewhere after the Second World War) and the men gave one another knowing laughs and hand-pumped each other the same way their fathers had done when purchasing tractors.

Inside the Mall the excitement was brought to a low simmer so the customers could spend their boom money with dignity and calm. This was a time when everyone still wore hats, and they were tipped at other felt fedoras and straw boaters in mute brotherhood. All the trousers had breaks, the shoes leather soles. They shopped like this and for the first time in the history of shopping, every footfall, each purchase or "*ohhhh,*" was accompanied by an echo.

Looking back, holding the colorized photograph of this moment, the hidden tragedies of these nameless people have gone and will continue to go, unnoticed. They have been bleached of their cruelty, of their petty concerns and betrayals, their failures. All that is left to see is a group of people one generation removed from the uncertainty of farmwork, war, and immigration; the only emotion allowed them is hope, made (like the merchandise they are forced to consider) out of plastic.

These are the things Simon will never know, that could offer some solace. Not that everyone wants the same thing, or feels the same way, nor even harbors the same crime. How many, after all, have driven their dying nephew through the streets?

Rather, it would have been a comfort to know that the city, the Mall, the buildings and streets, much like the reservation up north, have been designed to sluice not just his happiness, but everyone's, into predictable channels. A stable home, caring parents, a good job, close friends, quiet nights. It would have been good to know that our modern existence is designed to ask only for these meager returns, when, beyond the dim dome of lights, off the trail a few yards, just around the bend, lurk much larger, much meaner alternatives. How poorly we are prepared to do well.

34

Betty is sitting at the kitchen table playing cribbage with Boo, who is trying to peg off a four-day binge, when she sees headlights sweep the room and an unfamiliar car crunch into the driveway. She knows something is wrong. She pauses and shuffles the cards, making sound around the silent agony and quiet shame Boo is trying to work through. She looks up in time to see Simon jump from the driver's seat and run around to the car's back door. She bangs out of the house and runs down the wobbly front steps when she sees Simon's blood-spattered T-shirt and Lincoln's limp body in his arms like an offering.

Her light blue robe flutters and she runs like an unfrescoed angel while a low wail, half-groan and half-scream, builds and pours from her mouth. She has eyes only for Lincoln.

"Oh my God. My baby, my baby."

She is hovering. Her hands are cupped on his long face, searching for chill, for a sign. She has to stand on her toes and reach up to clear the platform of Simon's arms, which do not shake or tremble.

She coos over Lincoln as if he were a newborn, nervous that the roughness of her hands might hurt him.

Simon doesn't say anything. His eyes are lowered and he looks at the open door. He moves quickly, lurching up each step.

Betty is right behind. "You okay, you okay?"

Simon moves toward the couch and Boo steps ahead and sweeps the beer cans and newspapers onto the floor. Simon sets Lincoln down and tears the blanket hanging over the back and covers him with it. Betty rushes to his side and looks in his face and feels his forehead.

"What did you do, Simon?"

Simon holds the phone receiver in one hand and looks at her. "Ma. He got shot."

"How could you?" Her voice is vicious.

"Ma."

"He ain't even Lester's age."

"Ma."

"How?"

Boo is listening obliquely as he fills a glass with water, drinks half of it and hands it to Betty who pushes it to Lincoln's cracked lips.

Simon dials 911.

"Got someone here who's shot." Pause. "Hunting." He gives the address and hangs up.

Betty is glaring at Simon. "I couldn't have raised you."

"Ma. I didn't do it."

"I couldn't."

"Ma." His voice cracks and he stands as if still holding Lincoln's blood-drained body. His shoulders heave but he doesn't lower his arms.

Boo approaches him and gently presses Simon's arms down to his sides.

"You'd better get goin, Simon."

Simon looks at Boo.

"I'll cover for you, Si. We'll make it all right."

Simon looks at Betty and Lincoln. Lincoln moves his head slightly and Betty whispers to him. The light from the kitchen makes it halfway into the living room before falling short. They are partially lit. Betty in her blue robe and Lincoln swaddled in his red-and-black jacket—this is the image Simon will take with him: Betty ministering to Lincoln's wrecked body. That is what he will take with him in lieu of an explanation, instead of comfort or understanding for himself. He runs into the thickening night.

Boo and Betty hear the car start and the gravel spit from under the tires. The transmission kicks down twice along the highway and then fades out of earshot. They are alone with Lincoln for only a few minutes before he dies, Betty anchored to his lifeless body, her hands resting on his shoulder, the curve of his baby-smooth cheek, his hand. She doesn't want to stop touching him. She thinks that maybe if she touches him he will come back. Her touch, perhaps, could spin time backward.

It doesn't work. The medics rush in, all arc lights and language, a whole symphony of orders and ritual. Betty and Boo stand at the margins of the activity. It doesn't last long. The ambulance driver tells Betty that he will have to take Lincoln's body to the coroner's for an examination. *Standard*, he says, searching her eyes for an answer.

Standard.

He repeats it a few times and looks at Boo, who nods. They take the body and leave.

35

Betty doesn't get out of bed for a week. One-Two came up on the bus for the funeral, mostly silent, but helpful in invisible ways. He knows that she doesn't want assistance and he tries not to anger her. After the hushed funeral where the perplexed relatives gathered, not sure what they were mourning, Betty covered herself with as many quilts as she could arm-load onto the bed and crawled under that colorful patched cave and didn't budge except to sneak off to the bathroom while One-Two and Boo slept. People came to see how she was doing. Not because they cared for or knew much about Lincoln; he had been a quiet transplant that grew in everyone else's shadow and escaped notice or serious attention. Betty's was the real tragedy and they came for her. She refused to see anyone and had One-Two lie for her, telling the visitors that she was sleepy, that she was sleeping. They dead-eyed One-Two, knew that she was doing what she had never allowed herself, in all her life, to do. She was taking it hard.

No one heard from Simon, though the police found the car. He had torched it by dumping chain saw mix on the front seat. The police circled the vehicle looking for tracks but found nothing except the empty red plastic gas can thrown in the weeds by the railroad tracks. They added the car to the long list of burned wrecks they already had.

After the funeral Betty came back, hung up her black dress, dressed in her house clothes and got into bed. One-Two checked on her but she faced away from the door and seemed to be sleeping. He and Boo played cribbage all night. Boo was half loaded and whenever One-Two got up to check on Betty, he came back to find Boo's pegs had crept up the board and rounded the corner. Boo wouldn't look at him. Instead he busied himself with the foil wrapper of his cigarettes or palm-swept ashes off the kitchen table. One-Two pretended he didn't notice.

The next morning One-Two cooked breakfast and tiptoed the tray of steaming eggs and oatmeal in to Betty's room.

"Leave me alone."

"Betty. You gotta eat."

"I don't gotta do nothin."

One-Two didn't argue. He retreated with the cooling food and creaked the door shut. He looked at Boo. Boo shrugged and took the breakfast.

"Food's food," he said, as he spooned half the eggs in his mouth. "Food's food."

At lunch One-Two cooked venison loin in Crisco. For supper he offered her mac with stewed tomatoes. Each time she waved it away, as if she were shooing summer flies. He knew better than to argue.

He tried tempting her out of the room with smells. He tried roast rabbit and partridge on a bed of wild rice. He cooked onions. He went to the bridge one afternoon and caught walleye pike and fried it. He made spaghetti. Bacon.

She refused to crawl out from under the armor of quilts. "Whatever you're burnin in there sure gives me a headache."

He called her bluff by baking cornbread. She upped it by taking the last blanket off the back of the couch while he and Boo slept. Boo was getting fatter by the day, but One-Two didn't have the heart to eat while Betty was starving, so he began to shed weight.

When he saw the food tactic wasn't going to work, he began fixing anything he could think of that needed mending, and some things that didn't.

He shored up the front steps and screwed them to the house so they no longer wobbled. He took all the screens off the windows and the door except for the ones in Betty's bedroom windows, and sat in the living room and patched them while listening to "Wheel of Fortune" at top volume.

On the fourth day he got sick of television and made a trip to the hardware store for some solder and spliced the broken cord to the eight-track tape player he found underneath the winter boots in the hall closet.

The only two tapes that still worked were Boo's old Kiss tape that One-Two didn't dare play, and "Marvin Gaye's Greatest Hits." The rest of them, by ABBA, Kenny Rogers, and Jim Croce, had all been soaked by the boot slush that gathered on the floor of the closet.

One-Two played Marvin Gaye so much that Boo began to sleep in his car. By the sixth day the tape player broke for good, but by then One-Two could sing all of the songs from memory in a raspy monotone. He was crooning "How Sweet It Is" outside Betty's window while he raked up the dead leaves, cigarette butts, and dog shit that had been collecting in the lee of the house since it was built. Betty yells at him out the window.

"Either fix the damn tape player or hoof it to the church for choir practice. You got the most god-awful voice I ever heard."

He leans the rake against the house and switches to a hum as he dusts his boots on the new doormat and walks straight into Betty's room.

"There ain't no fixin it."

Betty sighs deeply and sinks back down under the lead weight of the blankets.

"There ain't no fixin it," she muses.

"I can get a new one."

"There ain't no fixin it," she says with greater conviction.

"I can get a new one. It ain't no big deal."

"I don't know, One-Two." She turns her head to face him. "I just don't know," she repeats, her voice sinking to a whisper.

One-Two sits down on the edge of the bed. "You gotta get up, Betty."

"I don't got no reason." One-Two says nothing. "There ain't no fixin this," she repeats.

"No. Maybe not," he says. "But this ain't all there is. There's more. Lots more."

He looks at her quickly, ready for the solar flare of her anger. Instead, her eyes are getting wet, and for the first time since he's known her, she begins to cry.

"What else? What else is there? What else?"

One-Two starts, then stops, clasping and unclasping his hands. "Irma."

"She's gone."

"Her baby."

"Never met the baby."

"They're around, Betty. They're around somewhere. There's Simon."

"He's gone, too."

She shakes her head and leaves it turned away from him. She tries to sigh, but it comes out jagged, cut into steps by her silent sobs.

"It ain't enough, One-Two. I tried so hard, with all of them, but it wasn't ever enough."

"You enough."

"That ain't true."

"You're enough."

"You don't know what you're talking about."

"I do," he says softly. "I do know."

She looks at him. She reaches from under the covers and puts her hand on his.

"You're a good man, One-Two."

He nods, to let her know he hears what she is saying, but he is looking down at their hands. She doesn't take hers away.

"How long we know each other?" she asks.

"Twenty-three years."

She looks at their hands, too. Marble from adjacent quarries, the veins running from one to another. They sit this way for minutes. They hear cars passing on the highway. It is warm, and the ground thaw sends the smell of mud through the open windows. She reaches with her other hand for the box of Kleenex and blows her nose. They hear Boo start his car and turn on the radio.

"I can fix it."

"Can you?"

"Maybe. I don't know." He is uncertain. He looks up from their hands and out the window. He does not miss the city. "I ain't ever been much help to you."

"You're wrong, One-Two."

"Naw. I never kept none of this from happening. Simon. Irma. I can clean a gutter, but I ain't much use beyond that."

"It'd be nice to have some music," she says.

"Music's nice."

"One-Two? You did the best you could. You did your best by me."

"You think?"

She holds his hand tighter. "I know." She pulls her head back and takes in his face from a new angle. The afternoon light streams in the window and lights the dust, the wind-borne pollen.

"One-Two? I don't know your real name. Never learned your real name."

"Never? In all these years?"

She shakes her head.

"Sinclair," he says, blushing slighty, his heart racing.

"Sinclair," she says, the two syllables dropping down like eggs in a nested palm. "How about that." Her thumb traces his index finger, running the smooth brown skin like water over rock. "How about that. All of these years."

36

Simon races the engine. He is used to the octane rush of Irene's car, knows the sweet spot, when to let off and when to hammer it. He follows the highway north and then cuts off on a service road. The night hasn't rolled over yet and the darkness peels off the highway in front of the car and breaks over the top of him, great pages of night sky.

He pulls off the road, dust racking the air. The turnaround is littered with beer cans and piles of charcoal from party fires, midnight gardens sprouting wire and soot-darkened cans. Spent .30-.30 casings are stuck in the sand like buried treasure. He grinds the car to a stop and gets out, not shutting it off. Simon takes off his shirt and is surprised at how cold it is. He douses the seats with chain saw mix and unrolls the window three inches. He soaks the shirt in the gas and trails it down the outside of the car.

Without waiting, he lights a cigarette. He stands there and smokes, just a few feet and scant seconds away from an explosion, savoring the tension, the feeling of change that comes with intractable action, like death, like a first kiss. He rubs the cigarette out with his foot and lights another match. He holds it to the bottom of the shirt, and when the first finger of fire catches, he sprints across the railroad tracks.

It takes four, maybe five seconds for the fire to crawl inside the car. There is a whoosh as the fumes catch. The windows blow out. Glass falls to the ground like hail.

The fire is quick. The seats and carpeting catch and smoke billows out into the sky, lit not by moon or star, by satellite, or magic, or anything. Just soot into a greater, more wicked darkness.

He knows it will burn down, that the paint and hoses will burn, the gas tank will catch, that there will be nothing left. He turns from the car and faces the tracks. He breathes in deeply, like a sprinter. The landscape around him is dim, lit only by the growing fire. Sections of the track glow like eyes, the steel throwing off night shine. Simon pulls in more air. Once. Twice. He begins to run.

He stumbles on the crushed rock mounded between the sharp-smelling timbers. He catches his stride, timing each footfall with another piece of wood, ready to shift if he hits more rock. His chest hurts and his legs burn, but he is running.

Trees grow close on either side of the tracks, twisted blue-black tamarack. They fall away as the grade passes a swamp. Simon looks to his right and sees the edge of the sky crusted with yet another dawn. He looks back at the tracks. It is lighter and he sees that the gravel is studded with pieces of broken iron, old spikes, nameless, igneously puddled metals, dropped like scales from the underside of passing trains. Weeds grow up to the edge and as he passes he notices that among the winter-broken thistle, goldenrod, and sage there are shoots of greenery struggling through the husks of their dead parents, larval and waxy.

He puts on more speed and everything stretches and falls away. The swamp looks dead, like a blast zone, the tracks dawn-lit bones. Underneath it all, he knows it will explode, it will grow and turn, and soon there will be colors that will make you cry. There will be the felt of new lily pads, funnels of jack-in-the-pulpit. Orioles will blast from the woods like sunlets, buntings like skylets.

But the ground on which he runs will hold no print. His passing will never be marked into the earth. You move stones with your feet but there is no impression, no remnant of your life, your action. Whatever you do is not accommodated, it is simply dropped onto the hard earth you pass. You will be forgotten. Your feet, your hands are not words and cannot speak. Everything we accumulate—our habits, gestures, muscles trained by the regimen of work, the body remembering instead of the mind—it is of no use.

His feet speed up. There are eyes, witness to the mad dash, the stretch of muscle, the shock to tendon and bone. There is no noise, just the atmospherics of the woods shaking off night travels, settling down to notice the passing. The pockets are emptied, cigarettes and lighter clank down onto the gravel, crushed from smooth rock into shards, pieces that have no character and hold nothing. The tracks play out straight and level, so flat, that looking down them you can see the earth curve, bending to the north, bending in every direction away from where you run. The level ground becomes a summit, every direction an unchecked fall.

The arms mill efficiently, the legs are finding themselves and the breathing evens out. The body is made to do this, waiting for the chance, but it doesn't know, can't know, whether you're running to or from. All it wants is to get you there. There are eyes, and they watch as you run.